ELK GROVE VILLAGE PUBLIC LIBRARY
3 1250 01050
W9-BEK-609

A Novel

Tamar Ossowski

For Noah, Ben, and Chloe

This book is a work of fiction. References to real people, events, establishments, organizations, or locales are intended only to provide a sense of accuracy and authenticity. All other characters, and all incidents and dialogue, are from the author's imagination and are used fictitiously.

Skyhorse Publishing books may be purchased in bulk at special discounts for sales promotion, corporate gifts, fund-raising, or educational purposes. Special editions can also be created to specifications. For details, contact the Special Sales Department, Skyhorse Publishing, 307 West 36th Street, 11th Floor, New York, NY 10018 or info@skyhorsepublishing.com.

Skyhorse® and Skyhorse Publishing® are registered trademarks of Skyhorse Publishing, Inc.®, a Delaware corporation.

www.skyhorsepublishing.com

10 9 8 7 6 5 4 3 2 1

Library of Congress Cataloging-in-Publication Data is available on file.

ISBN: 978-1-62636-037-2

Printed in the United States of America

Franny

The second time Matilda asked where we were going, my mother turned the radio up louder. It had been an hour or maybe two or maybe more—I didn't know because, at that moment, all I could hear was the tapping noise she was making against the steering wheel. We were stopped in traffic, which made her drum faster and harder, and then I felt it coming like a volcano about to erupt, the letters, mostly A's and R's sitting inside the rounds of my cheeks, readying themselves to pop out. Big and unwieldy, making my lips ache, but then just as they were about to slip past, Matilda reached over to hold my hand. I closed my eyes and thought about electrical storms. Matilda told me that I was born during one and that the first time she saw me, the lights flickered, and in that moment of darkness, my sister leaned over and whispered, "I missed you."

Like I had just returned from a trip.

I squeezed her hand tighter and she turned toward the window. I tried not to think about leaving our grandmother's house or how our mother stuffed our things into garbage bags that got so big and misshapen, she could barely drag them out of the room. I had watched as she packed the blanket my grandmother made for my ninth birthday. It was pink and soft and had a big F embroidered in the center. Now those garbage bags were crammed inside the trunk and I imagined my things swirled together tightly with no room to breathe.

The car stopped in traffic and the sound of engines rumbled through me. Matilda was still staring out the window and I could feel the letters slowly creeping back. They were steady and strong and constant and I wanted them to come and make everything happening fade away like the tiny dot on a television screen that disappears when you turn it off. Effortlessly, they slid across my tongue, this time smooth and silky and not bulky at all. I closed my eyes until they were all I could see, floating randomly, innocently in the darkness. Matilda took a long, exaggerated breath and, suddenly, the car came to an abrupt stop.

My mother pulled over to the side of the road and, as gently as if she was powdering her nose, folded into herself and began to sob. Matilda got out of the car and seconds later was in the passenger seat. Matilda and my mother had an alliance to which I was never invited.

The radio played. The car filled with the voice of an enthusiastic DJ commanding his audience to dial in and win a shopping spree at Wal-Mart. My sister hovered over our mother, who was crying so softly that I was no longer sure that she was. Equally as quiet were the words she said when she finally spoke. "Forgive me."

F-O-R-G-I-V-E M-E

Alone in the backseat of the car, I broadened my shoulders and tried to convince my body that it was brave. Matilda's arms were folded across her chest. Even though sometimes it's hard for me to tell when something is wrong, this time I knew. I knew it when the fighting between my mother and grandmother got so loud, I could hear the words without pressing my ear up against the door. It was my mother's voice that was the loudest.

"There is no other way!" My mother yelled and then grumbled something that sounded like bullets being shot underwater. Their bitter exchanges continued over the next few days, my mother's voice humming like a sewing machine, chasing my grandmother from one room to the next. She was relentless until finally one night she reached into her purse, pulled out a brass-colored key, and laid it on the table. My grandmother swiped her arm across the surface, sending it flying to the floor, and then she ran out of the room.

That night their fighting was too quiet to hear.

Matilda and I stayed in the kitchen, watching television on the small black-and-white perched on the counter. We sat in red vinyl chairs until it was time for bed; we turned up the volume so loud that it made the air around us shake. In the morning, we acted like we always did. My grandmother was making toast and I remember breathing in the smell.

I wondered what my grandmother was doing now while I sat in the backseat of my mother's car, counting the number of times her shoulders bounced up and down. My sister reached over to twist the radio dial, first slowly and then faster, until all I heard were electrical bleeps and broken, cracked words. My mother wiped her face with her fingers and then pulled back into traffic. This time, instead of tapping out the rhythm of a song, she gripped the steering wheel tightly and focused with a determination that reminded me of a heavy rainstorm. We turned streets and passed neighborhoods that grew less familiar until finally we pulled up beside a small white house. We got out of the car, my mother first with Matilda and me trailing behind. I reached out to hold my sister's hand.

"Where are we?" Matilda asked.

My mother kept walking, as if she didn't hear.

"Why are we here?" Matilda now asked, this time the shake in her voice broke up her words and made it sound like she was out of breath.

"Everything will be fine," my mother answered as she used a brass key to open the door. "Just come inside."

How do I describe what I smelled the moment I entered that house? Simply put, I smelled art. It smelled of paper and charcoal and glasses tinged with colored water. It smelled of sweat and risk and inspiration. The old wood floors creaked as we inched closely behind my mother. She turned to us and smiled and then I heard a voice coming from the other room. It was soft and gentle and then the woman to whom it belonged entered the room.

She said her name was Leah.

Matilda stopped dead in her tracks the moment we laid eyes upon her, but she never told me why. Leah's hair had shards of light that glistened even though she wasn't standing in the sun. Her lips were the shade of pink that mine sometimes got after I sucked too many cherry-flavored Lifesavers. Her voice was so melodic that, as she spoke, I got lost in her music and forgot to pay attention to what she was saying. Her name was beautiful, too. Like my mother's, it had a silent H, except the H in Therese's name hid behind the T like it was scared to be noticed. The H in LeaH stood proudly at the end, and if you listened very closely, it would make itself heard.

"You must be tired from your trip," Leah said.

Matilda stood in front of me. "Who are you?"

Leah smiled and then looked down at the ground. "I am an old friend of your mother's."

When she looked back up, I realized she was staring at me. I felt my sister shift so that she covered me even more. "Why are we here?"

"We are having a visit." My mother smiled and then whispered something to Leah, who then led us upstairs into a room the color of cucumbers. It took a few minutes for me to notice little painted pixie fairies on the walls—each standing on her toes and fluttering her wings as if she were about to go soaring around the room. I eased myself onto one of the beds and Matilda sat opposite me, her eyes fixed upon the fairy directly above my head. After Leah and my mother left, she came and sat beside me. She held my hand and we sat together, silently.

Side by side.

I don't remember when I fell asleep, but when I woke the room was caught in that space between darkness and light. The kind of color that makes you wonder if the day is just about to begin or end. Matilda was curled up on the bed opposite mine so I tried to be quiet, but secretly hoped my movements would wake my sister. She barely stirred.

Downstairs, my mother was curled in the same position on the couch in the living room. I found my way into the kitchen, which was entirely white from the cabinets to the countertops to the floor. I walked over to what I thought was the door to the pantry and nudged it open and inside, with her back to me, sat Leah. The room was small and on either side sat two long tables. She turned and motioned for me to come in and then, without saying a word, handed me a watercolor set.

I sat at the table beside her and held the brush in my hand. Next to spelling, my favorite thing to do was paint and, when you're nine, part of the magic of painting is that you can also color water. I spent the first fifteen minutes watching the paint spiral and float into the water in my jar and turn from red to orange to brown. I listened to the sound my paintbrush made as it scraped against the fibers of the sheet. I filled the page with broad strokes of rainbows and clouds and butterflies and then I looked up to see what Leah was doing.

There was an orange on the table. A very large piece of paper was clipped to her easel and she was drawing it in such enormous scale, it didn't fit into the confines of the sheet. Her work was so detailed I could see each and every bump on the fruit's surface. I looked around the room and, for the first time, noticed other samples of her art—everyday items blown up to cartoon-like proportions. I saw a hairbrush and a can opener and a slice of pizza. All enormous and exposed in such an intimate way that even though I didn't understand what I was feeling, I felt myself blush. It was only days later that I realized that all of her work was in black and white. Otherwise, I might have found it strange that she had a watercolor set to give me.

She peered over my shoulder. "That's beautiful." She pointed to a swirl that looked surprisingly like a wave in the ocean. My favorite parts of art were the things that happened when you didn't mean them to, and I tried to nod, but she was too close and I could feel my face turning red.

"Want something to eat?" She put down her pencil and stood. I followed, waiting to be told what to do.

"What kinds of things do you like?"

I didn't answer, and then I saw my mother standing in the doorway rubbing her fingers across her forehead like she was trying to erase something from her brain.

"Eggs?" Leah asked.

My mother nodded and jumped up onto the counter. She and Leah whispered to each other, but I was too busy folding my napkin into the letter V to pay attention. When I looked up, Matilda was standing in the doorway rubbing her forehead in the same way that my mother had. I watched Leah crack the eggs and then I heard her say something about an art museum and my mother say something about shopping. Their voices started to jumble inside my head, so I tried to focus on how much prettier an egg looked raw than cooked and then the letters came spinning and I watched them dance until it was quiet and peaceful around me.

The next thing I remember is waking up in a bed in the room with the pixie fairies. In the bathroom, I squeezed toothpaste onto my toothbrush and watched it seep into the bristles, and then I started in the back and scrubbed each tooth three times before moving on to the next. I wondered when my mother found the time to pack my toothbrush. Today was Thursday. I had math tests every Thursday. Were we going to go to school? How long were we going to be gone on our trip? I didn't like missing my math test. I was on my eighteenth tooth and had yet to come up with any reasonable answers to my questions. So I rinsed, spat twice, got dressed, and went downstairs.

Everyone was at the table, my mother and Leah sipping tea from mugs. There was a bowl of cereal waiting for me. I liked that we were finally having breakfast at the right time instead of for dinner, like we had done the night before. It made me uncomfortable when things happened out of order, like eating breakfast foods at dinner time. I poured the milk and listened to the crackling sound of the cereal, which always reminded me of beginnings, and then waited for it to lose its crunch.

"Franny, do you remember that today we are going to the museum?" Leah asked.

I was grateful that I had a spoon in my mouth and could escape without offering more of a response. I didn't like things that were loud and museums were loud.

“Matilda and I are going to do a little shopping. Why don’t you finish up and get going, and we’ll give you a fashion show when we get back,” my mother said.

“We’re going to buy new clothes?” Matilda suddenly seemed interested in her excursion with our mother.

“Among other things. Why don’t you finish up, and we can get going.”

I skimmed the surface of the leftover milk with the bottom of my spoon. Part of me wanted to take Matilda’s hand and not let go, but then Leah went to get her coat and brought mine, as well. I slipped it on and Leah put her hand on my back and Matilda waved and then the choice, if there even was one, was made.

My mother turned and hugged me. “Have fun and don’t worry about us!” She smiled and pulled me close. “Leah will take care of you.” She squeezed the top of my shoulder so hard it hurt and then she whispered something that I didn’t understand because I was too busy rubbing my nose in her hair because I loved the smell of her shampoo. She pulled me back a second time, but then Leah held out her hand and I took it. When I turned back around again, my mother was gone. Leah and I walked out the door and into her car.

Dangling from the mirror was a crystal that sparkled in the sun. I fixed my eyes on it, watching it turn the sunlight into hundreds of strands of magical light. Neither of us said a word. Leah turned on the radio and we listened to the music. It was the longest time I had ever spent not spelling in my head.

When we got to the museum, Leah led the way up the steps and I couldn’t help but notice the large groups of school children pinching and prodding each other.

“It’s okay, Franny.” She put her arm around my shoulders and, even though I didn’t usually like being touched, I stuffed my hands into my pockets and moved in closer to her. The museum noises flickered in my ears and then blended into one big vibration that bounced around the inside of my head. She took my hand and led me through the exhibits, but I didn’t look at the paintings or the people; I just stared down at my feet because the noise felt close enough to touch. Letters appeared like doorways offering escape, but I held on to Leah's hand instead.

She took me to see Monet's paintings. I had seen them in books at the library, but all I remembered were images of lilies and haystacks. Leah pulled me along and I kept my eyes down, counting steps until finally we stopped in front of a painting. "This one. It's my favorite."

She waited until people moved and then, just as the guard looked away, took my hand and ran my fingers across the lower half of the painting. I closed my eyes, connecting through the oil and canvas, feeling the heat of her hand over mine. When we pulled away, she wrapped herself around me, her breath on my neck, slow and controlled, as if she was asleep. I forced myself to look back up at the painting and then suddenly, instead of shadow, there was light. The letters slipping clumsily from my lips stopped and the rattling inside my head calmed and I felt the painting in a different way than when she had let me touch it. I breathed in the color and smell of quiet and then the light dimmed and the ache in my neck released. Leah was watching me, her face soft, like it had been washed in rain.

"You see what I see." When I didn't respond, she pulled me in closer, put her nose in my hair.

We drove home submerged in calm, but as we got closer to her house, I started to feel it—the buzz in my head getting louder and bigger, a static hiss that happened when things around me moved too fast. Leah pulled up to her house and I ran out of the car. I covered my ears and quietly rocked back and forth while I waited for her to fish around in her bag for the brass-colored key. She slipped it into the lock and, with a click, the doorknob turned.

It was the way the pillows on the couch were arranged. The way they all had perfect V's plunged into their middles, as if someone had walked up to each and given them a swift karate chop. It was my mother's style of fluffing cushions before she left a room.

And that is when I knew.

I knew they were gone, and I knew they were not coming back.

Matilda

The air between us felt electric and my ears turned red from the heat. We drove slowly at first and then picked up speed once we reached the highway. Music from the radio filled the space between us and it was so loud that, for a moment, I forgot that Franny wasn't with us, sitting and spelling in the backseat. When I finally looked up at my mother, I could tell she knew where she was going. The scenery became more rural, and soon we weren't getting any radio stations. Without the music, the sound of the road took over and my mother's smile grew even more determined. I pretended that she was a stranger who had abducted me and kept myself busy trying to come up with ways to let someone know I needed help.

I imagined rigging up the radio and sending waves to the nearest police station or making her stop at a gas station and then using my blood to scribble a message on the bathroom mirror. I mouthed "help me" anytime we passed another car on the road, which wasn't very often. It amused me for a while, but then I got bored. There were only so many ways I could think of to summon help, and it got harder to think about what I would do if I ever did escape.

Trees passed by in a green blur, moving me farther from my sister, so I closed my eyes to shut out the view and I thought about my grandmother's yellow house. The one we grew up in with a staircase filled with photographs of my mother getting older the higher you climbed. The house that held no father, for me or for her.

It was the one thing we had in common.

I remember when my grandmother pulled me up those stairs and into her bedroom and whispered the story to me, as if overhearing it would somehow hurt my mother, as if she did not already know that she was in the middle of it.

That she had always been in the middle of it.

My grandmother dreamed of having a child. Every prayer, every birthday wish was the same and ultimately went unanswered. It was all she could talk about and soon my grandfather tired of her and began spending nights away from home. Eventually she gave up on both prayer and hope until one morning her passion for conceiving was replaced with a passion for consuming Hershey bars. From the moment she woke, all she thought about was Hershey bars, and finally, because she could not control her newfound obsession, she went to see a doctor. He ran some standard tests, but found nothing that a bottle of vitamins could not cure, so he sent her home and told her to get some rest.

As the months passed, she began to feel something inside of her. At night, she lay awake trying to figure out what could possibly be invading her body with such determination. She decided what was growing inside her was, in fact, a large and fatal tumor. She refused to go back to the doctor, convinced he would just confirm her fears, and secretly planned her funeral while adding Hershey's with almonds to her grocery list.

Eventually, my grandmother woke feeling such intense pains that she knew the end had come. She asked a neighbor to drive her to the hospital and fifteen hours later, a perfectly healthy little girl was born. That is the way my mother arrived into the world—disguised as a cancerous growth. There was no secret in the selection of my mother's name. My grandmother, grateful that she wasn't dying after all, named her new child Therese, after Teresa of Avila, Patron Saint of bodily ills.

A nurse called my grandfather to share the exciting news, but he wanted nothing to do with my grandmother, deciding that she must have betrayed him to conceive. That night, he packed his things and disappeared for good. My grandmother bought a bag of Hershey's kisses, had a good cry, and got down to the business of raising her daughter. I had heard the story of my mother's birth so often I knew it by heart. It was my story I was more interested in—and the one that my mother kept secret from me.

My mother kept many secrets from me. Like why she treated my sister and me so differently, and why our father's name was one that could never be spoken, and why on one sunny afternoon in October she decided to pack up all our things and leave our grandmother's house. I remember watching as she frantically dug through drawers, gathering our things, while Franny and I stood in the middle of the room—mostly because we didn't want to get in her way. I knew I needed to do something to make it all stop, but I couldn't and I didn't and then it was too late and the next thing I knew we were driving away in her car. I turned to look back and watched the house where I had grown up shrink away. She held the steering wheel tightly and focused with such intensity that it made her look angry. After what seemed like hours of driving, we pulled up beside a little white house that was so dainty, dolls might have lived inside. My mother used a key she wore around her neck to let us in, and when we walked through the doorway a woman appeared and I suddenly felt overwhelmed by a sense of familiarity. But the harder I tried to remember, the deeper the memory hid. She led us to a green room with fairies and I just held on to my sister because I didn't know what else to do.

I helped Franny get under the covers and eventually we fell asleep, but when I woke she was gone. I walked to the top of the stairs and listened to their voices blending together. In the kitchen, Leah was standing over a frying pan and my mother was sitting on top of the counter, her legs dangling down and her arms hugging her chest. Franny was at the table folding her napkin into triangles.

"Hungry?" Leah asked.

The table was set for four, and Leah was scrambling eggs. It never occurred to me to wonder why she would be making what appeared to be breakfast for dinner, as though we were at the beginning of something instead of the end. Later, I spent hours reliving the details, replaying the moments, over and over again.

"Matilda, would you like to go shopping tomorrow?" my mother asked.

"For what?"

"I thought it might be fun to get some new stuff."

Franny stiffened. I saw a tremor pass over her lips. Our sisterly Morse code.

"What about Franny?" I asked.

"Maybe Franny and I could spend some time together. Would you like to go to an art museum?" Leah turned to look at her.

Franny held the fork in her hand and used the tines to trace designs on her plate.

"She won't like that." I slid in next to my sister. Franny never looked up from her plate, but I knew what she was thinking because I always knew what she was thinking. She looked so pale, I could make out the little blue veins beneath her skin, and I reached over to hold her hand. When I looked up, Leah was staring at us, but then quickly turned back to the stove. I squeezed my sister's hand tighter.

That night, in what I thought would be our new room, Franny fell asleep before me. I listened to her breaths, deep in and out, like what I imagined a newborn baby might sound like. In the morning, I woke before she did and went downstairs. She came down after and started eating her cereal and I wondered if Leah knew that she only liked it soggy.

My mother brought up the idea of shopping again and, because I really wanted to go this time, I said nothing when Leah suggested taking Franny to the museum. I waved goodbye to my sister and then went back to eating breakfast. When my mother returned to the kitchen, I looked at her face and only one thought crossed my mind.

Some mornings I put my shirt on backwards.

I picked ones with big stiff collars that sliced into my chin and openings that dipped down my back. I wanted it to be obvious to anyone who saw me that I had done it on purpose. I practiced my look in the mirror, emptying my eyes of emotion and arching my eyebrows. Slowly, I would walk out of the room as though I had a book balanced on my head, trying desperately not to shake the expression. Inevitably, I would spin the shirt around, slipping it back into its proper position because I never had the courage to go out into the world backwards. That morning, when I glanced back at my mother, I recognized her look—the one I had practiced and failed to achieve.

We went upstairs and she told me to collect my things. I looked around the pretty green room with the pixie fairies innocently watching me and then I disentangled my belongings from Franny's. I gathered some clothes and books and hair barrettes—things my mother had hastily thrown together when we left my grandmother's house. When I was done packing, I sat down on Franny's bed to talk to the pixie fairies. I knew it was silly and childish, but I made them promise that they would look after her, especially at night. It made me feel better to imagine them hovering around the room while she slept.

My mother was waiting for me when I came downstairs. "Where are we going?" I tried again. She simply shook her head. "Mom. Please." And even though I didn't mean to, I could feel tears slipping down my face, making me feel worse.

But it didn't matter because she didn't look at me. She fluffed up the cushions on the couch like we were waiting for company to arrive and then took my bag and walked out of the house. I wanted to disappear, and I even looked around for a second, wondering if I could hide in a closet, but then I heard her calling and something in her voice made me know there was no place I could go where she would not find me. I got into the passenger seat of the car, purposely not putting on my seat belt because I didn't really care if something bad happened. Maybe I even wanted it to because I could not envision anything worse than leaving my sister behind.

I started to imagine what she would think when she realized we were gone. I glanced at the clock on the dash; I didn't know what time we left Leah's. I wondered how long we had been driving and how much farther we had to go and then, just as I was about to start crying again, the crunching sound of gravel startled me out of my head. She slowed down as we passed a sign that read EMERALD WELCOMES YOU.

"We're here," she said.

"Where's here?"

"Emerald. It's just what we needed."

"What are you talking about?"

"A place to settle down. We'll be happy here. You'll see."

"Why here?"

She was quiet for a few minutes. "Someone told me about it once, and I thought it sounded perfect."

She drove on and then pulled up alongside a row of attached town homes. She turned off the ignition, held the keys in her hand, and tilted her head back on the headrest. A white pickup truck drove up beside us. An older man got out, thrust his hands into his pockets, and began jiggling their contents. My mother puckered her lips in the mirror, folded a tuft of black hair behind one ear, and climbed out of the car. He was still busy digging in his pockets when she tapped him on the shoulder.

Even from a distance, I could see his features soften. His hands moved in a clumsy way, like they weren't attached to his body. Her back was to me, but I knew exactly what she was doing. One eyebrow was slightly arched and her mouth was poised in a half-smile, making her cheek look round and full. She put both hands on her hips and curved her shoulders inward.

He was no match for my mother.

Within minutes, she talked him down several hundred dollars and an hour later we were unloading our things into our newly-leased town home. It was sandwiched between two others units, which eliminated the possibility of any natural light and made it feel colorless. The only saving grace was a small porch off the back of the living room. My mother was so involved in unpacking that I managed to sneak out onto the porch without her noticing.

I found an old plastic chair a previous tenant had left behind, but it was caked in thick black grime, so I sat on the wooden planks instead. Everywhere I looked, I saw green. It was still warm, but the air now had a snap to it. I closed my eyes and reinvented the porch in my mind, filling it with people I wished were there. I saw my grandmother and Franny sitting at a picnic table eating hamburgers. I pretended that it was windy and the napkins were flying away and that ketchup dripped onto my plate and a bee buzzed by my ear. It took a few minutes before I realized that the sounds I was hearing were not in my head.

I opened my eyes and heard it again, a soft chirp coming from the other side of the wall that divided our porch from our neighbor's. I peeked around, not sure what I would find, and there was a girl, very small but probably my age.

The first thing I noticed was her hair, which she had tried unsuccessfully to tie back with a ribbon. It was honey-colored, but what was more striking was that her eyes matched the hue of her hair. They were the most yellow-brown I had ever seen. She smiled, pointed at one of the trees beyond where we were sitting, and made that sound again. An orange kitten appeared from behind a bush. He walked toward her in that loping, unsteady way kittens walk, and she scooped him up and nuzzled him with her cheek. He lifted his paws over her shoulder and started kneading her hair. "You just move in? I'm Laverne. But everyone calls me Lavi."

The way she said it sounded like "Lovey" and reminded me of what Mr. Howell called his wife on *Gilligan's Island*. "Yeah we just got here today. You live here, too?"

She nodded, stroking the kitten, who had found a home in her hair. "I've lived here for almost two years with my mom and brother. It's not too bad. You gonna be starting school here?"

The question jolted me back into reality. I had no idea why or what I was doing here. I didn't like looking as though I'd been thrown off guard, so I shrugged my shoulders and nodded my head. Luckily, Laverne didn't seem to need much more from me. I figured she would assume what she wanted to and whatever that was would be fine by me.

"What's your name?" she asked.

I paused. Were we on some secret mission, my mother and I? Should I have just said the first name that came to my mind? I hated my name and was always thinking up potential replacements, something glamorous and mysterious. Quinn or maybe Scout. A name that would leave someone speechless. A name that would make me feel like I could wear my clothes backward. I took a deep breath. "Matilda."

"Oh. That's a nice name. Like 'Waltzing Matilda'?"

"What?"

"The song—'Waltzing Matilda.' We learned about Australia last year. It's their national song. Something about stealing sheep. It's kind of sad. Not your name, the song."

It was nice to hear that Lavi didn't think my name was sad, and I was glad that I had been honest when I told it to her. There was something about this girl that made it hard to lie. We sat on her side of the porch for a few more minutes, listening to the rumble of the kitten as it purred and burrowed into her hair. Then I heard a car drive up and a door slam, and Lavi unhooked the kitten from her shirt and placed it on the ground.

"I'll see you around," she said, but she wasn't looking at me. Her focus was on the kitten, watching as it scurried behind the tree from which it had come. She seemed distracted, but finally turned to me and smiled. "See you at school, Matilda."

I nodded and made my way back to my side of the porch. My mother had turned on the radio and was humming to the music. I wished she would sing louder. I wished she hadn't brought us to live in a place that was so empty. I wished she could make it so that I didn't have to hear the screams coming from the unit on the other side of the wall.

Therese

Therese turned the radio up louder, hoping to drown out the noise of the neighbors. She hated living so close to other people. She enjoyed her privacy and the fact she could hear the sound of muffled voices coming from next door made her angry. She wondered where Matilda was. Maybe she had gone off to explore. Maybe she needed some time to figure things out. Part of her wished she could have explained, but Matilda would not have understood.

In fact, no one would really understand, but Therese always followed her instincts, and no matter how angry Matilda appeared at the prospect of leaving Franny behind, she was not about to divulge to her twelve-year-old daughter why they were on the run. It was too difficult to explain how she knew about things, about people. In fact, she barely understood it herself since she was only six years old the first time it happened.

Sitting in the dentist's chair, she watched his eyes dart back and forth across her face, and they reminded her of pebbles. Just as she was about to turn, a bolt of electricity pulsed up her wrists and around her elbows. She blinked as the energy buzzed warmly around her ears and wondered if this had ever happened to anyone else. He stared blankly back at her, seemingly unaware of what was going on.

It kept whizzing through her, oddly exhilarating, overwhelmingly revealing and luxuriously out of her control. After it was over, she replayed it in her mind and when it came time to leave, she kept her face down so that he would not see the reflection of his secrets in her eyes. He was too busy peeling off his plastic gloves to notice. Everyone was stunned two weeks later when he was arrested for beating his wife.

Everyone, except Therese.

She called it "sparking" because the flickers reminded her of the shocks she got when she danced around the living room rug in tights. She taught herself to focus and then braced herself for the electrical spark that followed, allowing her to see the world through another person's eyes and gain a glimpse into their soul. When the conditions were right, and her focus was strong, few were unsparkable.

It was with surprise, then, that one day that she found herself distracted. She was at the supermarket picking things up for her mother, and he was organizing apples in a bin with the precision and thoughtfulness of an artist. The white apron tied around his waist fit snuggly, reminding her of an enormous loincloth. Later, she decided what distracted her most was the way he held each apple so delicately in his big thick hands, as though each one might crumble at his touch.

When he saw Therese, he smiled with a grin she could tell he had practiced in the mirror. His eyes were the color of silver and gave the illusion that they were transparent—that if she looked closely enough, she could see into his head. But she had forgotten to look that close and, before she could turn back and try, the moment for sparking was gone.

"Want a bite?" He lifted one so close to her face that she could feel the warmth of his fingers against her cheek. She tore a plastic bag from the roll at the side of the display and threw two apples inside. Then she smiled, turned, and walked away.

To her mother's surprise, she offered to do the grocery shopping every week. In the produce department, she taunted him by hiding and then willing him to turn and spot her. As the weeks passed, he became more and more adept at a sport he never knew he was playing. It seemed he could sense her presence within seconds, and she quickly grew tired of the game.

Therese was confused about her attraction to the grocer. She was always successful with boys, but this time things were different. This time the stakes seemed higher. There was something special about him, and she never questioned her instincts.

His name was Tim, and he loved chocolate shakes. They met after work and went to the Friendly's across the street from the supermarket where he always instructed the waitress to make his shakes extra thick. It fascinated Therese to watch him struggle to get the drink up through the straw. His cheeks would sink in and his lips would purse and it seemed as if all he cared about at that moment was getting the sweet taste into his mouth. He spent a long time studying the menu, and then when the food came, he ate it slowly, many times just taking the first few bites even as she neared the end of her meal.

He lived on the other side of town with his mother, but when she dropped him off at home he never invited her inside. The house stood out from the others on the block because every inch of it, including the trim and basement windowpanes, was painted a dark crimson red. She guessed that other people probably thought it was strange, but she thought it was sweet: a house permanently decorated for Valentine's Day. Whenever she asked him about it, his skin would turn pink, and he would find a reason to change the subject. His behavior fueled her curiosity even more.

Her biggest weakness was an insatiable need to uncover secrets. It drove her to search through her mother's nightstand drawers, listen in on phone conversations, and open mail that was not addressed to her. She practiced softening the arch of her eyebrows and leaving her lips partially open so that her face looked gentle and warm. Girlfriends would confide their deepest hidden secrets and no matter how shocking or dull, she would remember to keep her face in the same position. It was delicate work, secret cracking, and she was positively consumed by it.

Experience taught her that secrets hid behind discomfort. Instinct told her that Tim was hiding some big secrets. She stayed up nights plotting and scheming and understanding that she would not be able to rest until she saw what lay inside that house. Sometimes, when she knew he was at work, she would drive by and park across the street. It sat like a red jewel among the beige and white houses surrounding it and occasionally someone inside would move a curtain. She rarely noticed any other sign of life.

She asked questions, first directly and then in a more underhanded way, tilting her head and fluttering her eyelashes slowly up and down. "Maybe after work we can go to your house and you can make me those meatballs you are always telling me are so delicious?"

His eyes narrowed and his face got red. "How about I make them and bring them to you?"

"A whole pot of meatballs? Don't you think that's silly?" She tilted her head in the other direction, making sure to moisten the bed of her lip with her tongue.

"You aren't coming over. Drop it."

So she did.

The next day she was in the bathroom putting on lipstick and practicing her look. That was all she needed to break most men, but Tim was different. He was different in so many ways. Why hadn't she realized what she was getting into that first day in the supermarket? She couldn't stop thinking about his little house and that maybe in addition to holding his secrets it might also be the way into his heart. She stepped farther from the mirror to admire the red on her lips. The doorbell rang then unexpectedly, and by the time she came outside, no one was there. On the top step sat a pot full of homemade meatballs still warm from the oven.

She decided it was time to have sex.

She chose an afternoon that her mother was not home and he came over after work, his hands still dusty from unloading a shipment of Idaho potatoes. She hooked her thumb into the back of his jeans and playfully pushed him toward the kitchen sink until they were standing side by side, thighs rubbing.

She pumped soap out of the dispenser and rubbed the white pearly liquid into the grooves of his hands, trying to look concentrated while she leaned over knowing that her breast was touching his chest. Still clinging to his hands, she slipped them under the running water and allowed the suds to pool in the corners of the basin. She stopped rubbing his fingers to make circles on the rough skin of his knuckles and he tilted his head back slightly.

Therese leaned in and gently kissed the space that connected his neck to his shoulder. Surprised that his skin was so delicate, she let the tip of her nose rest against his softness. Suddenly, he grabbed her waist with his slippery hands. She felt spots of wetness forming on her blouse and seeping through to her skin, but when she pushed him away, he pulled her in harder. When he put his mouth on hers, all she could smell was the dirt she had worked so hard to cleanse him of. That was how it began—she would tease and he would restrain and then he would leap at her with such fury and intensity, she could feel the desperation in his movements. He drew her in with the same level of concentration that he used with his chocolate shakes.

Every Tuesday afternoon they met at her mother's house. It became their routine until she began making excuses for why they could no longer meet. Tuesdays passed like pages in a book and still she waited, hoping that his addiction to her would prove so powerful that he would relent and invite her into that little red house.

Each day she waited, knowing that it was killing him inside, but still he held his ground. It seemed that keeping the contents of that house out of her reach was more important than any desire she could ignite within him. She felt angry and hurt, but trusted her instincts and knew that somehow the answer would come. Then, one day she woke and realized that the nauseous feeling she was experiencing each morning meant that she had finally won. She laughed at the simplicity of her situation. Then she plotted how she would share the news: She was going to bring his child into the world.

She went to see him at the grocery store where they first met, coming up beside him, rubbing the underside of his elbows the way that he liked. Instinctively, he ground his back into her. She had clearly deprived him of a great many Tuesdays and enjoyed his sense of neediness. He went to the storeroom to get his things and together they walked to the Friendly's across the street.

They sat in their usual booth, and while Therese ran her finger along a crack in the Formica, Tim studied the menu with grave intensity. "Maybe the fish and chips? What do you think?"

Therese sighed. She didn't understand this ritual of his—why he had to insist on getting something different each and every time they came. It irritated her immeasurably, but she refused to allow it to taint the mood she was in. She could not wait to share her news and Tim's culinary adventure was not going to deflate her enthusiasm. "I was thinking about your house."

The menu rose a bit higher until all she saw were his eyebrows. She had encountered this response many times before and, in the past, nothing she would do or say made any impact. Today was different because today she was getting inside. For some reason, a picture of the father she had never met flashed before her. She blinked twice and forced the image to disappear. She swallowed quickly, trying hard to delight in the moment. "I just thought that maybe you could show it to me so that we could decide to stay or look for one of our own. You know, for when the baby comes?"

She couldn't see his face. Instead, the menu loomed over her and all she could make out was a large smudge of brown sticky goop—the likely remains of a spilled Coke. Instantly her mouth filled with bile, but she swallowed it down, refusing to allow anything to ruin the euphoria of her victory.

Finally, the menu lowered.

She had won. She knew it before he said a word, by the way his shoulders sloped just a little bit lower. She knew it when he paid the bill, leaving behind cold fries and an uneaten plate of fried fish.

The next morning, while still relishing her victory, a phone call interrupted her breakfast. Her friend Joan had taken a job as a clerk at the local hospital and often called with stories about who was leaving the gynecologist's office or who was checking into the psychiatric ward.

"Therese, are you sitting down?"

"Yes, Joan. What is it?"

There was a pause, which happened either for dramatic effect or because, in her excitement, Joan was gagging on her own saliva. Therese prepared herself to hear the latest update on who had just had a mammogram and waited for Joan to resume.

"You know that guy from the supermarket? The one you've been seeing?"

She pressed the phone so close to her ear that a dark red circle formed. "Yes," Therese said. Her voice was sharp, like a hand slapping a face.

"I was walking by the ER, and I saw him there. I overheard some of the nurses talking, and they said he was in a car accident. I think he's okay, but maybe you should get down here. Anyway, I just thought you should know."

Was he going to call her? Had she earned the right to be one of the people contacted in case of an emergency? She quickly dismissed any pangs of sentimentality and instead thanked Joan for the information, promised her a lunch, and quickly got off the phone.

She went into the bathroom to fix her makeup and then brushed her teeth, her mouth waking with the motion and taste of mint. As she drove, she wondered whether her news had contributed in any way to Tim's accident. She caught herself smiling in the rearview mirror, thinking how funny it was that things always had a way of working themselves out.

Therese walked into the hospital and smiled at the man at the registration desk. She recognized him from the few times she had met Joan there for lunch. "I'm here to visit a patient."

"Patient's name?"

"Timothy Yaga."

She edged closer to his desk and smiled, shifting her weight to her left hip and tilting her head to one side. A strand of hair came loose from her clip and rested along the side of her face. She twisted it, slowly, enjoying the feel against her finger.

"Second Floor. Room 212. Elevator all the way down the hall to your right." He hesitated. "Why don't you just go ahead and use the employee elevator. It's closer and much less crowded. If anyone gives you a hard time, you tell them to come see me. Name is Jim."

"Thanks, Jim."

She started to walk away and then stopped and turned. She kissed the palm of her hand and, very gently, as though she was sending him a butterfly, blew in his direction. He grinned and looked down, but she had already seen the redness creep into his face.

The second floor was busy with nurses carrying charts and orderlies pushing carts. No one paid much attention to her, and she found Tim's room easily. She took a deep breath, fixed the hair that had fallen out of place earlier, and pushed open the door.

He was lying in the bed with a blanket pulled up to his chin. His forehead was bandaged, and she could see him twitching beneath, so she knew he was awake and just ignoring her entrance. Her attention was drawn to the other side of the room where an enormous woman wearing a hot pink dress was sitting in a chair. Therese composed herself and extended her hand. "I'm Therese Wolley."

"Barbara Yaga." She didn't look at Therese and instead spit something into a paper cup. Therese was prepared for the various turns this meeting might take and the fact that Tim probably hadn't mentioned her to his mother. "I'm a friend of Tim's. He called from the emergency room when he was admitted. He wanted to make sure that you would be taken care of. He talks about you often. He loves you very much."

Her details about Tim's relationship with his mother were basic, and she had to prevent herself from adding anything that would raise suspicion. "He asked me to move in with you for a few days to make sure you aren't alone while he is here. He is such a good son. You must be so proud." She watched Tim's face for a reaction when she spoke to Barbara, and wasn't surprised to see his eyebrows furrow in frustration. She'd lied and he knew it, but would he call her out in front of his mother?

It was clear that years of smoking had turned the woman's face a lighter shade of the tobacco she seemed to love. The large jowls that hung on either side of her mouth jiggled delicately when she spoke. "Timmy is a good boy."

Tim's eyes were still closed, feigning sleep, but she could see his teeth grinding through the thin, pale skin of his cheeks. Therese couldn't tell if he was furious or irritated or maybe just mildly impressed. He lifted the worn green hospital blanket up to his ears. While Therese began to work out the details of her new living arrangement, he pulled it completely over his head.

Franny

Leah walked over to a bookshelf beside the fireplace stacked with board games. She pulled out a familiar maroon box that was so old, the corners were worn soft as tissue paper. I followed her into her stark white kitchen and sat at the table.

I opened the Scrabble game and ran my fingers across the wooden tiles, flipping them over and rubbing them between my fingers. Touching the letters made them feel more real than when they were just randomly floating around in my head.

Leah let me go first. I took my tiles: Y-C-C-O-E-N-L.

I was lucky and managed to use them all in my first turn—C-Y-C-L-O-N-E. I chose some more tiles and slid them into the rack.

Leah used the E in CYCLONE and spelled R-E-D. New word opportunities appeared with each tile flip. After my fourth or fifth turn, I lost myself in our game and the next time I looked at the clock, I realized that two hours had passed.

I guess it was odd that I didn't break down in tears or try to find out if Leah had known all along that my mother was planning on running out . . . and leaving me behind. Maybe I should have demanded she tell me where my mother had gone, but I was just so used to things happening to me that none of these thoughts came to mind. Instead, after our Scrabble tournament, Leah prepared dinner and I went upstairs to change my clothes.

I was alone in the room where I had last seen my sister only that morning. Her bed was unmade, but beside that, not a trace of her was left behind, like she had never even existed. I laid my head on a pillow and that's when I felt it. Matilda's journal hidden beneath the blanket. I opened it and ran my finger along the jaggedness the ripped pages left behind and then I saw it, scribbled quickly in the upper corner.

"I will come back for you."

I pulled out the purple pen that was tucked into the binding and carefully traced over the words she left for me. I slipped the book under my mattress and that night, when I closed my eyes, I dreamed of fairies.

When I woke the next morning, Leah was sitting on the bed across from mine.

"Hi," she said as she tucked herself under the blanket.

Instinctively I buried my head into the pillow.

"We need to run some errands. Why don't you get ready and come downstairs."

I did as I was told and got dressed, but abbreviated my usual teeth brushing ritual. My mind felt numb and I didn't want to give it opportunity to wander. Leah was in the middle of preparing breakfast when I came down.

She wore a robe covered in fuchsia and canary flowers and the stroke of her movements against the white canvas of the kitchen looked like a living painting. As I ate, she sat beside me and calmly stirred her tea. Every few minutes her spoon hit the porcelain and it reminded me of bells. The room was quiet except for the sound of her tea music.

"Is she coming back?" I mumbled.

She slipped her lower lip into her mouth and sucked it. "I don't know." She put down her cup and left to get dressed. I reached over and picked up her spoon, dropping tiny amber colored orbs around the saucer.

We got into her green car and I thought about the last time I was there and how drastically my circumstances had changed. As if on cue, Leah reached up and twisted the crystal glass hanging from the mirror and sprinkled me with hundreds of magical twinkling lights. The rainbow-rimmed circles bounced on the dashboard as we drove and before I knew it, we were walking into the entrance of a department store.

I felt overwhelmed by the racks of clothes that stretched before us. I mostly wore Matilda's hand-me-downs and, if not, my grandmother shopped for my clothes and brought them home for me to wear. Like she did at the museum, Leah took my hand and together we inched our way through rows of pants and shirts and prominent displays of white and pink underwear.

Leah looked through the racks and pulled out things she thought would fit. I busied myself by staring at a tag hanging from the sleeve of a dress, rearranging the letters into different words in my head. After Leah collected an armful of clothes, she handed them to me and I went inside the dressing room while she waited outside. I tried on a gray sweater so soft it felt like a kitten. It had designs around the wrists that looked like O's. I tried on a few other things and when I came out of the dressing room, Leah slipped her arm around my shoulders.

Next, we went to the drugstore. She left me alone to browse among the notebooks and pens and pencils. I loved the smell of new notebooks and the way the scarlet line kept all the words in their proper places. I chose three with different colored covers and then started thinking about going to a new school. A sick feeling grew inside of me and spread to my arms and legs, making them feel so heavy that I was scared if I didn't move soon, I might be stuck in the stationery aisle of that drugstore for the rest of my life.

She came from behind, warming me as though I had just come in from a snowstorm. Her hair tickled the back of my neck and I could feel her heart beating against me. She eased the notebooks into her basket and slipped her hand into mine. We walked to the magazine rack where she pulled her hand away only so she could throw something into the basket she was carrying. As we were leaving, I saw what she had chosen—a thick, soft-covered word search puzzle book. On the way back to the car, I realized that since breakfast, we had not exchanged a single word. I sat in the passenger seat with my word search book, curling the corner of the cover lovingly between my fingers.

The next afternoon, I was busy working on a puzzle when the doorbell rang. Leah went to answer it. I was so involved in what I was doing that even though I heard her voice, it was so far in the back of my head that she startled me when she put her hand on my shoulder.

"Franny." Her fingertips brushed the back of my neck as she spoke. They felt cool, like autumn. "There's someone here to see you."

When I looked up, my grandmother lowered her face close to mine. I didn't realize how empty I was until her face was all I could see.

"How are you, Franny?" Her hair was parted down the middle and hung like two big S's on either side of her head. I snuggled into her chest, which looked like two cement slabs but was deceivingly soft. A whimper came up through my throat that I thought would stay hidden in the folds of her blouse, but she heard it and dislodged herself from me. She put her face to mine. "Franny, how are you?"

I knew this time I needed to answer.

I looked into her eyes, which were blue like the color of wind, and then suddenly I began to cry. She rocked me back and forth like I was a doll. When my lips finally stopped trembling, my head felt thick and heavy. As if on command, my eyes closed and instantly I was asleep.

I dreamt of falling and when I woke, I was still in her arms, but now we were both sitting on the couch. I felt disheveled and clumsy, like I had just traveled a long way. I was sweating and she pushed the hair that had gotten stuck to my forehead away. When I shivered, she brought me closer in to her body.

"Franny," she whispered. "You have to be a brave girl. I promise that I will come and visit you again. Is Leah kind?"

I nodded.

"Good," she continued. "You are safe here, Franny. I know that you miss Mommy and Matilda. You'll see them again, I'm sure."

I started to fidget. I don't think I really understood until that moment what it actually meant to have my mother and sister disappear. I was going to have to figure things out for myself, by myself, from this point forward. It had taken nine years for my mother to understand who I was and what I needed. And when she left, she took all of that with her. I was back to square one, and left in the care of a woman I barely knew.

"Do you know why? Why she left me?"

She looked at me but didn't answer, and for a minute, I wondered if I had even asked it out loud.

"There is something I want you to have. Something your mom must have forgotten to pack." She fished in her bag and pulled out a white envelope folded in half. She opened it and spilled its contents into the palm of her hand. Two gold hearts with each of our names—Franny and Matilda—engraved into them. It was the fancy jewelry that we were only allowed to wear on special occasions. My grandmother strung both onto a thin pink ribbon. She handed them to me and I held them between my fingers, snapping the charms together over and over and finding satisfaction in the way that the metal hearts clicked against each other.

"You keep that one for Matilda and give it to her when you see her."

"I promise."

She went into the kitchen and she and Leah whispered so that I couldn't hear. Then, my grandmother got her coat, hugged me, and went to the door. I watched her get into her car and fumble with the keys. After she left, with the sound of the car engine still humming in my ears, I wondered why it had never occurred to me to ask her to take me with her.

I thought about talking to Leah more about where my mother had gone, but by the time I figured out the right words, I was already in bed. The next morning, Leah told me we were going to school and then the letters started to come so fast that it was all I could do to finish swallowing the cereal in my mouth.

My new teacher's name was Mrs. Fern Ficsh. The C was silent. Whenever anyone said her name, it created a soft whooshing sound in the classroom that reminded me of the ocean. Leah came with me and introduced me to Mrs. Ficsh. They whispered as she led me to my seat.

The tables were set up in twos, and the girl I shared my desk with had thick blond hair and glasses. She was too busy arranging her things to notice when I sat beside her. First, she took her pencils out of their case and lined them up in perfect order, each sharpened to the same point. She had a hardcover three-ring binder with a picture of a white kitten on it, two glue sticks, one pair of scissors, one box of colored pencils, one pack of index cards, and a brand new pink eraser. I figured out that her name was Evelyn because each and every one of her belongings, including a mitten that had fallen from her coat pocket, was labeled with her name.

eVelyn.

The "V" held up the other letters, like one of the spokes in a spider's web. It looked delicate and ethereal, but in reality, it held all the power. I liked Evelyn right from the start. I think she liked me too because I was quiet and didn't distract her from her organizational duties.

Mrs. Ficsh spent the morning teaching us about maps and globes. She asked us to draw a map of our homes. Evelyn's box of colored pencils came in handy and, without thinking, I drew out the rooms of Leah's house. I followed Evelyn to lunch and sat beside her at a table near the window.

"Did you just move here?" she asked, taking a bite into a peanut butter and jelly sandwich, the edges of which were perfectly sliced off.

Nodding, I played with the wax paper Leah had used to wrap my sandwich.

"Do you like to read? Because after we finish eating we can go to the library. Most of the other kids go outside for recess but the librarian lets me sit and read for the whole time. Do you want to come?"

I nodded again.

Evelyn didn't seem to mind that she was the one doing all the talking. We finished eating and walked past a table of giggling girls on our way to the library, but Evelyn kept walking, her eyes set on the exit. When we got to the library, the woman behind the desk smiled. Evelyn walked over to a bookshelf near the corner and I watched as she bent down to the lowest shelf and counted till she reached the twelfth book from the left.

She opened it to the middle, began to read, and instantly I could tell that she had forgotten I was even standing there.

For the first time that day I felt alone. I wandered along the perimeter of the library, admiring the display of books like they were puppies in a pet store. Their clear wrap reflected the fluorescent lights in the ceiling and reminded me of stars. I walked around the room twice before making my choice and then I sat on the floor cross-legged and leaned my back against the shelves. I opened *Mary Poppins*, enjoying the satisfying creak the binding made, and took a whiff of the pages. They smelled a little like every person who had held it before me. I was completely lost in the world of the Banks children and what it must have felt like to wait for Mr. Banks to come home at the end of the day when I felt a hand on my shoulder. It was the librarian, motioning that the bell was ringing and that it was time to go. Without a second thought, my fingers glided over the bindings on the bottom shelf until my book found its home—bottom shelf, twelfth from the left.

Matilda

My mother dropped me off in front of a big brick building on the first day of school. She reached across and squeezed my shoulder, but I didn't look at her.

All of my life, I was the strong and tough one. I was there to make sure that Franny was safe and protected. When she looked lost in her own head I always knew how to bring her back. Kids never bothered her because they knew if they did, I would find them after school. I did everything I could to make her feel like she was the same as everyone else. I played that role for so long, I almost forgot what it felt like to be standing alone in a crowd of kids, unknown and forgotten and having to start from the beginning.

I swung my backpack over one shoulder and ignored the uneven feeling it created. I held a blank notebook in front of my chest like a shield and walked the steps up and into the building.

Many of the kids turned and stared and then ignored me. This was a college town where parents taught for several semesters and then moved away; these kids were used to seeing families come and go. I was walking along in the hallway, lost in that noise that only happens in a school hallway, when I felt her next to me. She was walking beside me, her hair desperately trying to evade the rubber band she had chosen to contain it.

"Hi," Lavi whispered. Her soft voice sailed over the chaos and settled effortlessly inside my ear. A half-smile shifted my tough girl look.

"We're in the same homeroom. I'll show you around." She led me to a room at the end of the hallway, and I sat down and slid my backpack underneath my seat. Lavi was whispering to the girl behind her, so I busied myself with decoding the scribbles on my desk as though they were ancient hieroglyphics. I learned that Nicole loves Danny, that Stephanie sucks, and that Joey is #1. I looked up just as a man shuffled in with a beaten up leather bag and an attendance book under one arm.

From the neck up, Mr. West looked menacing. From the neck down, he looked absurd. His scalp was completely shaven and his handlebar mustache was dyed jet black to match his shiny black goatee. This terrifying-looking head sat on a body that resembled an enormous egg that narrowed at the neck, exploded at the waistline, and tapered again at the ankles. I was mesmerized. The other children quieted down upon his arrival.

"We've gone over this. Silence—that is what I demand when I walk into a room. You will respond only when your name is called. As you know, if you respect me and obey my rules, we will not have any problems."

As he wrangled into the chair, his belly shifted so far upwards that his belt looked as if it was splitting him in two. I wanted to laugh, but I didn't, and my classmates were equally reserved.

"Susan Abrams?"

"Here."

"Tonya Bonitelli?"

"Here."

"Michael Browning?"

"Here."

That was how it went that first morning. That was my introduction to Mr. West's seventh-grade class. I sat in that room unknown, ignored, and fated into the hands of this tyrant. As each stranger's name was read off his list, my heart sank deeper. By the end of roll call, I understood how much I really hated my mother.

And as the weeks went by, it did not get any better.

The hours spent at school passed like days. Each minute felt as futile as trying to put back together the shell of a cracked egg. I became practiced at looking like I was in one place, when really I was somewhere very different. With Mr. West, however, there was little hope of entering the kind of daydream that was worth slipping off into.

"*The Gift of the Magi.* I expect that you have all read it. Please open your notebooks."

There was a shuffle of books and then quiet as everyone spread their things onto their desks. The unspoken rule was that the student with the highest stack of papers could avoid the eye of Wicked West as he had come to be called. I read the story the night before in my new bedroom, which had a slanted roof. I pushed my bed into a corner of the eave so that when I stretched my arms up, I could touch the ceiling. It made me feel really big and really small at the same time. It was the first time I could remember having a bedroom to myself and I couldn't help but enjoy the solitude that came along with it.

"Miss Wolley, can you answer the question?"

Hearing his voice forced my breath to quicken and I hoped I didn't look like I was panting. Quickly and with as little inflection as possible, I responded. "Could you repeat the question?"

"Certainly, Miss Wolley, but perhaps in the future you could try and stay with us so that I need not waste my or the class's time on useless repetition."

There was scattered nervous laughter in the middle section of the room. It came from the kids who were worried that sitting in the front would put them face-to-face with the enemy and sitting in the back would identify them as defiant. I was proud that at least I had taken a stand when it came to choosing my seat. Last row, third in from the window.

"I would like to know, Miss Wolley, how you define the concept of irony?"

"It's when you expect one thing and get another."

"Simple, but mildly interesting. Can you give the class an example of irony?"

"When you work all night on a homework assignment and then the teacher asks you something completely unrelated."

More snickering this time from my comrades in the last row.

"Amusing. This is a story about two people so much in love that they each sacrifice their most meaningful possessions so that the other can benefit. Tell me then, Miss Wolley, does this story suggest a different theme than the one of irony?"

I took a deep breath. I felt calm and relaxed and didn't feel taken off-guard anymore. "This is a story about how being in love makes you stupid. It makes you think stupid thoughts and make stupid choices."

He smiled and then put his face next to mine. The fluorescent lights in the ceiling made his mustache take on a blue tint and he came so close that I could see the small balls of spit that landed above his lip when he talked.

"Fascinatingly ordinary."

He turned to the board and clapped it with an eraser. White dust exploded into the air and then he began to write. The class settled down to copy his notes.

He knew he'd given me the biggest insult of my life.

The hour passed in a blur, but even at the end my face still felt flush. Our last class of the day was gym. I got my things together and slung my jacket over my shoulder, but on the way to the locker room I stopped in the bathroom where the mirror confirmed that I looked like a newborn pig, pink and swollen. Within a few minutes, she was standing beside me. I didn't want to turn to her so I just kept looking straight ahead into the mirror.

"He's a jerk. You can't listen to anything he says. I think it was good. The way you stood up to him," Lavi said.

I was grateful for that mirror and for a minute I imagined that my reflection was a separate person. I could just let her do the talking. Unfortunately, neither of us had very much to say. "I need to get out of here," I mumbled, as much to Lavi as to the Me in the Mirror.

"The day is almost over. We can do something after."

"No. I mean now. I need to get out of here now."

Lavi looked uncomfortable. She crossed her arms in front of her belly and methodically drew circles around the skin of her elbows.

"We can sneak out easily if we leave now. Leave it to me," I said.

Without giving her any more time to decide, I grabbed her things and pushed her out of the bathroom. There were still kids in the hallway, mostly those who waited until the last second to get to their classes. We mingled among them and then I guided Lavi around a corner and through a side door. We turned the block and lost sight of the school within minutes. As we neared the park, I saw two of my back-row friends smoking cigarettes beneath a tree. They waved to us and Lavi moved closer to me.

"So what do you want to do?" The wind lifted itself gently through her hair.

"I don't know. Maybe we could go in there." I pointed to a storefront.

"You mean Royal's? I don't know if that's such a good idea."

"Don't worry so much, Lavi. It will be fun."

A bell attached to the doorknob ringed in our arrival. An older woman at the counter looked up. At the same moment, her bifocals slipped off her nose and dangled precariously from their chain. She retrieved them and slipped them back over the bump on her nose.

"Hello, Laverne. Who is your little friend?" She raised her eyebrows, making the skin on her forehead ripple.

"This is Matilda. A friend from school."

"What brings you girls in today?" Her voice pierced the air. She reminded me of someone, but I could not think of whom.

"Matilda just moved here."

"Take a look around." Her arm swept across the counter and I could see blue spidery veins running from her wrist to her fingertips.

I left Lavi staring intently at a display of neon-colored thermoses and inched my way toward the back, stopping occasionally to touch a rubbery pink eraser or look at a new board game. The shelves were crammed with random things and it took some time to make my way. I could hear their voices in the front of the store where I had left them.

"How is your mother?"

I pictured Lavi head down, hands searching for her elbows.

I hurried farther down the aisle. I passed photo albums, colored pencils, and a display filled with pastel-colored stationery.

"And your brother? We haven't seen him around much."

For a moment I even wondered if Lavi was still there, but then I heard Mrs. Royal again. "Tell your mother to stop in some time and see me."

"How much for this thermos? The one with the footprints all over it," Lavi said.

I lingered by the stationery for another minute. And then I saw it. A box filled with paper the shade of purple so perfect it made your eyes glaze over when you looked at it. Without hesitation, I slipped the stationery into my backpack and quickly headed back to the front of the store. Mrs. Royal handed Lavi a bag just as I walked back up the aisle.

"Thank you Mrs. Royal." I smiled as I herded Lavi to the front door. "You have a very nice store."

"Come back any time girls!"

She was too busy wiping the smudge marks off her bifocals to notice the little bulge in my backpack.

Franny

The letters arrived promptly every week.

Leah placed them on my pillow but never asked any questions. They were lavender, addressed to me and postmarked from a small town I had never heard of. One time I thought about looking it up, but the idea of me going to find Matilda seemed silly. I was always the one being taken care of, not the other way around. So instead I stared at the envelope, tracing the swirl in the F of my name, which was so exaggerated it looked like a lollipop from a carnival. I tucked the notes away inside a manila envelope pasted to the back of Matilda's journal. My sister filled her letters with little tidbits of her life, things she ate for dinner, and what color she wanted to paint her room. She wrote like she talked and I would read her letters over and over before going to sleep, pretending I could hear her voice. I had gotten into the habit of using the purple pen to trace her words and soon the pages became so worn they began to fall apart in my hands, but it didn't matter because I had already memorized most of them. Especially the last line of each, which never changed. "Remember my promise."

I must have looked more distant than usual at dinner that evening. Engrossed in trying to spear as many peas as I could onto the tine of my fork, I dropped number five when Leah caught me off-guard. "Do you miss her?"

"Who?" I mumbled.

"Therese. Do you miss her?"

"I guess."

This was the first time Leah had brought up anything about my mother's disappearance. It startled me and I wasn't sure how to react.

"Therese used to pose for me."

I tried to imagine my mother posing for Leah. What had Leah seen in the curves of my mother's face? My teacher once made us spend a month drawing trees. He told us that once we could draw one from memory we would own that tree. Was that how it was for Leah?

"Do you want to see some of my drawings?" she whispered, as though she was exposing something to daylight for the first time.

Even at nine, I understood the extent of the gift Leah was giving me. To show me images of my mother from her eye before she was my mother.

Before she deserted me.

I nodded carefully, fearful that showing too much enthusiasm might make Leah change her mind. We got up from the table and I followed her, expecting her to take me to the room off the kitchen that was her art studio. Instead, she led me upstairs to the bedroom opposite mine. She patted down a corner of the duvet and motioned for me to sit. Her room was the color of hot chocolate and made me feel like I was wrapped in a blanket. She got down on her knees and searched underneath. The mattress creaked as I shifted. It sounded like a cat and I pretended that Leah had one living in the springs of her mattress that she snuggled with at night.

She pulled out a large worn maroon portfolio and released the rubber band that held it together. Then she slipped out the drawings stacked between sheets of tissue paper and arranged them on the floor so I could see. There were ten all together, all portraits of my mother. There was something about the very last drawing, something about her expression that made me feel that if I reached out to touch it, I would feel flesh instead of paper. Her back had been to Leah, but she turned her head so that her eyes were visible. She looked like she was caught in the middle of thought and I wondered how Leah was able to capture her in that kind of a moment, almost like she knew what my mother was thinking.

"You like that one," Leah said and pointed to the one I was staring at.

I nodded.

"I do too. I remember that day." She was quiet and looked down at her lap. "Therese means a lot to me." She reached back to retrieve the layers of tissue paper and suddenly an envelope appeared.

"What's that?" I asked, pointing to it and hoping that her generosity would continue.

She unhinged the flap and revealed its contents. Photographs of my mother smiling and laughing. In one photo, she was sitting at a kitchen table, her fingers laced around a coffee mug and she was looking straight at me. Leah put the drawings back into the portfolio. She returned the photographs to the envelope and handed me the one that had caught my eye.

That night I studied it, trying to understand what it was that bound Leah to my mother. Why it was that Leah was whom she had chosen to leave me with. I slipped it into Matilda's journal when I was through, but not before noticing that there was something very familiar about the setting. It was Leah's kitchen. Except instead of being stark white like it was now, it was painted all the colors of the rainbow.

I wished that I could ask Matilda what she thought about Leah and her sparkling white kitchen, which at one time had been more colorful than an entire box of crayons, but Matilda was not here and I had no idea how long it would take for her to make good on her promise of coming back for me.

So instead I turned to Eveyln. I had never had a friend before but with Evelyn, it was easy because she did all the work. She told me where to sit, what to say, and even invited herself over after school. One afternoon, as Evelyn and I sat on the porch waiting for her mother to pick her up, I decided to try and ask her about Leah's kitchen, but the words just jumbled up inside of my head, so instead I stared at the birds singing in the trees and started spelling what I heard—Twee Too Twee Too Twee.

"Leah's nice, Franny. You're lucky to live here," Evelyn said as if she was reading my mind.

Her backpack was propped between her legs and she made a pleasing clicking sound every time she ran her finger along the teeth of the zipper.

I nodded, focusing on the new song the birds were attempting. Cha Cha Cha Weeo Weeo Weeo.

"Is she an artist?" Evelyn asked as she pulled at a stray thread that clung to her pants.

"She teaches art at the college. Leah told me my mom used to be a secretary there. That's how they met."

"That's cool."

"I've seen some of her pictures. They're nice. Big."

"Oh yeah? I meant it's cool that your mom was a secretary. That's what I want to be when I grow up."

My mother had never complained about her work, but she always made it clear that it wasn't very exciting. I couldn't imagine someone would dream about growing up to become my mother. "Why?"

"Why, what?"

"Why would you want to be a secretary?"

"Oh, that. I guess I like the idea of being able to organize all day long. I think I would be good at it. But more than that, I like the secret part of being a secretary."

I turned to her. "Secret? What do you mean?"

"The word 'secret' in the beginning of the word secretary. You know, like secret business."

My eyebrows were frozen in place. "That's what you want to do when you grow up? Be involved in people's secret business?"

"Yes. That and also make sure that everything is always put away in its right place."

The sunlight was strong but laced with chill. I brought my knees in closer, hugging them. "What kind of secrets do you think a person who is a secretary would be able to uncover?"

"I bet lots of things. Like who is calling the boss who shouldn't be. Like where the boss goes when he takes a really long lunch. Like if the boss is stealing. Yes, that is definitely what I want to be when I grow up."

I imagined adult Evelyn, hair pulled back in a bun with glasses hanging off the bridge of her nose, stenography pad in hand. Then I thought about my mother. "Do you think maybe my mom discovered a secret and that's why she had to run away and leave me here?"

Evelyn shrugged her shoulders. "Maybe that's what happened. She came across some big secret and had to run. Maybe she couldn't risk your safety. Maybe Matilda was in on it or something. Did she leave behind a clue? Did she give you anything before she left?"

I thought about the two hearts my grandmother brought me because my mother had forgotten. I held them every night before going to sleep. My fingers rubbed over the gold so many times that I worried they might soon lose their shine. I thought about the journal filled with my sister's words. Her promises.

"No. She didn't leave me anything." My arms were wrapped so tightly around my knees that my shoulders began to ache.

"We'll figure it out, Franny. Don't worry. I'm always right about these things. I can just feel that it has something to do with a secret."

Evelyn's mother drove up and as she stood, her bag brushed across my fingers. A gale of wind appeared from nowhere and the two large maple trees across the street began to shake, spraying their helicopter seeds into the air. They spun with such purpose that for a moment it looked like they were alive. The sun disappeared behind a cloud and suddenly I felt overcome by a large, dark shadow. In that instant my stomach lurched and I felt lightheaded. I don't think I could have moved even if I wanted. I didn't know what exactly was so frightening to me.

All that I knew, without question, was that Evelyn was always right about these things.

Therese

Therese couldn't contain her excitement. Finally, she was going inside the little red house. She knocked on the door several times before Barbara came to let her in.

"It's you," she grumbled and turned back to the living room.

Mail was strewn across the floor, probably where it landed after Barbara lost interest. There were bottles of nail polish everywhere, some strategically covering cigarette burns on the Formica in the kitchen. The sink was filled with dishes that gave off a sickly sweet odor. She tried to cover her disgust but there was no need because Barbara hadn't given her a second look and had already returned to the living room and her spot across from the television.

The couch had so many colors weaved into it that it just looked gray. It cratered inward beneath her thighs and molded to her back. In front of her sat a tray table with an ashtray surrounded by bullets of charcoal-colored ash that had missed their mark. An episode of *General Hospital* was blaring from the television.

"How's it going?" Therese tried discreetly removing a pile of magazines from the only other seat in the room.

"Shhhhhhhh!" Barbara hissed. "This is the good part. That bitch Bobbie Spencer is switching test tubes so she can win Scotty back from Laura. She's going to trap him into being with her by pretending to get knocked up. What a whore."

Therese blinked, her face starting to ache from her forced smile. It wavered for just a moment, but she recovered quickly. She folded her hands in her lap and waited for a commercial. She started to speak again, hoping that Barbara wasn't as invested in children singing about how much they'd like to buy the world a Coke. "How are you doing with groceries?"

The large lump on the couch shrugged and pointed a perfectly painted red fingernail toward the refrigerator. Therese stood, made her way back to the kitchen, and opened the fridge. Inside were white Tupperware containers labeled with masking tape—meatloaf, tomato soup, and fried chicken all in Tim's writing. Food he had prepared for her for the week that had now gone bad. Nausea affected her mostly in her ears, and even though she felt dizzy and unsteady, she managed to throw everything out.

"What are you doing?" Barbara howled from across the room. Where she was seated, she had a clear view of the kitchen and Therese. "That's the food my Timmy made for me!"

"I'll go to the store now. What do you want?"

"I don't know. Timmy does the shopping. He knows what I like."

"I'm going to visit him today. Want to come?"

"I don't like hospitals. You find out when my Timmy will be coming home. And don't stay too long. I don't want you tiring him out."

Barbara turned back to the television. As Therese walked to the door, she took another look around and saw that the house had lovely arches separating the rooms and large windows that were covered with sheets. The floors were wood and with a good scrub they would return to their original honey color. The house had potential, the only problem being the very large obstacle bolted to the couch.

For the first time she started to feel pangs of doubt and it confused her to suddenly question the correctness of her path. She returned to the kitchen, closed her eyes, and took in a deep breath but, never having tried to spark a house before, all she could smell was must and nail polish. She settled her mind and became so focused she could almost hear Barbara exhaling puffs of smoke in the other room. Still, there was nothing. She envisioned hiding places and secret phone calls and the many lies that had simply been absorbed into the walls. She waited, refocused, and three seconds before she was about to give up, she felt it. It wasn't as clear as when it happened with a person, but there was no denying what she sensed. Beyond its shabby and dilapidated interior, it held secrets and there was no way she was going to turn back and give up now. Pushing her lingering doubts aside, she got into her car and drove to the hospital.

On her way in, she winked at Jim sitting at the front desk. He waved to her and she pretended not to notice the coffee cup he tipped over in the process. At the gift shop, she picked up a magazine and a pack of Wrigley's Big Red. When she walked into his room, he was propped up in bed watching television. His selection might have differed from his mother's, but his enthusiasm did not.

"C'mon, man! Mushrooms!! Mushrooms!!"

He tried to shake the remote control, which didn't give him much satisfaction since it was tied to the arm of the bed. In the meantime, Richard Dawson stared hopefully at a clearly perplexed contestant and repeated, "Name a topping you eat on pizza." The contestant looked dumbfounded and finally whispered, "Tomato sauce?" Richard Dawson snickered and shouted "Survey says . . ."

Therese never got to hear what the survey said because at that point Tim flung the remote so hard it slammed into the side of the bed and cracked. "Damn."

"Rough day?" she asked, easing herself onto the side of his bed and rubbing his knee with her hand.

"I guess." He slid himself up farther so that her hand now rested on his ankle.

She removed it and put it in her lap.

"I dropped my stuff off at your house and saw your mother."

Perhaps it was just her imagination, but his face seemed to take on a grayish hue and then, as if on cue, the telephone rang. Tim reached over to the night table to answer it. "Hello? Yes, Ma. Yeah, okay. Uh huh. I don't know. Bye, Ma."

He tried to hang the phone back up, but the cord became twisted. After he pulled several times, the whole base fell to the floor. Therese slid off the bed to retrieve it.

"She wants cigarettes. Marlboro Lights."

"I'll get them for her. I brought you a magazine."

"Thanks."

"What are the doctors saying? How much longer?"

"Just a few more days. They want to monitor me to make sure everything's stable. I'll get out of here soon."

"Thank goodness it was nothing more serious. I can't believe it happened while you were driving. You were lucky not to have hit anyone."

"Yeah. Lucky."

"Don't worry, I'll take care of things." She leaned over and kissed him on the forehead. He turned away, occupying himself with the cracked remote control.

Halfway down the hall she remembered that she had forgotten her gum. She walked back to his room and stood outside the door for a minute while she adjusted her skirt. And then she heard talking.

"Hi, Ma. I know you miss me. It will be okay. I promise I won't leave you."

The loyalty in his voice pushed at her chest and she hated herself for the tears that came. She thought about how different Tim was than the others. The words he was speaking to his mother rang in her ears, a picture of her own father slowly appearing like an image from an old Polaroid before her eyes.

Her hand was still on the doorknob, but she never went back into the room. Instead, she walked away, leaving her Big Red and her doubts behind.

Matilda

Sometimes my feelings fly around inside of me and I can't catch them. Other times, they find me when I am not looking. My stomach sinks and the space where it once was fills up and it feels like my insides will come shooting out of my mouth. Those are the times I hate to be alone.

Lavi and I were in the habit of buying french fries at McDonalds and bringing them home to eat after school. We sat in her kitchen on stools, hooking our feet around the legs and pouring salt into piles on small paper plates. Lavi liked the crunchy ones and I liked the soft, mushy ones, so most times we would just buy a large and share. She was lost in thought, using the tip of her fry to draw a heart in her salt pile. "My dad hates ketchup."

I looked up, surprised. It was the first time she had ever mentioned her father.

I found a soft one and dragged it through the ketchup, watching as it folded under the weight of the thick red sauce. She was quiet for a few minutes. "He comes back and forth. A lot."

I nodded, concentrating on a fry that was perfectly browned on the outside, but still soft on the inside. I had assumed that Lavi's father, like mine, was permanently out of her life.

"What about your dad?"

That was an easy question to answer. I didn't even need to think. "Nothing. I know nothing."

She stopped making circles in the salt long enough to catch me rummaging at the bottom of the container in search of more limp fries. "What do you mean 'nothing'? You must know something. His name? Where he lives? How long your mom knew him? Something?"

"Nope." I shook my head. "I know absolutely nothing." I started licking my fingertips. Long ago, I learned that my mother would reveal her secrets when she was ready. As a result, I stashed away my curiosity like a bill that wasn't due to be paid and didn't give it much more thought than that.

"Do you think he was a jerk? Like he was mean to her or something?"

I was about to share the one tiny shred of information I had managed to discover. I was going to tell her that my mother told me never to see or speak to my father, but before the words came out, the front door flew open and in walked Lavi's brother.

At sixteen, Daryl was lean and compact. Even when he smiled, his face looked compressed, as though it was too painful for the muscles to move into position. He sauntered in and tossed his books onto the counter.

"Hey," he said, clicking his head back once in acknowledgment of our presence.

"Hey," responded Lavi.

Daryl's hair was buzzed short, which made him look like he was on leave from the military, and the faded fatigues he wore added to the illusion. I didn't know much more about him because most times he would go into his room and slam the door when he came home. He had Lavi's coloring, but that was all. Everything else about him was the complete opposite. It was strange how two siblings could be so different. My mind wandered to thoughts of Franny, so I didn't notice when Lavi's mother walked in a few minutes later.

She was never home during Lavi and my french fry feasts, so this was the first time I had ever seen her. Her hair was curly like Lavi's, but the color had faded and it looked dry and wiry. What were probably once pretty tendrils now poked out from her hairnet like stiffened old fingers. She worked at the diner in town and still had on her apron, which was splattered with pale orange grease stains. Her eyes were wild and round and she was trying to speak, but all that came up were sputters of bubbled saliva. She didn't seem to realize I was even sitting there.

"How could you?" she wailed, sending sparks up my spine.

"Leave it alone, Ma," Daryl said, walking behind the kitchen bar and rummaging in the cabinet underneath.

"But you promised me. You promised." I watched as her face caved in and rage was replaced with despair. She began to sob and her shoulders shook as she cried into her hands.

"Stop it, Ma." He was still rattling around in the cabinet. I looked over at Lavi, who was staring down at the counter twisting a french fry between her fingers. Lavi's mother whimpered and suddenly Daryl snapped up from his crouched position. "Did you hear what I said, Ma? I said stop it!"

He pounded his fist onto the counter; it landed on a packet of ketchup and the thick, red sauce sprayed all over the white kitchen cabinets. The loud splat it made when it hit echoed through the room and I watched as the thickest part oozed down, leaving behind a pink watery trail. Lavi startled me by reaching for my wrist. She led me to the sliding glass doors and pushed me out. "Go home, Matilda," she whispered.

I pictured her in that house. I could hear the shrieks coming from inside and then I promised myself that someday, I would do exactly as she said I would find Franny, and I would go home.

But thinking about home made me sad. My favorite places to cry were in the shower or in the dark, but because my mother spent a lot of time in the bathroom, I started sneaking out at night to sit on the back porch. Even though the dark terrified me, I enjoyed the freedom I felt when I wasn't surrounded by walls, so I sat in the white chair with a flashlight in my hand and I cried.

I missed Franny.

I missed watching her listen to the sound cereal made when it mixed with milk and the way she would spell in her head without realizing that her lips were moving and giving all her secrets away. I thought about her toothbrush sitting in its cup and I wondered if she remembered to make her bed and then I thought about the way her face must have looked when she realized she was alone. I wrote her letters every week, but I didn't say much. Mostly I wrote so she wouldn't forget me. Maybe I wrote so she would forgive me. I sat in the white plastic chair with my arms crossed and tucked into my armpits, hoping the rhythm of the crickets would distract me from all of it.

The chill in the air felt good and the sky was clear with stars pulsing above me like millions of blinking white Christmas lights. Then I heard the sound of the sliding glass door opening on the other side of the porch. I twisted my wrist into a shard of moonlight and read my watch. 2:30 a.m. Who would be up on Lavi's side of the porch at this time of night? I heard the muted sound of ice cubes hitting each other. Whoever it was sat at the edge of the porch and then I saw shoes: army boots going halfway up the shin with laces spilling out on either side. I was pretty certain he didn't realize I was there, and for a moment I contemplated sneaking back inside. But I didn't. Instead, I stood up and crossed to his side so that I faced him directly.

If he was startled, he didn't let on. He acted as if it was completely normal to see me in the pitch-black hours of the morning and looked up and grinned. "Hello, Mytilda." He drew out the "a" in my name, making it sound like I was his possession.

"Hey, Daryl." I wrapped the blanket tighter around myself.

The light was on in the living room and it streamed onto the porch, making the setting feel unnatural, as if it was a scene from a play. He held the glass in his hand and swirled it around, amused by the ice cubes chasing each other. "Do you like milk?"

"No."

"I like it with lots of ice cubes. I like it so cold that it hurts when it goes down." He continued to swirl the glass and stared into it as if it were about to reveal some deep hidden truth. "You and Lavi have become pretty good buddies."

I didn't want to sit beside him so I leaned up against the divider.

"She tells me it's just you and your mom. So where's your dad?" He drew himself away from his glass and turned to look at me.

"I don't have a dad. It's just me and my mom."

"Your mom's a real looker. Can't imagine why it is she couldn't keep your dad around." He snickered.

I felt my cheeks turn red. I wanted to ask where his father was. Why it was that I heard screams coming from his house. I wanted to tell him that he didn't scare me. I wanted to take that glass and smash it into his face. But I said nothing.

"Matilda, what are you doing out here at this time of night? Get inside right now."

My mother was standing behind me with her hands on her hips. She wore a silk lavender robe that tied at her waist and stopped above her knees. When she tilted her head, a piece of hair fell in a perfect wave against her check. Her face still held the sweetness of sleep and the softness took me by surprise.

Daryl seemed to be enjoying himself because suddenly his eyes were open wide and he licked his mouth. His lower lip hung down like a fat pink worm. "Hey there, Miss Wolley."

She looked down at him and I recognized her expression. It was the one she got when someone tried to cut her off on line at the bank. "From now on, if you want to speak with my daughter you can do so at a more reasonable hour."

She waved at him. Maybe he thought she was waving goodbye. To me it looked like she was shooing at a gnat that was annoying her. He waved back and smiled.

She took me by the elbow and led me back to our side of the porch. She didn't let go until we were safely inside and then pulled me towards her and whispered in my ear. Her words came out in soft little puffs that made the hairs on the back of my neck stand up.

"Stay. Away. From. That. Boy."

I went upstairs and got into bed. I fell asleep quickly that night, and the last thought I remembered having was that maybe Daryl wasn't that bad after all.

In fact, maybe, he was absolutely perfect.

We didn't speak much after that night. Maybe she felt badly about it or maybe she was just tired of making macaroni and cheese—or cooking for two, in general. Whatever the reason, when she came home from work a few days later, she insisted that we dress up and go out for a nice dinner.

I wore a black t-shirt and jeans with a hole in the knee, chosen specifically because I knew it was an outfit she hated. I waited outside while she got ready, amusing myself by staring into the bark of an enormous oak tree. It was only when I got close enough that I realized it was crawling with angry and determined black ants. From a distance, it looked like any other tree.

She finally came outside smelling of peaches and looking like a flamenco dancer with her hair smoothed and tied behind her neck. We got into the car and drove in silence but I could tell she was distracted, as if she wasn't seeing the road ahead. I stuck my finger into the hole in my pants and wiggled it around.

The restaurant was at the top of a hill and it felt like we were driving through a mountain of trees to get there. For a second, I wondered if maybe she had actually picked a place I might like—but then I got a better look. It was a steak house with its name burned in big black letters across the entrance. It was supposed to look like a log cabin, but instead of real wood, the logs were plastic. Inside, strands of white Christmas lights weaved around two fake Ficus trees, the leaves of which were covered in dust. All it did was remind me of the stars in the sky and how much I would have rather been outside and alone. We were seated at a table beside the only redeeming aspect of the restaurant—a working fireplace crackling and spitting orange sparks that drowned out the country music seeping from the speakers embedded in the wooden paneled walls. She looked over the menu, nodding her head every few minutes.

The waitress came over. She wore a light brown suede skirt with beaded fringe that dangled above her knee and clinked together every time she moved. Pinned to her chest was a big cowboy hat that read DEBI.

"What can I get you ladies?"

"I'll have the Pioneer Prime Rib and a large Bug Juice."

She scribbled in her note pad and I wondered if she thought the names of the meals were as stupid as I did. They both turned to me.

"I'll just have a burger, thanks," I said and flipped closed the menu.

"One Pioneer Prime and one Bronco Billy coming right up." She took our menus and walked away, tugging down her skirt and waving to the bartender as she passed.

"I know things have been hard for you, Matilda, but let's try and have a nice night, okay?"

I was about to tell her how hard things had been for me. I was about to tell her that I hated what she had done and I hated where we lived and I hated steak houses. I felt it all well up inside me, but then suddenly we were interrupted.

"Terrrryyyy!" a male voice crooned. He walked to our table and put his hand on my mother's shoulder. The other he kept in his pocket to jingle his keys.

She smiled warmly. "Hello, Professor Royal."

"Terry, I had no idea that you would be here tonight."

So now she was Terry. Never in my memory had anyone called my mother Terry.

"Yes, I remembered your recommendation and thought I would bring my daughter." She motioned across the table to me.

A woman suddenly materialized beside him and extended her hand. "Let me introduce myself. Mrs. Dorothy Royal. Nice to meet you." The spidery veins looked terribly familiar.

"Nice to meet you, too, Mrs. Royal." My mother shook the tips of her fingers. Professor Royal folded both hands behind his back, which made his belly jut out and hit the side of our table.

"Hello, Matilda," Mrs. Royal said.

"You know my daughter?" my mother asked.

"Yes, she came into my shop a few weeks ago with her friend."

A memory I would have preferred to forget.

"I haven't seen you since, Matilda. Please know you are always welcome."

She dipped the spectacles on her nose in my direction and for a second I thought that maybe she could see me sinking deeper into my seat. Or worse—she had x-ray vision and knew exactly where the little box of purple stationery was hidden.

"She mentioned your shop. It sounds lovely. We will have to come together some time." She raised her glass to the Royals and I watched as the bug juice came dangerously close to spilling.

"Have a wonderful evening, Terry," Professor Royal said as he led Mrs. Royal to their table.

Debi came over with our meals. I piled as much of the fixings onto my hamburger as I could; when I finished, I could barely fit the sandwich into my mouth. My mother held her fork in her hand daintily, as though it were a feather. A slice of onion slipped out from the bun and slapped on to the table loudly. She looked up, but didn't say a word. I couldn't help myself. "So now you're Terry?"

She smiled and shook her head. "He's just someone I work with, Matilda."

"I see that, Mom. I just didn't know that now you are Terry. It would be nice if you let me in on these kinds of things every once in a while." A pickle escaped from my hamburger and I finally put it back on the plate and gave up on the possibility of being able to eat the monstrosity I had created.

She was quiet for a few minutes. "Matilda, I have and always will take care of you. And that is all you need to know." Then she sliced into a piece of steak that was so rare, it almost looked blue.

"What about Franny? Do you always take care of her, too?"

The sound of her knife as it scraped against the plate screeched in my ear.

"C'mon, Terry. Did it just get too hard? Is that why you left her behind like a pair of old shoes?"

She stared down at her plate and for a second it looked as if she closed her eyes. "You don't understand," she whispered.

"I'm pretty sure I do." I pushed my seat away from the table and stood by the coat rack, waiting for her to finish and pay the bill. I wished I had the courage to walk all the way home in the black night air, but I didn't really know where I was so I waited as she ate every last bite on her plate. For a moment, as we drove home, the silhouette of her face against the dark night looked soft and I wanted to say something to fix it, but just as I was about to speak, her lips pursed and her knuckles hardened around the steering wheel and I realized that I had just run headfirst into another one of my mother's very well kept secrets.

Therese

Therese fumbled with the key.

She could hear the television and then the loud crashing sound of metal, which was followed by a ringing noise. She imagined the object that had fallen was spinning on the floor, growing slower, sloppier, and quieter with every rotation. When she finally pushed the door open, she found Tim on his knees collecting popcorn that had landed like shrapnel all over the living room floor. Therese put her bags down and joined him, but he would not look at her, instead whispering quietly that he had told his mother about the baby. It was the sound of apology in his voice that made her cringe.

Barbara was standing now, her arm raised and pointed at Therese, "Don't think it ends here." She stormed into her bedroom, her weight sloshing back and forth from the force of her exit. Therese looked back at Tim. The red marks on his face were in the perfect shape of a hand. She reached out, but he pushed her away so she left him alone.

Barbara kept to herself for days, and the house felt different without her at its center. Therese and Tim developed a routine. Every night she sat on the kitchen counter, legs dangling, while he did the dishes. She liked watching him cook and was amazed that he never used a recipe; he made up the steps as he went along, mixing ground meat and adding water and breadcrumbs until it reached the consistency he liked. His big hands became delicate as they rolled perfectly round little meatballs the size of golf balls. The house smelled of onions and tomatoes and basil and sometimes she would forget that it wasn't just the two of them.

She tried to help him clean up afterward, but when she joined him his movements became awkward. So she left him to his chores and returned to the counter to watch. Sometimes he brought her fresh fruit from the store, which she ate while he cleaned.

"How long have you been cooking?" Her teeth slid across the shiny skin of her apple and then embedded into the white flesh.

"As long as I can remember. It's never been something my mother was good at and it comes pretty easily to me."

A stray fork fell to the bottom of the sink, creating the sharp tinny noise of metal on metal.

"You are good to her."

"She's given up everything for me. It's the least I can do."

Therese crunched loudly into her fruit. "Has it always been just the two of you? Where's your dad?"

"We don't talk about him." Suddenly he spun around and pointed a soapy finger in her direction. "I mean it, Therese. Don't go sticking your nose where it doesn't belong! You leave Mama out of this. Don't start asking her all your questions."

"Okay, okay!" she shouted, lifting her hands into the air as though he had just pulled a gun on her. He turned back to the sink and shifted his focus back to washing the dishes. She stood to leave, the mangled remains of her apple lying brown and limp on the kitchen counter.

He hadn't told her very much about his mother, but she was good at sensing things, and her instincts told her that whatever was between them was heavily unbalanced. There were no pictures of Tim as a child; in fact, she had yet to see evidence that he had even been one. Sometimes at night while he slept, she could hear him murmur, but when she touched him he would pull away.

His secrets consumed her.

The next day at work, she was so busy thinking about Tim and his mother that when the shock came, it took her by surprise. Its intensity ripped down her arms, forcing her to knock over the cup of pens she kept on her desk. She shifted onto the edge of her seat, stretched out her legs, and tried to kick the pens that had fallen closer with her foot. When that failed, she got down on her knees and crawled underneath the desk to use her fingers to search along the floor. She was so involved she didn't realize someone was standing in front of her desk waiting for her to reemerge.

It was intriguing to experience someone from the feet up. The edge of the desk cut off her view so that she could only see the woman below the knees. Therese edged in closer, examining the uneven hem of the woman's skirt. The material was a long, billowing silk that seemed to float as though a breeze was coming up from the planks of the floor. The shoes were pink with pale ribbon laced up the ankle. "Are you okay under there?" The sound of the voice matched the gracefulness of the feet.

Therese pushed back and emerged from beneath the desk.

Was she real? Therese shook off a compelling desire to touch her.

"Therese, can you get Professor Dugan the C12 forms? Human Resources asked her to fill them out," said Maryann, the secretary seated behind her.

Therese moved carefully and began looking for the papers, never completely turning her back, fearing the woman would disappear. Her hair looked like it should have been on a doll's head instead of a person with curls of yellow satin ribbon too perfect to be real.

It took longer than it should have to locate the papers, partially because she could not take her eyes off their visitor. When she finally handed them over, she gave in to her curiosity and used her other hand to tug hard on a tendril that looked especially flawless.

"Ouch!" Professor Dugan shouted, rubbing her scalp with the pad of her thumb.

"Sorry. Just making sure you're real."

"Maybe next time you could ask?" Professor Dugan continued to rub the back of her neck, but this time she smiled.

"There is just something about you . . ."

The woman was silent.

"We're going to be good friends," Therese said as mild sparks danced up and down her forearms.

"We are?"

"Yes," nodded Therese, finally certain of herself. "Very good friends."

The woman's eyes lit up. "Then you should probably know my name. It's Leah. Leah Dugan." She turned to leave and as she did, she winked and waved her pen in the air as if it were a magic wand.

Therese replayed the scene over and over in her mind. That day she forgot to answer the phone, open the mail, or lock her desk drawer when it was time to go home. Hours later, after agonizing over every detail of the exchange, Therese still wasn't sure if the woman, who had fallen in such a jolting way into her life, was really only just a figment of her imagination.

She began taking her breaks at 2:15 in the afternoon because that was when Leah finished teaching. They got mugs of steaming hot tea from the faculty lounge and found a spot to sit. Their favorite place was a small room off the main entrance that had once been used as a library. It was still surrounded by bookshelves and had a fireplace on one end that the janitor always remembered to light. The desks were replaced with large leather easy chairs and, on most afternoons, she and Therese had the place to themselves.

The beginning of the friendship passed quickly; before they realized it, they were in the middle of it. Miscommunication or awkwardness did not exist between them, just the intimacy of connection. Some days they sat beside each other in silence, and other times they spoke over each other, finishing each other's sentences. Almost always, they would sit close enough so that Leah could lay her hand on Therese's belly. They talked a lot about babies and Leah confided how much she wanted to have a child. Sometimes there was desperation in her voice and Therese couldn't help but wonder if this was the same way her own mother had sounded. When she tried to encourage Leah, all she would say was that she did not know if she was capable of caring for another person. Therese sensed the depth of her wounds and the stories came slowly, and affected Leah physically, almost as though she was reliving them with each word. They were about a father who, when Leah was nine, betrayed her innocence. The number rang in Therese's head. Dressed to the nines. Nine lives. Cloud Nine. But for Leah, nine was when her world fell apart and, even though Therese had never met her own father, she felt an instant bond. Sometimes they would hold hands and not speak at all. Those moments were both the saddest and happiest for Therese.

They spent a lot of time talking about the baby, and Therese confided that her favorite part of pregnancy was the frequent flutters she experienced throughout the day. Sometimes she wondered if she had swallowed a caterpillar and that a beautiful Monarch would float out of her instead of a baby. Leah sat close and Therese loved that she smelled like wild flowers. She laid her head on Therese's shoulder and closed her eyes, smiling each time the baby kicked her hand.

One day they were sitting in their usual position, the sound of crackling bark coming from the fireplace. Normally, Therese would stare into the flames, drawn in by the vibrancy of the colors, but today she was tired. She closed her eyes and tilted her head back, sinking into the softness of the leather. It always seemed that when Therese was calm, the baby was energized, and today it was twirling and twisting and swirling and then, suddenly, Leah pulled her hand away. Therese jumped, startled by the sudden separation.

"What?" Therese asked, looking alarmed.

"Nothing," Leah said.

"Tell me."

"What is Tim like? I mean really like?"

Therese lifted her body upward and, as she began to speak, Leah reached out to hold her hand, like a child about to cross a dangerous intersection. "I've told you. He works at a supermarket. He likes to cook. He is devoted to his mother."

"I need to know more. What kind of man is he? When you look into his eyes, what do you see?" Leah clutched her hand tighter.

"Why are you doing this to me? Why are you asking me this?" Therese pulled her hand away and lifted the mug of tea that was sitting on the table beside her. The warmth that was so comforting moments ago now made her feel hot, suffocated. She tried to shake the memory of the first time she saw Tim—tried to erase the fact that she was so overcome that she neglected to spark him. She couldn't admit to Leah that when she looked into his eyes now, she wasn't really sure what it was that she saw, but that her instinct told her he was hiding something. And her instincts were never wrong.

"Because I need to know that both you and the baby will be safe with him."

Therese began to unbutton her sweater. Her fingers felt clumsy and fat, but she finally managed to slip the last button through its hole. "What are you talking about?"

Leah turned away. As she stared off into the distance, her body seemed to collapse into the frame of the couch. She looked small, like she might suddenly disappear. Her lovely golden curls were suddenly flat and limp and stuck to the side of her head. She closed her eyes and winced as if what she was seeing was simply too horrible to bear. When she finally spoke, her breathing was labored and her voice sounded like she'd just swallowed fire. "Just make sure you know who he really is. Because Therese. You are going to have a girl."

Then she laid her head on Therese's belly and wrapped her arms as tightly as she could around her waist.

Franny

Dear Matilda,

I've been trying to write every night. Sometimes I just write the date at the top of the page and draw pictures. Other times I write "Dear Matilda" and pretend that I will send you my letter.

I named one of the fairies in my room after you. Leah told me the story of the night they came. She kept hearing a scratching noise in the room but every time she walked in and turned on the light, the noise would disappear. She looked around but all she could find was a small little hole that not even a mouse could fit through. So she turned off the light and fell asleep. When she woke up it was dark and she forgot where she was and she got up to turn on the light but then she got a feeling that maybe she shouldn't. So she sat back down and she waited. And then she saw them.

Flying all around the room coming from that little crack in the wall that not even a mouse could fit through. They flew past her nose and over her knuckles. She said it tickles when they fly close to you. The next thing she knew they all flew back to their spots on the wall and didn't move again. I keep waiting for them to fly for me. After I finish writing I try and stay up for as long as I can but I haven't seen them yet. One time I thought I saw the one closest to my pillow turn her head. That's the one I named after you.

I made a friend at school. Her name is Evelyn and I like having her around. I've told her about you and she wants to meet you.

I know you will come for me soon because you never break your promises.

Love, Franny

Franny

I didn't mail my letters.

I believed so strongly that my sister would return, I simply copied them into her journal to save. But as the weeks passed I started to worry. Was she really going to come back for me?

Maybe Leah sensed my concern because even though she was spending more time at the college, she started taking me with her on weekends. The art building was my favorite and she let me look inside the rooms. I poked around the storage closets and she would let me have an eraser. They were different than the hard pink ones I was used to because they were gray and stretchy and fun to roll into different kinds of shapes.

She took me into the art studio where students were working at their easels. It always got quiet when she walked into a room and some of them looked at her with the same expression that Matilda had when she first met Leah. The studio had a center area where Leah told me the model sat. Easels were clustered together in different groupings and the light was the kind that made the dust flying through it sparkle like glitter. I liked the quiet of the art studio and how even if there were people inside, they were too engrossed in their work to notice me. The sound of pencil moving across paper calmed me.

One day we walked down a hallway and I smelled something that seemed familiar, but was different than the smell of charcoal and paper that I had grown used to. I was so curious that I couldn't help but peek inside the room I assumed it was coming from. Immediately, I felt a waft of warm air hit my face and then my eyes focused on an enormous shimmering rectangle.

A swimming pool.

I had never seen an indoor pool before. The possibility of being able to swim any time you wanted amazed me and the whole rest of the day, I closed my eyes and tried to conjure up that smell.

The next afternoon, Leah was late getting home. When she walked through the door, she handed me a brown paper bag. Inside was a bathing suit with the tag still dangling from the strap. After that, we went once or twice a week. A modern athletic complex had been built several blocks away so the pool at the college was almost always deserted.

It didn't take long for us to develop a routine. Leah always brought her sketchbook and sat on the bleachers watching me. The first thing I did was slip in up to my chest, holding my breath and feeling the funny sensation of being half wet and half dry. I liked running my hands around and making big angry circles and then lifting them up high to let the water drip down, making tiny splashy ones. My hands looked softer and cleaner underwater.

Once my body got used to the temperature, I would flip over on my back so that I could tilt my head and let the water fill my ears. The bathing suit Leah had chosen for me was turquoise and I would pretend that I blended into the pool so well that no one would ever be able to find me. Floating was easy and soon my lips would stop spelling and then it would get so quiet that I could forget that I was in a swimming pool in a room in an art building in a place far away from my sister and mother.

I would stay submerged for as long as I could.

Leah didn't seem to mind. She didn't tap her foot the way that many of the grownups in my life did. She looked up at me from time to time, but mostly she was busy with her sketchbook.

One day I stayed in for so long that every fingertip on my hand shriveled. Leah was engrossed in her work and didn't notice me coming out of the water. I sat down and watched her draw and then for some reason started thinking about oranges—specifically the one she was working on the very first time we met.

"Why do you draw things so big?"

She looked up for a minute then back down. "Because not everything appears as it is and if I draw really big I know I won't miss any of the details. It's my way of getting to know something."

I didn't say anything.

"I don't like surprises," she added.

I nodded because I completely understood and then I looked over at her paper. The sketch was of a young girl being pushed on a swing and, aside from the drawings of my mother, it was the only image of hers that I had ever seen that wasn't blown up to enormous proportions.

"That's me."

She nodded.

"How come you didn't make me big?"

She smiled and then whispered so softly I couldn't be sure that I heard correctly. "Because I already know you."

That night I didn't write a letter to my sister and it made me feel happy and sad and confused, so the next morning as Leah and I were eating waffles, all I wanted to think about was the maple syrup that drenched each bite.

"Can you say the alphabet backwards?"

"What?" I mumbled, enjoying the sweetness that filled my mouth.

"The alphabet. Can you say it backwards?"

I contemplated another bite but instead took a breath.

"Z Y X W V U T S R Q P O N M L K J I H G F E D C B A."

Leah was quiet.

"That's amazing, Franny. How do you do that so fast?"

"I see the alphabet. I see letters. In my head."

My cheeks got warm and I felt like I had opened the front door without first asking who was there. I had spoken too easily and without thought and I wished that I could take it all back.

"You see them? In your head."

I wondered if she was teasing me. But it was Leah. Leah with a silent H at the end of her name and she would never tease me.

"You are an incredible person, Franny. You see details that no one else notices."

I drew circles in the maple syrup. "What was my mom like? I mean . . . from before?"

She lowered her mug of tea. "Therese has always been determined."

"Were you good friends?"

"There is nothing I would not do for her. Nothing."

"Why did she leave me with you?"

Leah looked down and then shifted in her seat. "It's complicated, Franny. One day I will try and explain it to you."

I mashed the leftover crumbs of my waffle into the syrup. I probably should have stopped asking questions, but it was almost like they were sitting inside my mouth and I had no choice but to spit them out. "What about your parents? What are they like?"

Up went the mug. "I don't speak to them anymore."

Was Leah like me? Did her parents leave her, too? I couldn't look at her anymore so I looked down.

Leah laced her fingers around the mug. There was a pause before she spoke again. "My father hurt me, Franny. He hurt me when I was a little girl." She looked like she wanted to say more but instead took another sip of her drink. "It would be great if everyone was like your letters. That way you could always predict what they were going to say and do."

I nodded and looked back down at my plate. It had designs around the rim. Little yellow flowers that looked distorted under the film of syrup.

She reached over and took my chin in her hand, tilting my face so that my eyes were on hers. "You are a very special little girl."

I turned away from her because the one thing I did not want to be was Special. When teachers at school told me I was special all it meant was that I had to be taken out of the classroom to sit in small offices to talk about why I was special. It made me feel different from the other children when all I ever really wanted was to blend in and disappear so that no one would notice me. So many times I wished I could be invisible so that I could make the world stop moving so fast, stop sounding so loud, so that I could just spell to my heart's content. One time I heard two of my teachers talking about me and they used the words "on the spectrum." Later, I asked my grandmother what they meant. She said that a spectrum is a beautiful band of colors like a rainbow and that was a perfect description of me and, even though I wanted to believe her, I didn't. Deep inside, I was pretty sure that being special was the real reason my mother had left me behind.

She probably said it to make me feel good but it didn't. It made one whole side of my body go numb. For the first time in a long time, I started to feel it on my lips. I shook my head, trying to make it stop but I couldn't. The letters slipped past and I let it happen. I let them pour out of me, too overwhelmed by the moment to make them stop. They popped out of my mouth like gumballs dropping out of a candy machine. Big, ugly letters. Steady, mean, constant, and loud enough for Leah to hear.

S-P-E-C-I-A-L.

That afternoon I tried ignoring the Things that were swirling inside of me. Things that used to have color but were now so muddled they looked like the paint water I used the first day I met Leah. It felt like the closer I got to her, the farther I moved from my sister. And no matter how I tried, I could not seem to think of one without the other.

I am not sure why I decided to do what I did. I don't think I realized the consequences, but moments are so fleeting that sometimes it's hard to know their value. If I had, I never would have taken such a risk.

Leah was working later than usual and Evelyn was engrossed in a school project. I felt a little ball bouncing in my stomach and as the afternoon wore on, the ball got bigger. I tried walking into different rooms, but that only made it bounce more.

Not only did I miss Matilda, but I missed my mother.

I was dreaming of her at night. Quick little visits. She never spoke, and when I reached out to touch her, she turned and walked away. Some nights I would wake up to the sound of random letters spilling from my lips, shaking me from my dreams. The sadness came so slowly that I didn't notice until it was too late and then it was all I could feel.

I was alone in the house that afternoon, the bouncing ball in my belly so loud that I could hear it in my head. I went into Leah's room and sat on her bed. Then I crawled underneath and pulled out the maroon portfolio. I unhooked the string that held it together and pulled out the drawings Leah had made of my mother. I sat on the floor and spread them around in a big circle so that everywhere I turned I saw a different image of her. I pulled my knees in close, wrapped my arms around myself, and rocked back and forth until the bouncing ball finally stopped. I collected the drawings, put them back inside the portfolio as neatly as I could, and slid them back under the bed.

Things would have happened differently if it hadn't been so cold that day. I was wearing my big gray sweater, the one Leah picked out for me with designs around the wrists that looked like a bracelet made of O's. I slipped the portfolio under the bed but one of the loops got caught on something. I struggled for a few minutes, fumbling to pry myself loose, and that's when I felt it. A second manila envelope stuffed between the slats of the bed. I don't know what compelled me to loosen it from its hiding place but that's what I did and then I opened it.

More drawings. But these weren't of my mother.

These were images of Leah.

Her features drawn with amazing delicacy, as if the artist didn't want to press too hard against the page because doing so might hurt her. Lovely, clean lines that suddenly disappeared when it came to her hair and then the gracefulness was replaced by angry thick black strokes that crept toward her cheek like the hands of a gloved robber. They were random and brutal and frightening and in the corner of each drawing was a name. Lionel. LIONel.

The bouncing ball started bouncing again. I wished I had never opened that envelope. I quickly stuffed the drawings back in, but the bouncing got bigger. And when I looked up again, she was there, standing in the doorway.

Looking through me.

She didn't say anything that night, but her eyes were different. They were dull, diluted. Like when my grandmother mixed too much milk into her tea. It was as if something inside of her was frozen and I wished I could take her out into the sun, like a grape popsicle melting and running down my arm, but nothing I did made it any better. She still took me swimming, but didn't bring her sketchbook. Instead, she sat on the bleachers, legs crossed at the ankle and hands folded in her lap. She stared vacantly down at the deck of the pool, counting squares, towels, puddles, I did not know. I did what I could to make her smile. I jumped and splashed and made silly faces. She turned to face me, but it never seemed like she saw me. I didn't know what else to do so I stopped doing anything.

We went about our routine. I came home from school and we made our meals. I stood beside her peeling potatoes or snapping green beans or ripping lettuce. When I first arrived, she taught me how to do things in the kitchen with her hand over mine, but now I was on my own. Few words passed between us. We ate at the table in that stark white kitchen, both of us lost in our thoughts. If I accidentally touched her hand, she would jump back.

She took a few days off from work and I think she slept while I was at school. Evelyn and I sat in the library during lunch. She read books, but I just thought about Leah at home, lying in that bed with those terrible drawings stuffed into its springs. She was always awake when I came home from school. I rushed in each afternoon like a nurse checking to see if her patient's fever had broken, and she greeted me at the door, but each day was the same as the last. At night I talked to the fairies, begging their forgiveness for the hurt I had brought to Leah. I took the gray sweater that I loved so much and stuffed it into the garbage bin outside. When I slept I dreamed about the angry black strokes of her hair and sometimes they would reach out to strangle me and I would wake up gagging.

I knew she wasn't sleeping at night. Each night, I closed my door and climbed into my bed. She waited until she thought I was asleep and then she went into the bathroom and turned on the shower. I listened to the water running through the pipes in the walls, the sound of waves rushing around me like liquid wind, but it wasn't enough to muffle her sobs. I didn't know what to do, but I knew I needed to do something because I wasn't willing to lose her. I thought about talking to Evelyn, but I didn't want to share Leah's secret with anyone. As hard as I could, I wished for Matilda because she always knew exactly what to do.

Days and nights passed and Leah slipped farther away. Finally, one evening I waited until she was in the shower and then I snuck downstairs. I opened the door to her art studio, which was so cold and dark that, for a moment, I wondered if the room missed Leah as much as I did. I found a large pad of paper and ripped out a sheet. There were pieces of charcoal lying on the table so I sat down and started to write. The letters were big and black and each time my arm moved, the darkness rubbed itself onto me but I didn't care. Even though I didn't know what to say, my hand moved anyway.

I took the paper and ran, feeling it flutter behind me as I went upstairs and straight into her room. Kneeling in front of her bed, I felt underneath, then took them out and spread them around me. My hands were covered in black and I left fingerprints, perfectly gray ovals that reminded me of grapes all over the drawings. I didn't care that I was ruining his pictures of her. I stamped my hands over them harder, tears splashing down on to the paper, making the spots where they landed ripple and fading the angry black lines to gray.

And then more because I could not stop.

I smudged and I pounded and I fought until I forgot where or who I was and then suddenly I remembered because I felt her beside me. Her hair was wet, and when it touched my cheek it cooled me. She was rocking me, kissing the top of my head. When she spoke the words got lost between us, but I understood.

"I will never leave you again, Franny."

I don't know how long we stayed that way, but when we separated I was still clutching the paper. And when I let it go, it dropped from my hand and crumpled to the floor. The black letters were now covered in a delicate swirl of gray and it was hard to read, but I could still read what I had written.

F-O-R-G-I-V-E M-E

After that night she came back to me. At the pool she waved from the bleachers every time I popped out of the water. She took me to the grocery store and let me pick out things that I liked. I chose bright green lollipops that made my lips pucker so much that I looked like a fish when I ate them. She thought it was funny that I loved them so much. I liked to see her smile.

We sat in the living room together, me on the couch and she in a rocking chair, moving back and forth, floating through the stillness that surrounded us. Then one night she turned on the radio and a melody that sounded like bells streamed around us and I saw that she had her sketchbook in her hand. It took me a few minutes to realize I was her subject. She was looking at me closely, her gaze brushing down the slope of my nose and slipping across the curve of my lips. No one had ever paid such close attention to me before and it made me feel stiff. I was scared that if I moved too much, she would lose interest in me and then I would go back to being who I was before. So I stayed perfectly still, my word search book laying flat on my lap.

"Franny, don't forget to breathe." She kept looking down at her page and then back up at me, her hand moving as if it wasn't under her control anymore. "Has anyone ever drawn you before?"

I shook my head but then I couldn't remember what position it had been in before.

"Just be yourself. Work on your word search book. Forget I'm even here."

Even if I wanted, I could never forget.

I tried to find the same position but nothing felt right, so I stared back down at the puzzle I was working on, waiting for the words to jump out at me like they usually did. Most people circled the entire word, but I circled each individual letter. It took me longer and looked more confusing, but I liked the idea of singling out every letter separately.

"Have you always liked letters?"

I nodded.

"It's okay to talk, Franny. Really, I want you to be yourself."

She got off the rocking chair and sat on the other end of the couch. Then she swiveled around so that she was looking directly at me, her sketchbook balanced on her crossed legs.

"I have always known how to spell." I felt the hotness creep into my face.

"That's kind of how I feel about drawing. I've done it for as long as I can remember and it's always been the one thing I could count on. No matter how bad things got."

The music on the radio changed and now it sounded like rain hitting the windowpanes of an empty house. Leah took a breath and then held the sketchbook close to her chest. She closed her eyes and her head swayed delicately to the music. I wished I could freeze that moment so that it would never end, the two of us with the music playing in the background, and a half-finished sketch of me in her hand. I wanted things to be easy, to hide so that nothing bad could ever happen. But something new and strange was growing inside me, taunting me until it was hard to breathe, and I knew I had to speak. I ignored the lump in my throat and took a deep breath.

"Who was he?"

The music was over and the announcer was naming the piece that had just played. I wondered if she'd heard me. Her eyes were still closed, but she stopped swaying. She lowered the sketchbook and was quiet for a few more minutes before she finally spoke. "Someone I thought I loved. He was sweet and passionate and then suddenly he wasn't. And I don't know how I didn't see it. I don't know how I missed the signs."

Her face was pale and her hair was stuck to the sides of her head. I don't know why, but suddenly I thought about earthquakes. I reached forward and took her hand and it felt cold, damp. Her eyes closed again and she kept wincing, as though what she saw burned her from the inside out. She shook her head like she was fighting something and then, suddenly, the shaking stopped and her head was still. Even though the music was still playing, I was surrounded by an overwhelming sense of quiet. Quiet so loud that I could hear it. Finally, she opened her eyes and we sat together on the couch holding hands. We must have fallen asleep that way because when I woke our fingers were still intertwined.

Matilda

I don't like being in cramped, loud places, so no matter how many times Lavi begged me, I rarely ate lunch in the cafeteria. Within the first few weeks of school, I figured out how to sneak into the auditorium and almost always ate my lunch there.

I packed the same thing every day—a peanut butter and jelly sandwich and apple juice in a thermos. I would sling my legs over the armrest of the chair, eat my sandwich, and stare out the window until it was time to go back to class. One time a janitor came in looking for something, but I slid down low and got really quiet and after a few minutes he left. My mother was keeping a more watchful eye on me, so sitting out on our porch until all hours of the night was getting more difficult. Instead, I sat in that big empty auditorium, thinking.

Mostly, I thought about Franny.

I wondered what she was eating for lunch. No matter how many times she tried, she never liked peanut butter and jelly. I think she hated feeling that her mouth was stuck together. Panic would fill her eyes, and I imagined that she feared she would never be able to pry her lips open again.

I loved it for all the reasons she hated it.

I liked how the peanut butter got thick and sticky and made it hard to swallow and then right at the moment you thought things were going to get worse, the jelly came to the rescue.

Franny and I, we always saw things differently.

I ate the last of my sandwich and then suddenly realized that there was a commotion growing outside the auditorium. I crammed everything back into my backpack, walked quickly to the door, and cracked it open just a bit. All I could make out were the backs of people's heads, so I slipped out and tried to blend into the crowd, acting as though I had been there all along. The last thing I wanted was to get caught and lose the only place in the school I could really be alone. I had nothing to worry about because no one paid any attention to me. They were all too busy whispering loudly about the red paint smudged along the corridor walls.

There were random smears here and there that reminded me of the finger paints I used in kindergarten. It would have been funny—except the streaks looked like blood and there was sense of brutality in the air, as though a battle had raged in this hallway. It took a few more minutes for me to notice that the person had also taken the time to inscribe a message across the door of Mr. West's classroom. Boldly, unapologetically, and in crimson paint, it read:

FAT ASS

At first I was shocked, but then I wanted to laugh. I admired anyone who could pull off a prank designed to humiliate a man who lived to humiliate everyone around him. Several teachers joined the group and tried to coax students back to their classrooms. Then, suddenly, it got quiet and the whispering and pointing all stopped as a man made his way towards the classroom.

Mr. West stood in front of his door, hands on his enormous hips, his goatee trembling and, even though I wished I didn't, for a second I felt sorry for him. With a roar, he leapt into the crowd and grabbed his prey. When he reemerged, it was with a struggling Daryl in tow.

"Get off of me, man!" shouted a furious Daryl without a hint of panic in his voice as he worked to slip out of the grip that Wicked West had firmly placed him in.

The group dispersed. Teachers herded kids back to their classrooms, but I stayed. So many times in my life I have allowed opportunities to pass me by and I was not going to allow that to happen again. That is what I told myself as my peanut butter and jelly sandwich turned to cement in the pit of my stomach.

"You little freak," Mr. West growled.

I saw his grip tighten, but Daryl didn't look scared. Instead, he seemed comfortable, almost relaxed. As if this wasn't the first time someone was close to smashing his skull into a wall.

"Did you think I wouldn't figure it out?" Mr. West put his face up close to Daryl's. I cringed, thinking about what his breath smelled like.

"Stop it!" I yelled.

For a moment, we were all stunned, myself included. I understood my words but . . . had that voice really come from inside of me? Did I have any idea what I was getting myself into?

"Get out of here," hissed Daryl.

"Get to class, Ms. Wolley. This matter does not pertain to you." He pushed Daryl harder.

"But he didn't do it."

Mr. West suddenly let Daryl go and turned to me. It was like a scene from a horror movie where the innocent young girl lures the killer away from her friend and then runs away screaming. Except there was nowhere for me to run.

"This paint is still wet. That means it had to have been done within the last hour."

Mr. West smirked. "Brilliant, Ms. Wolley, or should I call you Ms. Holmes? Now can you explain to me how that impacts the fact that this weasel defaced school property?"

I shuffled my feet for a minute and looked down because it was the best I could do to create dramatic effect.

"He didn't do it. He was with me the whole time."

I am not sure which of them look more shocked. The difference was that Daryl recovered more quickly.

"Oh, really? And where were the two of you?"

For a moment, I stumbled.

"We were riding up and down in the elevator."

"That elevator is designated for staff and for students with disabilities. Do either of you have a disability that I don't already know about?" He snickered, then grabbed Daryl's jacket and crumpled it in his fist.

"I guess you're off the hook this time, dirt bag. Thank your little girlfriend. You two will have a lot of time to spend together during detention next week." He tossed him against the wall as though he was a rubber ball, and Mr. West stormed off, leaving the two us alone in the hallway.

Daryl adjusted the collar on his jacket, picked up the books that had fallen to the floor, and continued down the hall. He never said a word to me. But it didn't matter; I already knew.

I knew that he owed me and I knew that it was killing him inside.

I got to detention early the first day. I had never been punished at school before and I certainly didn't want to make things worse with Wicked West. Daryl sauntered in at exactly three o'clock. He sat in the front row, slouched down in his seat, and stuffed his hands into his jacket pockets. That first day, he spent the entire time staring blankly at Mr. West, who pretended to be intensely engrossed in a newspaper.

The next day Mr. West gave us more homework than ever before.

Again, I made sure to arrive a few minutes early and Daryl got there right at three. He picked the same seat, took the same stance, and the staring contest began.

Mr. West shuffled through his papers.

I was trying to read the pages he had assigned in Romeo and Juliet, but it was complicated. I squinted down at the book; I didn't understand a word of what I was reading. It was so quiet in the room that I don't think I would have noticed it if I hadn't looked up at the right moment.

Mr. West had stopped what he was doing and was staring right back at Daryl.

He had this grin on his face. The kind that made you wonder whether he was going to slap you on the back and laugh with you, or slap you so hard your teeth were going to come flying out of your mouth. I couldn't see Daryl's expression, but his focus didn't seem to falter. Mr. West walked over to Daryl like it was just the two of them and I wasn't in the room anymore and for a second I wondered what it would feel like to really be invisible. He lowered himself down and whispered fiercely into Daryl's ear. "Got nothing better to do, dirt bag? Why don't you get started on your assignment?"

Daryl never moved his head.

One hand came out of his pocket and dove straight down into his backpack. Out came a binder. He flipped it open and slid it across the table so that it teetered at the edge, inches from slipping onto the floor.

I'm not sure how he had managed it, but Daryl had completed the entire assignment.

Mr. West was furious.

If I thought the homework assignment that day was bad, I had no idea what was to come. Each day the workload increased and each afternoon, Daryl flipped open his notebook to reveal the assignment in its entirety.

On the last day of our assigned detention, Mr. West handed Daryl a piece of chalk. He made him stand at the blackboard and write over and over, *"I am a liar and a dirt bag and I don't deserve to be here."*

Daryl did as he was told. He wrote until the board was so filled with words it looked more white than black. The dust got into the crevices of his jacket and turned it ashen and still he wrote. He never changed his expression, and when he finished he walked to the door with a snarl on his face, like an animal that had just chewed his leg free from a trap. I had never seen anyone look like that before, and for a second, even Mr. West looked shaken. But then he growled at me to get my things together.

The expression on Daryl's face was so frightening, I could not erase it from my memory. That night, I decided to take a risk and sneak out to the porch. My mother had gone to bed early with a cold and I figured I could get away with it. I'm not sure what I was hoping for—maybe I thought I would find him there, but even if I did, I wasn't sure what I would say.

Suddenly, I heard a noise, a scratching sound coming from the tree a few hundred feet from where I stood. I peeked over to Lavi and Daryl's side, but all the lights were off. Slowly, I inched my way over to the tree. I have always been scared of the dark; noises are louder and shadows scarier when the sun goes down. I got as close as my nerves would allow and then jumped as an orange streak raced by.

A cat. The same cat that Lavi was playing with the first day we met. I walked behind the tree to see what he had been doing. It was mostly covered in dirt, but the cat had managed to unearth a corner of a plastic bag. I dug around with my fingers, feeling the soil embed under my nails. Then I pulled hard and out came the bag.

Inside was a small canister of red paint, a paintbrush, and a bright yellow thermos covered with little black footprints. A thermos that I recognized immediately . . . I'd been present during its purchase.

I brought it into my bedroom, threw it into a drawer, and asked myself what it was I really wanted to know. Later that night, when I held it in my hands, I realized how much I did not want it to be Lavi's. But I didn't want it to belong to Daryl, either, because not only did I want to believe in him, I needed to.

I could not stop thinking about him. I felt shaken and stupid and gloriously happy. I found myself searching the hall for his beat up brown leather jacket. I sat in Mr. West's class, trying not to make it obvious that my eyes were glued to the big white clock on the wall. Somehow, I thought if I stared hard enough, I could make the light blue minute hand move faster. I knew which days I needed to pack up quickly and when I could take my time because I had memorized his schedule and knew exactly which corner he would be turning and when. It happened rarely, but if I miscalculated and missed—which happened rarely—I felt this sinking feeling in my stomach.

I was frightened by the fact that I was so consumed, so I tried not to think about it. I created lists in my head of things I needed to do. I daydreamed about running away from home and alphabetized all the reasons I hated my mother. But no matter what I did, eventually my thoughts would drift to him and I'd experience a breathless, floaty feeling, as if I had just spent the day blowing up balloons. As punishment, I pinched the tip of my pinky finger, hard.

I started to see Lavi in a different light, too. Now, instead of just being my friend, she was *his* sister. She had the potential to provide me with insights that no one else could. I tried to be inconspicuous because I didn't want her to see right through me. I didn't want her to see that all I wanted was him.

The red paint incident burned inside me because all it did was remind me that I had no idea who he really was or what he was capable of. Worst of all was the possibility that my mother was right about him. I said nothing to either of them after my discovery. I wasn't sure what to think, so I decided to keep it to myself.

One afternoon, Lavi and I were enjoying our french fry ritual, but I couldn't tear my eyes from the front door and was trying my best to act like I was paying attention to the conversation.

"What do you think about reincarnation?" Lavi asked as she grabbed a carton of milk out of the refrigerator. She poured two heaping teaspoonfuls of reddish powder into her glass. She loved strawberry milk, and I watched as it turned from white to bubble gum pink.

"What?" I thought I heard someone at the door, but it was coming from the next unit over.

"Reincarnation. Do you ever think about it? You know, who you might have been before you were you?"

Lavi always surprised me. It never occurred to me to imagine who I might have been before, especially since I was not even sure about who I was now. "Who do you think you were before?" I asked.

She stirred her milk with such intensity that a small funnel formed in the center.

"Don't laugh, okay?"

I shook my head and grabbed another french fry.

"I think I was a bird before."

"A bird?" Were those footsteps or was that just the pounding of my heart in my ears?

"Sometimes when I watch them fly, I totally know what it feels like. I even dream about it. I know it sounds crazy but it's almost like I've done it somewhere before. You know, two strong flaps and then just glide." She closed her eyes and tilted her head back. She looked so peaceful, her curls skimming the tops of her shoulders, her hands poised at her thighs, as if she really could soar into the air.

And then he walked in.

He had that same detached look he always had. He turned to me and, almost automatically, my lashes came down slowly over my eyes and my head tilted slightly to the left. I couldn't help myself and, thankfully, Lavi didn't notice.

"Hey," he said.

I thought I saw a hint of a smile, or maybe it was a snicker. He grabbed his things, went upstairs, and slammed his door closed like he had done hundreds of times before. But for me, this time was different. I felt something I couldn't describe, which made the feeling of breathlessness so intense, I started feeling dizzy.

"I think I know. What I was. Before."

But she wasn't listening. She was busy making another glass of strawberry milk. So I pinched the tip of my pinky really hard until it turned blood red. When the dizziness finally disappeared, I decided I needed some help.

There was no one else to ask.

As hard as it was to admit, my mother was the expert. We were unloading groceries and she was distracted, trying to fit the food into our very small refrigerator.

"Whoever designed this thing forgot that people actually eat." She stuffed a head of lettuce into the produce drawer, which was already almost filled to capacity.

"Do you remember your first crush?"

She was sitting cross-legged on the floor, trying to wrangle the drawer closed. "What?"

"Your first crush. Do you remember what it was like?"

She gave up on the drawer and turned to look at me. "Second grade. Bobby Warner. He had green eyes."

She went back to what she was doing and gave the drawer a hard shove.

"How did you know? I mean what did it feel like?"

She stood up and tried to adjust the refrigerator door, which was flung open so wide it looked contorted. She was after the landlord to fix the hinge because any time we opened it too far, it would hang down like a broken wing. "Know what? What are you asking me?"

"About the guy? You know, how did you know if he liked you back?"

That was the heart of the matter. I was pining away during the day and dreaming of him at night and still had no idea what he felt toward me. It had gotten so serious that when he was around, I felt like I couldn't speak. For the first time in my life, I got a glimpse into what it felt like to be Franny. I didn't understand the feelings I was having and I couldn't really talk to Lavi about it, but I had to talk to someone. So as much as it killed me, I chose my mother.

She was fumbling in a cabinet drawer, looking for something. "Got it." She pulled out a roll of duct tape. "Now what was it you were asking me? How do I know about men?"

She unrolled a piece of tape and, as it detached from the rest of the roll, it made a high-pitched ripping sound. "I just know. I get a sense. Know what I mean?"

"I guess," I answered.

She turned to me. "You do? You know what I mean? Do you get a sense, too?"

I was thrown by the plea in her voice. Like she was inviting me in. I could say that I knew and then maybe things would change between us. I thought about it for a second. "No, Mom. I don't really know what you mean."

"Oh." She shrugged and went back to taping the refrigerator door.

That was it. I could tell she was done with me.

"Is that what it was like with my father? You got a sense?" I knew I was breaking the rules. I knew he was a subject never to be discussed, but I was past caring.

She slipped the roll of duct tape back into the cabinet drawer. "Your father. He was different. And no, I didn't get a sense. That was pretty much the problem."

She turned back to what she was doing and I understood that we were now definitely done with our discussion. There was nothing left for me to do so I went back to unloading groceries. I was responsible for putting away the pantry items. I pulled out a can of soup and a bag of rolls, but there was something heavy at the bottom of the bag that I had to reach down deep to get. A can of SpaghettiO's. I hated SpaghettiO's because they tasted like tin, but Franny loved them. She was amazed that they could make letters out of pasta and they were her favorite.

I could feel the anger welling up inside me, pushing everything else aside. It rose into my cheeks and made my hands shake. "What's this?" I asked. I held up the can as though it was the key piece of evidence in a murder trial.

"Hmm?" She mumbled from behind the refrigerator door.

"This! What is this?" I shouted, this time waving it in the air.

She peeked from behind to see what I was holding. "Oh, that. Don't you like those, Matilda? I could have sworn that you did."

I tried to slow the rage building inside of me so I wouldn't be tempted to throw the can at her head. I took a hard, deep breath and tried to release the thought from my mind. I didn't believe her for a second; there was no way she no longer remembered that this was my sister's favorite thing to eat and not mine.

"No, Mom. I *hate* these."

"You do? Really? Don't worry about it. I'll bring it to work. I'm sure Margaret can take it home for her grandkids." She turned back to the refrigerator to finish what she started.

I turned back to the pantry and let my shoulders droop. All I could think about at that moment was Franny, and I found myself suddenly alphabetizing the cans, losing myself in whether corn should go before kidney beans, focusing hard so that she wouldn't see my shoulders start to shake as I began to cry. Later, I snuck back downstairs, opened the pantry door, and found the can of SpaghettiO's where I had left them, right beside the peas. I took it upstairs and put it in the same drawer that held the pretty lavender paper. After that, every time I opened the drawer, it rolled back and forth, hitting one side and then the next.

Reminding me.

That night, I woke with a start. The digital clock read 3:00. I should've been fast asleep. I should have been home with my sister and grandmother, but since that was no longer my reality, I gave up trying to predict what was going to happen next. I can't explain what pulled me to the window, but when I looked out, our porch light was on and I could see him standing there, staring up at me. We locked eyes and he coiled his finger back and forth, motioning for me to come.

Since she caught us together that one time on the porch, sneaking around had become more difficult. The second floor was carpeted and I knew where to step to avoid the creaks, but it took some time to get down the stairs. I supported my upper body by lifting myself up on the handrails and making sure that my feet barely touched the steps. I didn't want to risk searching for a jacket, so I went out in what I was wearing: a green short-sleeved t-shirt and old gray sweatpants with a rip at the knee. Far from the glamorous lavender silk robe my mother wore at night.

He was waiting for me, leaning against the divider with a bundle under his arm. I felt that nauseating airy feeling again. A spot at the tip of my stomach clenched and I thought I might explode from excitement.

"C'mon."

I followed. "Where are we going?"

"Just c'mon."

It was dark, but I ignored my fears and blindly followed him. I was too interested in finding out where he was taking me to worry about anything else. For weeks, I was plotting run-ins with him and hanging out with Lavi when I knew he would be around, but nothing had drawn his attention until tonight. For a second, I wondered if I was dreaming, but the chill in the air and the goose bumps running up and down my arms made me certain that I was no longer under the covers.

"Here."

If I was expecting some sweet romantic lovers' spot, I was sorely disappointed. The edge of the townhouse complex abutted a two-lane highway where the occasional tractor-trailer passed. He pointed to a spot on the ground and motioned for me to sit. It was cold and damp and I could feel the wetness seeping into the seat of my sweatpants. He unrolled the bundle from under his arm.

"What's that?" I asked.

"Jeans." He walked over to the middle of the road and laid them down. Then he came back and sat beside me.

"What are you doing?" I asked.

"You'll see."

We sat in the quiet. A street lamp across from us gave off the only light on the road. I could hear the sound of a truck in the distance and I could see two yellow headlights, like cat eyes, coming toward us. As it got closer, it got louder, and I realized I had stopped breathing.

The truck came barreling down, its headlights lighting a path and casting shadows onto the lump of fabric on the road, which almost looked as though it was alive. I watched as the wheels smashed down onto the ground, crushing the pants with their force, and then spit exhaust into our faces as it passed. The pants lay contorted, the legs spread into an unnatural position, helplessly awaiting the next assault, abandoned. Another truck came along a few minutes later, but this time I turned my head. After that, it was quiet and I kept my eyes turned away.

"You cold?" he asked.

I hadn't realized I was shivering.

"Here." He unzipped the worn brown leather jacket I had stared at all through detention weeks before. He tossed it into my lap and I slipped my arms into the sleeves. It still held the warmth of his body. I brought my knees up to my chest and tried to take an inconspicuous deep breath. He smelled like cinnamon. . . .

"So what was up with that story you gave West? About you and me in the elevator."

I shrugged my shoulders. "Just looked like you needed someone to help you out, I guess."

He picked a stick up off the ground and used his fingernail to crack the bark. "So you think I did it."

A truck rumbled in the distance. Like thunder.

"Didn't you?"

He'd torn the stick down to soft wood and was rubbing it slowly with his thumb. "Does it matter?"

He got up and walked to the middle of the road to examine the jeans, then came back and sat beside me. "One more."

I saw the headlights approaching, but now I knew when to turn to avoid the most brutal moment. When I turned this time, so did he. The truck zoomed by and the world shook and the air between us shivered. In that moment, I thought I saw something. Or maybe I felt it. Prickly, electrical sparks ran up and down my arms and then, as quickly as it came, it was gone.

He stood up and retrieved the jeans from the road. "We should get going."

We walked back in silence. When I got to the porch, I slipped off the jacket and handed it to him. "Thanks."

He nodded.

"I'll see ya."

He nodded again.

I snuck back inside and quietly made my way up the stairs. I thought about getting into bed, but I was so wound up I knew I wouldn't be able to lie still so I walked over to the window. He was still standing there, looking up at me. He held the jeans and his jacket close to his chest. I focused really hard on his lips, because I could see that they were moving but I couldn't hear what he was saying. I watched carefully and then suddenly I understood. I nodded my head and held my hand up to the window, his silent words ringing in my ears.

"I didn't do it."

I tossed and turned most of the night. When I woke, I decided it was time to have a talk with Lavi so I invited her over after school. We were sitting on my bed, our notebooks by our sides. Wicked West had assigned a poem that neither of us understood. I quickly lost interest and was staring at Lavi's ponytail which was resting on the page she was writing. She brushed it aside like it was debris.

"How are you going to answer question two? List three symbols and why they are used?" she asked.

"I don't care." I put the pen cap in my mouth and bit down on a familiar dent. She looked up to see if I was serious. "Lavi, it's a poem. You can pick any line and argue that it's symbolic of something. The assignment is stupid and West is an ass."

"You mean a fat ass." She looked back down at her notebook but not before I saw her smile.

I slid across the bed until I was sitting at the edge. "There's something I've been meaning to return." I stood up and walked to my desk. I opened the bottom drawer and pushed aside the can of SpaghettiO's to find what I was looking for.

"Here."

She was reading the poem and chewing on her lower lip.

"I think this belongs to you." I handed her the thermos with the little black footprints on the side that still had some red paint splattered on the lid.

"I was wondering where I'd left that."

And that was it. That was all she had to say.

I stood in front of her, arms crossed like a mother waiting for her naughty child's confession.

"Is that all?" I asked.

Her eyes sparkled and reminded me of ginger ale. "Yep." She went back to reading the book.

"Lavi, are you going to tell me or what?"

"It's none of your business."

For a brief moment, I was hurt, but then I felt insulted. "What's that supposed to mean?" My voice came out louder than I had intended.

"Which part did you not understand?" She closed the book and brought it up to her chest and I wondered if this was some kind of joke. One eyebrow was raised and her lips were pursed tight, as though she was sucking on something sour. For a second, I didn't recognize her. Then her face softened and she was the old Lavi again.

When she spoke, her voice cracked. "When were you going to tell me about your thing with my brother?"

I knew it wasn't possible, but suddenly it felt like the temperature in the room had risen by ten degrees. I walked to the window, trying to think of how to answer.

"Forget it," she said, obviously frustrated.

"Lavi, there is nothing to tell."

One of the things I liked best about my room was the way the sunlight warmed it in the afternoon. Now it cast a triangular wedge of brightness onto her head, making her hair twinkle as though it was sprinkled with glitter.

"Daryl and I are just friends." I sat in a chair, breathed out a heavy sigh, and hoped it made me look more irritated than guilty.

"Has my brother told you anything about Daddy?" she asked.

I shook my head. The way she said it made her sound like a little girl.

"Daryl's the problem. He's why my mom and dad aren't together. He always gets in the way."

I stared at her in disbelief. "So when you wrote that nasty thing about West and painted the entire hallway in red, did you know Daryl would be blamed or were you just hoping?"

"My father is back in town. This time Daryl isn't going to ruin it."

She stood up and walked toward the window. She turned her head so that she was looking straight into the sun. She didn't shift. She didn't squint. Just stared straight ahead as though it did not affect her.

As though she was blind.

Therese

Therese knew she was carrying a girl.

She sensed it weeks before Leah ever mentioned it. But why was Leah so frightened to tell her? Why hadn't the news brought her joy?

She shook off her concern and returned to her task. Tim was working late doing inventory and it was her responsibility to heat Barbara's dinner. She scooped out a helping of spaghetti and sauce and tossed it into a pot. Tim was adamant that it not burn, and he taught her to first fill a lid with water and add it into the pot before covering. He insisted that she stir every three minutes so that it didn't stick to the bottom. When she laughed, he brought out the kitchen timer and made sure she knew how to set it properly. Sitting obediently at the table, she reset it four times as he instructed. When it was heated, she slid the food into a large bowl and then balanced the basket of rolls he had prepared in her other hand. She brought it all to Barbara and placed it on the TV tray, but not before removing a half-eaten slice of chocolate cake that was still there from lunch.

Surprisingly, the television was turned off so that Barbara could devote full attention to consuming her meal. She twirled long strands of pasta into bundles, stuffed them into her mouth, and then used the roll to wipe the excess sauce from around her mouth.

"What do you think we should name the baby?" Therese asked, hoping to take her mind off thoughts of Leah.

"Huh?" Barbara swiped at her chin with a roll.

"The baby. What do you think we should name it?"

"Don't really care. Name it whatever you want."

"I was just wondering if you had any thoughts. How did you choose Tim's name?"

Barbara glared at her. "What do you mean?" She hissed. "Why would you ask me that?"

The fork dropped and landed onto a bed of spaghetti.

"Just making conversation, Barbara."

"I never had the luxury of sitting around thinking about names when I was pregnant with Timmy. Why don't you go ask your own Mama about picking names?"

She retrieved her fork and went back to bundling strands.

"My mother isn't really a help when it comes to this kind of stuff. She didn't even realize she was pregnant with me until the day I was born."

"What kind of idiot doesn't know she's pregnant?" she snickered.

"I suppose you knew the second it happened."

Barbara's face turned gray and, for a moment, Therese thought she might be choking. The color soon returned to her cheeks. "What are you trying to get at?" Barbara whispered.

"Nothing, Barbara. I didn't mean anything."

"Timmy never told you."

A secret.

Immediately Therese's face shifted and she smiled. A look she had practiced for so long that it had finally became natural. "What, Barbara? Tell me what?"

Barbara lowered her head so that she was staring directly into her bowl of spaghetti. "About his father."

Therese took a deep breath. "No, Barbara. He never told me."

"That's because I told him never to tell. He is a good boy." She picked at the rolls, pulling out pieces of the white bread with her fingers and rolling them into little balls.

Getting people to divulge their secrets was an art form, a dance. Therese knew exactly what to do next. She nodded her head, folded her hands into her lap, and waited.

"And he also probably didn't want people to know," Barbara said.

Therese held her position, counting the seconds to victory.

"That his father raped me."

Barbara was now pinching the balls, flattening them into circles and tossing them into the bowl of cold spaghetti. Therese's mind was spinning. She felt cold and her heart pounded so loudly in her ears that she wondered if Barbara could hear. Probably not, since she was in the same position, her face staring down into the bowl. What was it about Tim that she had missed? What was there, running through his blood? Was it something he spent his life trying to hide? Why had she not been able to spark him? She felt the baby kick her.

Hard.

She reached across and touched the top of Barbara's hand. "I am so sorry that happened to you."

Barbara pulled away. She lifted the remote from the TV tray and flicked the television on, but before the volume was at full blast, she said, "So now you understand."

Therese nodded. *Yes,* she thought. *Now I understand.*

The next day at work, it was all she could think about. She sat at her desk listening to the gardeners outside. Their leaf blowers were aimed low to the ground like rifles, blasting away the dried remains of winter. She covered her ears, trying to muffle the high-pitched hum that caused her pain between her eyebrows.

It was almost time to meet Leah.

She got a book out of her desk drawer, slipped it into her bag, and walked down the hallway. Leah was waiting for her in the foyer. The dark paneled ceiling was so high, even a whisper magnified into a roar. Leah's hands were tucked into the pockets of her jacket, and she smiled when she saw Therese approaching.

"I need to breathe some fresh air."

Therese nodded and they left the building to walk along the grounds. Little green tips sprouted through the mulch, still so tightly wound that it looked like they might change their minds and go back underground.

Leah squeezed her arm. "Over there." She pointed to a bench beneath a tree off the path. Once they sat, her attention was drawn to the groups of students rushing past.

"How are you?" Leah asked.

"Tired."

Just then, a young woman dropped her bag to the ground. She fell frantically to her knees to try to gather her belongings.

"Barbara told me. Everything."

The young woman located the last of her books, stuffed them into her bag, and ran off to catch up with her friends.

"Tim's father raped her."

The sun moved behind a cloud and what had been bright was now dark, as though someone had twisted the contrast button on a television screen.

"Leah?"

"Yes."

"What do you think about that?"

Leah shook her head and crossed her arms in front of her chest. She was staring down at the ground where the books had fallen. Now there was nothing but dirt and brown grass that had shriveled over the winter. She stared at it intently, like she was searching for something. "Have you thought of a name? For the baby?"

Therese removed the book she had slipped into her bag earlier, a book of baby names. "We should pick something meaningful."

Leah nodded.

"Do you like Dorothy? It's kind of old-fashioned," Therese said.

Leah dug into her bag and pulled out a yellow highlighter. She took the book and began flipping through it so fast, the pages sounded like they were ripping. She placed her finger at the top of each and then ran it down quickly.

"This one." She handed Therese the book, still pointing to the name she had found.

"Mathilda," Therese said the name aloud, eager to see how it felt on her lips.

Leah was quiet.

Therese folded down the corner of the page. "I would spell it differently though. No need for that extra H. It's silent anyway and will just confuse people."

"Whatever you think," Leah said.

They sat quietly together until it was time to go back to work. When she got home, Therese took the book out of her bag. The page was dog-eared and she found the name easily. Glaring at her, blinking in neon yellow highlighter, were the words that Leah had underlined.

MATHILDA
STRENGTH IN BATTLE

That night, Therese woke with the baby name book wedged under her chin. Saliva pooled under her cheek and left a wet stain on the pillow. Using her arms to support her weight, she swung her legs over the side of the bed and waited for the dizziness to end. She looked over at Tim's side and saw he wasn't there, but tonight there was only one thing on her mind.

Tuna fish.

She tried to limit herself to twice a day, but right now the only thing she could think about was a sandwich. She stood up, rubbed the slope at the base of her back, and made her way downstairs. She walked straight to the refrigerator where Tim left a fresh batch of tuna every day. He knew exactly how much mayonnaise and lemon juice to put in to make it creamy and tangy at the same time. She ate it open-faced on slices of untoasted English muffins. She had already tied the twisty around the end of the plastic bag when she changed her mind and pulled out a second. Scraping the remaining bits of tuna out, she spread it onto the bread and finished the sandwich before the dirty bowl made it to the sink.

Her belly felt taut, hard, as though it was encased in metal, and she rubbed it through her nightgown. A spray of acid grazed the round of her throat and then the baby shifted. She suddenly felt like she was suffocating. Sitting made breathing even more difficult, so she walked to the back door, hoping the night air might help. It was dark and cool and the feeling of being trapped disappeared for just a second. She walked outside and lifted her arms up toward the moon, enjoying the cold that wrapped itself around her spine, up through her neck, and into her scalp. She took in a long slow breath and thrust her belly out into the night, making it disappear into the blackness. She thought she heard something, but the sound was too muffled and incomplete to make it distinguishable. She walked closer to the shed and could barely make out a shadow.

Tim.

She crouched down low so that she was out of his sight. He had hung an enormous burlap bag of rice on two large meat hooks that were suspended from the ceiling. The bag drooped down looking misshapen, crippled. She watched as he hammered his fists into its middle. Again and again, fist over fist, his bare shoulders cupped with sweat. He reminded her of a boxer, hopping back and forth on two feet with his hands drawn in closely. Her heart pounded loudly in her chest, and she felt even more lightheaded.

Then, suddenly, he stopped. He threw his arms around the bag and buried his face into it. She watched as his back heaved like an enormous balloon, pulling the air in and out so sharply that she thought he might explode.

And then she heard his sobs.

She wondered what it would sound like if he chose to unleash it into the world. If instead of being absorbed by the bag, he had howled it into the black air. She crouched down lower so that he could not see her. When he turned back around, she caught a glimpse of the anger and despair in his eyes, so deep it almost made them appear hollow. The air got heavier to breathe and she felt clumsy and thick, but it was only a few steps back to the house and she knew she could make it without him spotting her. She turned and began to walk, but something made her freeze in place. Her breathing came more sharply now and each breath stung her lungs. She closed her eyes and willed what was about to happen to stop. *No,* she thought, *please, not now.* She clenched her fists and ground her teeth, but there was no preventing it. It started as a dribble, built into a stream, and gushed down her thighs. Within seconds she realized . . .

There was no going back.

"Push!" the nurse hissed, squeezing so hard her long red fingernails dug into Therese's palm. Her legs were in stirrups and her head was propped up. Every few minutes Nurse Red Nails shouted at her to push. With every contraction, her insides would crush, and she wondered if soon they would just come spewing out of her. Someone in the room told her to breathe. Instead, she screamed a sharp and angry wail that filled her mind with sound and made the hurt finally stop.

Then there was calm. She clung to the seconds of relief and convinced herself it would be over soon. A few more pain-free minutes passed, and her mind wandered to thoughts of Tim. After her water broke, she had fallen to the ground with the first contraction. He heard her and came running out of the shed. She could tell by the way he touched her that he was frightened. "Is it time?" he asked. She nodded. He lifted her from the ground and carried her to the car. She had felt his heart beating in his chest and had tasted his sweat on her lips. Salty. Like the ocean.

"I want a drink," she whispered. Her throat was sore and her voice was hoarse.

"Sorry, dear. Best I can do is some chipped ice." The red nails came close to her lips and slipped the ice into her mouth. They felt like cold pebbles. She kept them on the tip of her tongue, willing them not to melt too fast. She closed her eyes and was back in the car with Tim.

He made sure she was comfortable then raced back into the house to get the bag she had packed and left in the hallway closet. He didn't put on a shirt; he just slipped on the denim jacket that hung on the hook. As they sped through the black night, she watched him. His jacket was unbuttoned, exposing a strip of skin from his neck to his belt buckle. His hands were gripped to the wheel so tightly, she could see the bone through his skin. She thought about the night he proposed, thrusting a box with a small diamond ring toward her. He had taken her for a walk and surprised her with it. She surprised him by saying no. She knew how much it must have cost him. She had seen the folded up culinary school application in his sock drawer. But that wasn't why she said no. It was the wrong time, and she didn't know how to explain how she knew, so she just shook her head and pushed his hand away. He had seemed almost relieved. Now, here they were on their way to the hospital. He turned to her every few minutes, and she nodded to confirm she was okay. She closed her eyes and tried to force what she'd witnessed in the shed from her mind.

"Look at me and when I say push, you have to push!" shouted the doctor, who now had a plastic visor over his face. She wondered if he was scared her insides would come spewing out, too. She bore down as the next wave of pain hit. It crashed over her with such intensity that she was breathless with no voice left to wail. Then, it was quiet. Another big squeeze. Everything turned gray, and she heard a scream. It took several minutes before she realized that it was coming from her.

"It's hard work, honey," Red Nails said, her voice shooting like a dart inside Therese's ear. She shook her head hard, thinking that if it fell off her neck then the pain would stop. She imagined it rolling off the bed onto the floor, landing at the nurse's feet with a soft watery thud. She was in the middle of envisioning the look of horror on the nurse's face when another one hit. She pushed down with all her might and gasped as though she was choking.

"You're doing great, Therese. We're almost there," the doctor said.

"We're here," Tim had mumbled when he swerved into the emergency room entrance. He had pulled up close to the curb, jumped out of the car, and returned seconds later with a wheelchair. As they rushed away from the car, she looked back over her shoulder and noticed that he hadn't closed the car door. But before she could speak, he was wheeling her down the ramp. She held on tightly to the armrests as the glass partitions flew open.

The emergency room had been crowded, and people turned to stare. She quickly lost interest in her audience when a contraction started at the top of her belly, shot straight through her knees, and landed in the curve of her ankles. She wrapped her arms around herself and clenched. She leaned over, staring at the white and pink tiles on the floor. It was too painful to pick up her head. He pushed her toward the nurse's station, and she stared at the shoes they passed. The couches in the waiting area were vinyl, and the plastic smell had sickened her. She brought the collar of her nightgown close to her mouth and breathed in the smells of home, soil, and tuna fish. She rubbed her nose into her collar once again. Tim stopped in front of the nurse's station. "We're having a baby," he'd announced.

Now, the doctor was yelling at her. "You're having a baby, Therese!" As though it was a surprise. As though he wanted to make sure she understood the magnitude of what she was undertaking. She stared at him through the V of her legs and decided she wanted to slap him. She lifted her arm up to try, but stopped when the pain gripped her again. This time her mind swirled around in her skull, trying to find comfort in a voice, a touch, a face. She thought about Tim now in the waiting room, probably pacing and regretting the fact that he had no shirt underneath his jacket. Then she pictured him sitting on the green vinyl couch sipping lukewarm coffee. Which would he be doing? Then she thought about Leah. She wanted Leah.

"The head is out!" the doctor shouted. He held his hands down low and moved them around, but she could not see what he was doing. She felt ripped open. Exposed. She wondered if she would ever feel whole again. Half the baby was inside of her, and the other half was out. She was ready to give up, but her baby deserved better than to be stuck between two worlds, so she clenched her jaw shut and squeezed as hard as she could. Suddenly, she felt a release, as if a cork had popped and everything inside gushed out, like an exploding bottle of champagne. Her hips sunk into the mattress and she cried as each muscle in her body collapsed from exhaustion. The doctor lifted the baby into the air. "Here she is!"

The baby let out one long scream. It took several big breaths to create and it sounded like the noise a car engine makes in the winter when it refuses to turn over. The nurse swaddled her in a blanket so that all that was exposed was her face. Then, the nurse laid her onto Therese's belly and she quieted immediately. Therese brought her close. A spark ran through her as her daughter turned her head. They locked eyes and Therese sighed and wondered why everything in her life could not be this simple.

That night she dreamt of feathers, and when she woke Leah was sitting beside her. Therese stretched out her arms and pulled herself out of her dream. Tim. The pain. The baby. Her johnny was twisted, leaving her entire backside exposed. She tried to adjust it, gave up, and then turned to look into the bassinette. Matilda was wrapped in a pink blanket and looked like a cone of delicately spun cotton candy.

Therese lifted herself up and searched for a comfortable position in the hospital bed. Leah walked over to the baby and cradled the tightly wrapped bundle in her arms. It was quiet in the room except for the song that Leah was humming into Matilda's ear. She sang so softly that Therese could not make out the words, but Matilda cooed back as if she understood. Leah stopped singing, kissed the top of Matilda's head, and put her back in the bassinette. She sat back down in the chair, but without the baby, her arms hung down awkwardly on either side of her body. For a few minutes, neither of them spoke. Even though Leah was smiling, Therese could feel her sadness.

"Thanks for coming," Therese said, ignoring the throbbing pain that had just begun above her eyebrow.

"How are you?" Leah asked, rummaging in her pocketbook and looking more like her normal self.

"I'm glad it's over."

"I think it's only just begun," Leah said as she tossed something onto Therese's lap. "I brought you these."

Therese looked down at the package of Hershey's kisses.

The awkwardness that skirted them earlier moved in with more determination. Therese ignored it and ripped open the bag. "Want one?"

Leah nodded. She unwrapped the chocolate and then rolled the foil wrapper into a tiny silver ball. "Has your mother come by?"

"Not yet." Therese took a chocolate out of the bag and warmed it in her hand.

Matilda had fallen asleep and was making little snorting sounds. Therese smiled and tried to catch Leah's eye to see if she thought it was funny, too, but Leah was staring out the window. The late morning sky had turned from blue to a hazy gray, and Leah seemed lost in the clouds. Then, as if she found what it was she was searching for, she turned back to Therese. "Where's Tim?"

"He went home to get a few things." She felt cold and drew the blanket more tightly around herself.

"Where were you when it happened?"

"Have another." Therese passed the bag to Leah, who shook her head no.

"Where were you?"

"It was so fast, I don't remember," Therese said.

"You don't remember?" Leah's eyes narrowed.

Immediately, she pictured Tim collapsed into the bag of rice, his rage filling the shed so completely that part of the window fogged. She wanted to confess it all, to rest her head against Leah's shoulder and feel safe. She wanted to hear that it would all be okay, but she already knew what her response would be. A kernel of anger settled inside, and she tucked her legs beneath herself. "Sorry, but I don't remember. Maybe if you ever have a baby, you'll think to keep track of those kinds of things." She watched as each of her words hit its mark, making Leah flinch and pull back into her chair.

A few seconds later, Leah moved in closer and took Therese's hand. She hadn't realized how cold she was until she felt Leah's hand cupping hers, but the offer of forgiveness simply made Therese angrier. "I just want to make sure that everything is okay. For you. For Matilda," Leah said as she lifted Therese's hand to her lips and began to blow on them.

"I already told you there's nothing to worry about. Everything is fine. This is the way things are supposed to be." She pulled her hand away and used it to straighten the blanket. Leah looked down at the floor and moved her foot in a perfect circle, the silence between them broken up by the sound of the food cart moving along the hallway outside.

"What about Barbara?"

The nurses had been in and out of her room all night. She wondered where they were now that she needed them. She looked up at the clock and hoped that her lunch tray would interrupt whatever it was that was happening between them. Matilda stopped snorting and was now sleeping so peacefully she didn't look real. Leah was staring at her, waiting for a response. The gentle quiet that usually caressed them now felt oppressive and uncomfortable. Therese swallowed and then coughed, choking on the words sitting in her throat. Finally, she spoke. "It will be okay. She will warm up to the idea in her own time."

Leah inched forward again, appearing as though she wanted to speak, but then sat back and said nothing. The baby stirred and they both turned toward the bassinette, but Matilda quickly settled. It was just the two of them again. This time when Leah came close, she whispered so softly Therese could barely hear. "Be careful."

And then she was gone.

Therese reached over to the bed rail and pushed the help button. A few minutes later, a pretty blonde nurse appeared. "Do you need something, Miss Wolley?"

"Yes. A friend brought these for me, but I don't want them. Why don't you take them out front to share with the rest of the girls?"

"Are you sure?" the nurse asked, holding the nearly full bag of Hershey's kisses in her hand.

"Yes, I'm sure. Take them away." She rolled over and pulled the blanket over her head. The pit in her stomach made it hard to breathe. She wedged her head into the pillow and wept, the sound of her sobs muffled by the bedding, her tears buried under the thin layer of feathers.

Franny

Grapes were our favorite.

It was Tuesday afternoon and Leah dropped us off at the town library so we could do our homework together. Evelyn and I always sat in the adult section under the supervision of the librarian we liked, Miss Betty, who smiled politely when we walked in and then ignored us the rest of the time.

Evelyn and I plucked the grapes from their stems and tossed them into little plastic bags, which we hid in our backpacks. When the librarian wasn't looking, we popped them into our mouths. I liked the way they filled my hand and how the flesh of my palm protected them, like little eggs. When Miss Betty was working we could comfortably go through two bags of grapes each. Evelyn stuffed so many into her mouth, she looked like she had the mumps. She tried to speak, but her words came out half complete until, finally, she swallowed. "Think I beat my record."

I nodded, impressed.

"I think we should start investigating. You know, try to uncover your mother's secret."

Miss Betty was whispering loudly to a man with a large stack of books in his arms. Evelyn took advantage of the opportunity and slid her hand inside her backpack.

"Can you think of anything that might help us?" she asked, lifting her hand to her mouth and slipping three in before Betty turned to look at us.

I waited until two more people approached her desk before I spoke. "There is something."

Evelyn's eyebrow arched up and her eyes opened wide. Now she reminded me of a squirrel with her cheeks full of nuts. "What?"

"I'm not sure it's anything though." I was sure. Why was I lying?

"What is it?" she asked.

"Just a name."

Evelyn pushed her notebook and a colored pencil toward me. She pointed to the blank page. I took the pencil and started writing out the letters of his name. L-I-O-N-E-L.

"Who is he?" she whispered.

I shrugged. "Just a name I saw on one of Leah's papers. I thought maybe we could check it out."

She didn't look convinced.

"Do you think Leah might have something to do with this?" she asked.

I stared back at her, trying to convince myself that I was doing this *for* Leah. That maybe if I understood more about what happened to her, I would be able to help.

"Franny, who is this guy and what does he have to do with your mom leaving?"

I looked down at my lap and started playing with the drawstring of my pants, pressing the hard knotted end between my fingers. "I don't know." Another lie.

"You said his name was Lionel?"

"Yes."

"C'mon," she said, begrudgingly.

We went to the table that held catalogues of newspapers in binders. Someone had painstakingly covered each page in plastic but they had still yellowed with age.

"You take this one and I'll start here." She handed me one of the binders, but it was so unwieldy that I had to leave it on the desktop to leaf through. I watched Evelyn scanning each page, looking at photos and headlines, trying to find a link to Lionel. Lost, like the last piece of a puzzle. Why hadn't I been honest with her? I told myself it was because I was being loyal to Leah. But I knew the truth. I felt wobbly, like I was standing at the edge of something about to fall in. I was so used to being the girl that things happened *to* that this new feeling filled my insides with a sweet, dizzy whirl.

Evelyn's stack of books had grown smaller, and then I heard her sigh and knew she was close to giving up. We had been there for more than an hour and it was almost time to go home. She flipped through the last book and as she neared the end, the fizziness inside settled down and I felt relief.

But then Evelyn began shouting at me. Even Miss Betty turned to look.

"Franny!"

"You found something." Acid rose into my throat.

"This." She carried the large book to my side of the table and then dropped it down in front of me.

Evelyn's nose twitched when she got excited. I don't think she realized she was doing it, but when she pointed to the picture her nose was moving so quickly she reminded me of a rabbit. "Look!"

It was a black and white photo and even despite its plastic protection, it was faded. In it, a young man was pointing to a painting and the headline read: "YOUNG ARTIST TAKES TOWN BY STORM."

The painting had swirls of black and gray, like a tornado. In the center, he had painted an eye that was big and round with lashes that curled upward, making them look like the petals of a flower. He was smiling, pointing proudly toward his creation. Next to him stood a beautiful woman. Leah. *My* Leah. Even though the photo was old and blurred, I could see that she was smiling at him. The caption underneath the photo read "ARTIST. LIONEL KOZTERLAND."

Evelyn's nose was twitching. "That's him, isn't it?" she asked.

I didn't answer, but it didn't matter. Evelyn was busy scribbling into her notebook. I looked back at the picture then closed my eyes; I didn't want to see any more. Her lovely face hung on the insides of my eyelids and wouldn't disappear, no matter how tightly I shut them. I heard a faint humming in my ear that became louder and louder until finally it sounded like a roar. It became so loud, I wondered if Evelyn could hear. When I opened my eyes again, she was still writing in her notebook. She hadn't heard a thing.

I turned to look at Miss Betty. I wished that she wasn't so busy with the three people who had just lined up at her desk. I wished she would catch us with our bags of grapes, throw us out, and ban us from ever coming back. But she didn't even look up. So I closed the book and pushed it to the middle of the table and waited for Evelyn to finish.

That afternoon, Evelyn's mother drove us home and I sat quietly in the car until she pulled up in front of Leah's house. Even though I could see that lights were on, I used my key to open the front door.

When I got inside, I stood quietly. And listened.

She was in the kitchen, humming, and I smelled food cooking. A round itchy ball formed in the opening of my throat. I dropped my backpack on the ground and watched as Leah came out of the kitchen.

"I'm glad you're home." She helped me take off my jacket and hung it in the hall closet. "I thought we could have some fun with dinner tonight."

I followed her into the kitchen, my mouth now filling with an acidic metallic taste, which I tried to swallow. "Can I have a drink?"

"You know where everything is. Help yourself."

I walked over to the cabinet and got a tumbler. I didn't usually like soda, but poured myself a glass anyway, hoping it would help wash out the taste. I took a sip, and when I swallowed, I could hear the bubbles exploding in my ears.

"I thought we could turn our food different colors," she said.

I could tell she was excited, but all I wanted was to blurt everything out. I felt the strongest urge to tell her what Evelyn and I were up to and that I was scared about the changes I was feeling and that I knew I was heading somewhere I didn't feel brave enough to go. But I didn't say anything. Instead, I took another sip of soda and this time when I swallowed, the taste didn't bother me as much. Maybe it went away. Maybe I had gotten used to it.

On the counter, she had set up different bottles of food coloring.

"How about some green mashed potatoes?" She took the top off the bottle and handed it to me. "Three shakes." The magic formula.

I watched as the drops hit the creamy peaked mounds. The green looked vibrant, unnatural, out of place, and it made me feel sad to mix it, turning the potatoes into something they were not. But Leah was looking at me, full of enthusiasm, so I mixed.

At first, it started as a streak that I could follow with my spoon, but the more I mixed the more the colors blended into the white potatoes and soon it became a solid, uniform shade of apple green.

Then she passed me a bowl of macaroni and cheese. "Be creative."

I took two bottles this time, blue and red. Three drops each. Then I mixed. The result was the color of plums.

"Fun, don't you think?" she asked.

I nodded, mostly to please her.

She pushed over a container of vanilla yogurt. I took a red and yellow bottle and turned the yogurt into a bright shade of orange that reminded me of fire.

"Are you ready to eat?" she asked.

I crinkled my nose. The thought of eating green mashed potatoes repulsed me, but she had already put the food out on the table so I took my seat. My fork hovered over the plate.

"I have an idea," she said. "Close your eyes. See if you can taste the color."

I scooped up a helping of mashed potatoes, closed my eyes, and spooned it into my mouth. I waited for the burst of green, the taste of leaves, or grass, or cucumbers. But nothing came. Just mashed potatoes. When I opened my eyes, she was smiling at me.

"It tastes the same," I said.

"Really? Let me try." She plucked her finger into the potato, dipped it into her mouth, and closed her eyes. "Mmmm. Tastes green to me."

"It does?" I asked in disbelief.

She nodded.

"What does green taste like?" I asked.

"Franny, sometimes you have to be open to surprises. Things aren't always the way you expect them to be. Sometimes you have to find the courage to take a risk. Like eating green potatoes."

I ate another forkful, but it became thick and sticky in my mouth and I couldn't talk.

"Color is a risk," she said.

I swallowed. "Then why is your kitchen all white?"

It flew out of my mouth and then she was quiet. And even though I didn't know why, I knew it was a question I wasn't supposed to ask. I felt alone, like I was standing in the middle of an empty room while she hid in the closet. But I needed to know why she scrubbed the kitchen clean every night. Why every exposed surface was painted a stark and antiseptic white. Why, sometimes before we went to bed, she knelt on her hands and knees and scoured the floors with a sponge, going over one spot on the tile over and over again. Sometimes she scrubbed so hard, she made herself bleed, but I ignored the band-aids I saw on her fingers the next morning.

Now, she looked as though she had forgotten that I was sitting there and was quiet for so long, I briefly thought that maybe she hadn't heard me.

"You make me want to be brave."

Then, she took the container of fluorescent orange yogurt and dumped it on the floor; it sounded alive as it splattered around the table legs. She got down on the ground and spread it all over, like she was finger painting. When she looked back up, she was smiling. I watched as she continued to spread the bright orange goop on the floor, into the crevices of the grout. It seeped into the valleys of her fingers and turned her skin the color of apricots.

I thought about courage. Matilda was the brave one. Matilda wasn't scared of anything. But now, there was no Matilda.

There was just me.

Matilda

"Did you get my message?" Lavi asked, twisting a curl around her middle finger.

Her mother nodded, and then raced toward a customer who was lifting his coffee cup high into the air. We were sitting at the counter of the Good As Gold diner and Lavi had been rolling the corner of her paper placemat back and forth until finally it ripped. Her mother returned, grabbed a handful of straws, and stuffed them into the pocket of her apron. She picked up a rag. "What was so important?"

Lavi's voice cracked when she spoke. "Daddy called."

Her mother stopped wiping the coffee-stained counter. I hadn't seen her up close since the ketchup incident and she looked different than what I remembered. Her hair was pulled back and her uniform was clean and pressed. She wore a nametag that said SARAH but the H at the end was faded, as though someone had tried to scratch it off. She held the rag in her hand for a minute, twisted it, and then smiled. I felt a sudden pulse, a type of electricity, shoot through my arm. Someone waved at her and she ran off, coffee pot in hand. I watched as her hair bounced behind her, like a horse's tail.

"It looks pretty don't you think? I put mayonnaise in it last night," Lavi said.

I nodded, but all I could think about was the tingly feeling still running down my arm and to my fingertips so I turned to the dessert case to distract myself. The sugared apple pie glittered and the peaks on the lemon meringue reminded me of the star at the top of a Christmas tree. Lavi's mom returned, and seconds later she eased a slice onto a plate and handed it to me. I dipped my fork into the tips of white, which jiggled delicately in defiance.

"What do you think he wants?" Lavi asked, reaching out and grabbing her mother's wrist.

She stopped moving and, just as she was about to speak, I felt a breeze sweep up the slope of my neck. Then he slid onto the stool and turned toward me.

"Hello ladies. Looks like someone forgot to invite me to the party." Daryl grabbed the fork out of my hand and helped himself to my pie.

"Hey!" I shouted and snatched it back.

"Least you could do for forgetting to send out my invite." He took my napkin and used it to wipe the corners of his mouth.

"Daryl!" Sara had her hands on her hips, but she was grinning. Daryl smiled back. A coffee cup flew into the air and she was off again.

"So, Lavi, what brings you here?" He hooked his feet into the base of my stool and swiveled himself around.

"Not sure that's any of your business," she replied, now rolling the empty sleeve of her straw into a tight, hard coil.

"Actually it is," he said, bringing his knees up so that they sank into the outside of my thigh. I hunched down to avoid the line of fire.

"I'll ask you again. What are you doing here?" This time he hissed the words and they skipped over my back like razor-edged pebbles.

She didn't speak or look at him, just kept tearing little bits of her placemat off and rolling them into tiny pointed toothpicks. Then I heard her mutter under her breath. "Fat ass."

"What did you say?" He leaned forward, toward me and Lavi and I felt his kneecap against my thigh.

"All you want is for everyone around you to be as miserable as you are." Her face turned red and she pushed herself hard off the stool. She bent down to get her backpack, but as she stood to leave, he reached across me and grabbed her sleeve. The material collapsed in his hand like the petals of a flower and she winced.

"Stay out of this, Lavi." His knuckles turned white as he gripped her tighter. Then, suddenly, he let go. She didn't move, frozen, like she was still being restrained. Before I could let out a breath I hadn't realized I was holding, she was gone and all I heard was the door to the diner slamming loudly behind her.

Daryl stayed where he was, his feet still hooked to the base of my stool. Then, as though he just remembered something he had forgotten, he disengaged himself and stood up to leave. "Tell my mother I had to get going and I'll see her tonight."

I didn't look up, but I could feel the draft of his quick movements push past me like a wave. Sara walked over to the door and closed it. She came back and sat beside me.

"Thank you for being their friend, Matilda. I know that sometimes it's probably really hard." She smiled and I felt a sparkle run through me that reminded me of the millions of tiny pinpricks I often felt when my arms or legs fall asleep. I shook my head a few times until I was sure that I had erased whatever it was I thought I had felt. Then I looked back at my plate and focused all my attention on gathering as much of what was left of my pie onto my fork. I was so lost in thought when I walked out, I didn't notice he was outside.

Waiting for me.

He grabbed me as soon as I passed the blinking neon leprechaun in the window of the Good As Gold.

"We need to talk," Daryl said, taking me by the elbow and hurrying me along. I was more startled than scared, so I didn't have time to consider how he planned to get what it was he wanted from me. He led me to a small office building that had a For Lease sign in front and pushed me down the alley. He pointed to a rusted metal fire escape ladder.

"You want me to climb up there?" I asked, looking up at what seemed like the last place I would ever go, beside maybe the side of a highway in the middle of the night.

He smiled. "You'll be fine, Mytilda. I'll be right behind you."

Not terribly comforted, I contemplated my options. I could refuse and try and outrun him, but part of me was curious to find out what it was he wanted. The other part understood that the likelihood of outrunning him was unlikely. So I handed him my backpack and used both arms to lift myself up onto the ladder. As promised, he came up behind me, his arms never far from my feet. When we reached the top, I jumped off and he followed. I noticed that in the corner of the roof was a doorway. "Why couldn't we have come through the door?"

"Because I don't like doing things the easy way."

I didn't know how to respond, so I said nothing. He unzipped his backpack and pulled out a brown paper bag, then unscrewed the cap off a bottle and handed it to me. "Drink."

"You first," I said, pushing it back in his direction. Without hesitation, he tipped it into his mouth. After several gulps, he wiped his mouth with his sleeve and handed the bottle back.

Besides stealing some sips of wine from my mother's glass, I had never really had alcohol before. The first sip tasted fruity, but it burned going down and reminded me of cherry cough syrup. I choked a little and he laughed. "What is this?"

"Blackberry brandy. Good stuff."

I nodded, not knowing any better. The sweetness lingered in the back of my throat, but I could still feel the burn. I wondered what my mother would think of me now. I took a few more sips, this time ignoring the burning feeling, which I was slowly getting used to. He grinned at me; I was now a member of some private club.

"What do you know about Lavi and my father?"

So that was what he was interested in: finding out what was going on with his sister and her plot to reunite their parents. I would have lied to protect her, but I didn't need to because she hadn't confided in me. She didn't trust me anymore. The muscles in my body loosened and I felt like my bones were made of liquid. I tilted my head back, closed my eyes, and felt the heat spread into my cheeks. He reached over and grabbed my arm, shaking me out of my dream.

"I don't know anything, Daryl. Except that your sister thinks that your mom and dad should get back together."

He let me go and took another sip from the bottle. His backpack was still unzipped and there was a small notebook hanging out of it, so I reached over and took it. He tried to grab it back and, when I sensed it was important to him, I pulled it close to my chest and crossed my arms. He reached from behind, putting his arms around me and trying to get me to release my grip. He was angry, muttering things under his breath that I could not understand.

I tucked my head in and kept my arms tightly closed. After a few minutes, I felt his anger subside until there was no struggle left. I was sitting between his legs and he had his arms around me. His chest was moving up and down fast. His breath hit the tip of my earlobe and then he swiveled me around so that my head was resting in the crook of his arm, like a baby.

I was closer to him than I had ever been before and then his lips were on mine and I closed my eyes because it felt good and I didn't want it to stop. I don't know how long we stayed like that, wrapped up in each other, quietly rocking under the heat of the setting sun. When he separated himself from me, I unlocked my arms, which were still clutched around his notebook, and I handed it back.

"Aren't you going to look at it?" he asked.

"Not if you don't want me to."

"I don't." he snarled, the warmth of the moment instantly gone. "C'mon. We gotta go." He stood up and walked toward the door.

"I thought you didn't like doing things the easy way."

"Believe me. This isn't the easy way."

When I stood up, I understood what he meant. My stomach lifted into my throat and the clouds started spinning around my head. I put my hands out to steady myself, but that made it worse. He came over and took my arm and led me across the roof. I wanted to say something to turn him back into the Daryl whose breath I had felt against my neck, but every time I tried to speak, the words got jumbled up in my mouth. When we got to the door, he pulled a small screwdriver out of his pocket. He kneeled over the doorknob and eventually pushed it open. I followed him down four flights of stairs with a tight hold on the back of his jacket.

When we got to my house, he opened the door and pushed me inside. Through the window I watched him walk the path to his unit. When I was sure I was alone, I raced up the stairs to the bathroom. I got down on my hands and knees and heaved into the toilet. I wretched for a long time, holding on to the rim of the seat and watching as my insides emptied themselves into the bowl. I thought about leprechauns and cough syrup and lemon meringue pie and made promises to myself I knew that I wouldn't keep.

Afterward, I cleaned my face and got into bed. My mother worked late that night, and when she came home, I told her I had the stomach flu. I don't think she believed me, but I didn't care. I didn't care about anything.

Except Daryl.

When I wasn't thinking about Daryl, I was thinking about how much I missed my sister and my grandmother and that it had been a very long time since I could remember feeling anything else but sad. One night, as I tried hard to fall asleep, I rolled over onto my back and stared up at the ceiling. And that's when I heard it.

Footsteps.

Someone was walking down the stairs. I pulled the covers closer around my ears and looked over at the clock radio on my nightstand. 12:23. I rolled back over, hoping maybe it was all in my imagination, but then I heard it again. The only thing remotely weapon-like I could find in my room was a shoe, so I picked it up and walked along the outer edges of the carpet, trying to make as little noise as possible.

My mother's bedroom door was open, but something about the way the light filtered through the hall made me know she wasn't inside. I chewed the ragged skin around my thumbnail and crept slowly down the hall with the shoe in my other hand. When I reached the top of the stairs, I crouched down low because I could hear my mother's voice. I flattened myself out on the landing and leaned my head as far out onto the step as I could.

"Slow down." She was talking on the only telephone in the house, which hung on the wall in the kitchen. I pictured her winding the cord over and over, making little white nooses around her finger.

"You can handle this. It will be okay."

I had a mosquito bite on my ankle. As hard as I tried to ignore it, I couldn't resist scratching it. I raked my fingers across the skin, gently at first, but then harder and harder until it started to hurt.

"You will figure it out," my mom was saying.

She whispered something that I couldn't hear, so I inched myself closer, but then the shoe slipped out of my hand and went careening down the stairs. I watched as it fell, making a muted thudding noise as it hit each step. I only had a few minutes to decide what to do. I thought about tiptoeing back to my bedroom and crawling under the covers, but I was tired of being a coward. I sat up on the step, crossed my arms across my chest, and waited for her to come find me.

She hung up the telephone, walked to the staircase, and looked up at me. Her hair was folded around her head like she had been tossing and turning for most of the night.

"What are you doing?" she said with a sigh as she lifted her hand to her forehead and massaged her temples with her fingers.

"Listening to you." I walked down the stairs so that we were standing eye to eye. "Are you going to tell me what that was all about?"

"Nothing that concerns you." She turned and walked into the living room and flopped down onto the couch.

The room was dark, but I followed her and hit my toe on the coffee table, which made me even angrier.

"Maybe if you told me what was going on, I wouldn't have to eavesdrop in the middle of the night," I spoke it into the near blackness, not seeing or caring what impact my words had.

"Why do you always have to make things difficult?" She leaned back so that her head was resting on top of the cushion.

Once my eyes grew accustomed to the dark, I could see that both her hands were up, covering her face.

"Why couldn't you handle taking care of Franny anymore? Why did you dump her off at the first place you could find?"

"You don't understand," she said, her voice muffled as she continued to hide her face from me.

Maybe I was tired or still half asleep, but I was not willing to give in to her as easily as I usually did.

"I do understand. This is about you because everything is always all about you."

She dropped her hands. Even in the dark, I could see her face turn pale; I had caught her off-guard. She said nothing and that made me even angrier.

"I wish you would have just left me behind."

I wondered how long those words had been sitting inside of me, like a round of ammunition, waiting to be shot out.

"Oh, Matilda. I can't even tell you how many times I've wished the same thing. But for whatever reason, you are the one I am stuck with."

She walked back into the kitchen and then I heard the jingle of keys and the door slam behind her.

I don't really know where she went or how long I sat alone in that dark, empty room. All I know is that after a while I got up and went upstairs to my bedroom. I'd grown tired of waiting.

In the morning, the only evidence of the night before was an empty container of ice cream left on the kitchen counter. There was a big brown spot where she had left her spoon. I walked past my mother slowly, because I wasn't sure what she might do or say. I waited for her to apologize, to tell me that she didn't regret bringing me along and that she never wished she had left me behind. When that didn't come, I opened the cabinet and found the peanut butter. I took out a butter knife, swirled it around in the jar until I got a thick rounded wedge, and spread the peanut butter on a slice of bread. Still nothing.

As she started to pack her things, I cleared my throat and she looked up. Interrupted. "What is it, Matilda?"

I didn't know how to respond, how to tell her that I felt cracked open and needed her to glue the pieces back together. She handed me a permission slip for a school trip I had forgotten I had given her, and when I didn't take it, she left it on the table. I opened the refrigerator door and felt the cool air hit my face when I reached for the strawberry jam. When I pulled my head back out again, she was gone.

I crumpled the permission slip, tossed it into the trash along with my half-made peanut butter and jelly sandwich, and then because I couldn't stand being there for one more second, I left. Even though it wasn't warm enough yet, I put on a pair of flip-flops because I liked the sound they made when I walked in them.

Once I got outside, I didn't know where to go. Most people had left for school or work already and the air felt empty. I thought about walking toward the row of mailboxes at the end of the driveway, but it was too early to get the mail and, even if it wasn't, nothing ever came for me since no one knew where I was. So I walked in the grass, which was wet and made my feet feel slippery.

Maybe I ended up there because there wasn't any other place for me to end up. I was at the edge of the complex where Daryl had taken me that night to watch the trucks trample his jeans. When I looked down the hill, I saw him sitting on the ground, scribbling in what looked like the notebook I had tried to take from him that day on the roof. I tried to sneak up on him, but my flip-flopping gave me away. He turned towards me, the curl of his lip reminded me of a hissing snake. When he saw it was me, his face softened, but only for a second.

"What are you doing here?" he asked as he shoved the notebook into his backpack.

I had to rewind to the last time we were together to decide how to approach him. It was like losing my place in a book and skimming through the pages to find where I last left off.

"Thought this was a free country." I sat down, took my flip-flops off, and buried my toes into the soft, wet grass.

"No school for you today, Mytilda?"

"It's Maaatilda, and yes, it's an unofficial holiday." I leaned back against my elbows. "What's the big secret with your notebook?"

A car drove past and I wondered what we looked like to someone passing by.

"It's nothing." He pulled a blade of grass out of the ground and used the soft flesh of his thumb to flatten it.

I wanted him to confide in me. Tell me things he wouldn't tell anyone else. But I knew that first I had to offer him something that would make him know that I was trustworthy. "I have these dreams, sometimes."

He put the blade of grass in his mouth.

"It's always dark and I am screaming. Everything around me is swirling and then suddenly it all turns red."

A plane flew above us, but neither of us looked up. He didn't say anything, just stared straight ahead. "Does your mother know you're out here?"

I laughed and it sounded short and mean. "My mother wishes that I would just disappear."

"Then, maybe you should."

"Maybe I should."

He was quiet and I felt betrayed. Exposed. I started to get up to leave and that's when he tossed it at me.

His notebook.

As curious as I was to open it, something held me back. For a moment, I thought that maybe not knowing was better. I looked up and saw a van drive slowly past. On its side were the words JOSEPH'S PLUMBING and I wondered what it felt like to travel through the world with a sign that told the whole world exactly who you were.

I opened the book.

It was filled with drawings of big shoes and tiny heads like Daryl had been looking up from deep within the ground when he drew them. They were normal everyday people, except for the little corners of capes hanging from behind their backs. Tiny squares here and there, peeking out from pockets and jackets and zippers, all colored a bright sky blue. His notebook was filled with drawings of superheroes. Except that they were superheroes in disguise.

I closed the book and squeezed it tightly to my chest, but not like the last time when I was trying to take it away from him. "I think my sister would like it here."

He didn't answer. Just kept pulling at the grass.

"Except for before she was born, this is the longest we've been apart."

"Is she a part of your screaming dream?"

The tone of his voice and the fact that he was actually listening surprised me. "Franny is never a part of that dream. I am always alone."

"It's probably something stupid like your mom wouldn't let you eat candy when you were a kid." He snickered and Mean Daryl quietly crept into our moment.

I slipped my feet back into my flip-flops. I hated when I wasn't sure if he was making fun of me.

"What about your dad? Maybe he knows something." His voice was softer now.

"I don't know my dad," I told him.

He unzipped his backpack and held down the flap so that it looked like the tongue of a panting dog.

"Here," he said, handing me the familiar brown bottle.

"No."

He pushed it toward me, pressing the opening against my bottom lip. I took a sip and thought about promises.

"Who would know?"

"Know what?" I ignored the burn snaking its way down my throat.

"About your dad? Who would know about him?"

"Maybe my grandmother. But the only thing she's ever told me is that my mother wanted me to stay away from him." I was already starting to feel sleepy.

"Who else?"

I suddenly decided I needed to lie down in the sun and close my eyes. I felt warm inside and out and I was starting to forget my mother's words from the night before. "Probably Leah. I bet Leah would know."

My head felt heavy, so I rolled over and stretched my body out onto the grass. Trucks drove past and soon the rumbles incorporated themselves into my dreams, a steady rustling noise that sounded like door after door closing behind me.

When I woke, he was gone. Beside me was a note that said "MEET ME OUTSIDE THE GAG AT FIVE." I didn't hesitate for a second.

Well, maybe just a second.

I stood outside of the GAG and, when I didn't see him, I peeked over the blinking leprechaun to see if I could see her, but she wasn't there. Instead, there was a fat waitress at her station who kept getting stuck between customers' chairs. When I turned back around, he was standing beside me and I knew he had seen me looking. His hands were in his pockets and he was wearing a blue button-down shirt that hung past the waistband of his leather jacket.

"Find what you were looking for?"

I shrugged. I wasn't about to try and explain something I didn't understand myself so I looked down at my shoes. "Why are we here?"

He clicked his head in the direction he wanted me to go and I followed him to the corner.

"In here." He pointed to a telephone booth with a door that opened and closed like an accordion.

"You want me to go inside?" It was old and the panels of glass were scratched, which made it look like it was filled with fog.

He nodded.

I opened the door and cringed as a waft of pee hit my face. I turned to leave, but he was right behind me, using his chest to push me forward.

His ear brushed past my mouth and I breathed in the smell of his shampoo.

"Now what?" I planted my arms firmly across my chest, partly because I wanted to look annoyed, but more because there wasn't enough room to do much else.

"Here." He dug into his pocket and brought out a roll of coins wrapped in maroon paper.

"What's this for?"

He pointed to the telephone.

"Who am I supposed to call?"

"Leah." His whisper flew past my chin like a feather.

"Don't think so." I tried to push past him, but he wouldn't budge. "Let me out."

I unclasped my arms and pushed him harder than I meant to, harder than I knew I could. If it took him by surprise, he didn't react, instead he kept thrusting the roll of coins at me, like a gun at my side, poking me until I had to turn and face him.

Maybe I agreed because I thought that I might get to hear Franny's voice. Or maybe because of the way he was looking at me. When the operator asked me for the listing, I said her name slowly, "Leah. Leah Dugan."

He handed me a pen and then opened the palm of his hand so that I could write the number down. I held his hand open and wrote, watching the ink seep into the lines of his skin. When I was finished, he made a fist, like he got what he came for.

"Now call."

"Why? What is it you want me to find out?"

"Your father. Find out who he is."

I laughed. Because he thought the solution was so simple. Because of how the ink had rubbed off in his palm and made it look like blood.

"It's not going to help."

"Maybe it will."

"No."

"Maybe he can explain about the dream. The one with all the screaming in it."

I looked out through the blurry glass. I felt safe inside with him. Like we were invisible. Invincible. I should have asked him why it was so important to him. Why he needed to believe that my father could fix the mess I was in. But I didn't.

Instead, I unclenched his fist and punched in the numbers and pretended they were Leah's eye sockets. I pressed hard against the metal squares, poking and pushing until I heard a faint ringing in my ears. Up to the point that she answered, I wasn't sure if it was real or just my heart pulsing inside my head. She said hello more than once. I held the phone close to my ear, pressing it tightly to my chin. I counted for seven seconds and then right before I thought she was going to hang up I spoke.

"Hi."

I could hear her breaths on the other side of the phone. Like butterfly wings clapping together.

"Matilda?"

"Yup." I answered, as if I called every day.

"Is everything alright?"

"It's great."

"Matilda, are you in some kind of trouble?"

"How is Franny?" I asked. I twisted my fingers into the cord and then stopped.

"She's okay."

More quiet.

"How are you?"

Daryl looked at me for a minute and then opened the accordion doors and went outside.

"I'm fine."

"Is there something you need?"

"Why?" I had planned a heartbreaking beginning to this conversation, but that was the only word that came out, and when it did, it sounded muffled.

"Matilda, is there something you want?"

"Yes. Tell me why."

"I don't know what you want."

"Why are you covering for Therese?" Calling my mother by her first name made me feel rebellious.

There was a few seconds of silence. "Your mother loves you, and even though it may not seem like it, she's doing what is best for all of us."

"My mother is a bitch."

The words slipped as effortlessly from my lips as they did through the holes in the receiver. Leah was quiet again. Daryl crossed his arms behind his back and was softly hitting his fingertips against the glass. I closed my eyes and held my breath until it matched the rhythm he was tapping.

"What's in it for you, anyway?"

"Excuse me?" As if she didn't understand.

"I said, what's in it for you?"

"I heard you the first time." Her voice was flat, which for some reason filled me with rage.

"My mother gets to live like the world revolves around her and you get to have the daughter you've always wanted. Is that what this is all about?"

There was a quick gasp that reminded me of what I sounded like when I got hit in the stomach with a dodge ball in gym class—the wind, totally knocked out of me. Then there was silence.

"That's enough," she said.

But it wasn't. It bubbled up inside of me and I knew that it would never be enough.

"Enjoy it while you can, because I am coming back for my sister. She doesn't belong to you and I am going to come back for her."

"Goodbye, Matilda."

I slammed the phone down hard, disconnecting from her first. I inhaled deeply, gloriously impervious to the stench of pee, but my body betrayed me, and I felt a sliver of weakness start to make its way up. I wiped my eyes with the back of my sleeve and shook the door to let Daryl know I wanted to get out. He eyed me up and down, seemingly expecting my expression to somehow give it all away.

"Well?" he asked as I brushed past him.

"Well, what?"

"Did she tell you? Your father's name?"

"No."

"His name is Tim. Timothy Yaga. I looked it up."

He smiled, shaking his head back and forth, enjoying my obvious look of surprise.

"You knew? Why did you just let me waste my time calling Leah?"

"Because I thought maybe you should hear it from someone who's actually involved in this whole thing," he said with a slight shrug.

I didn't know what to say, though I knew what I *wanted* to say. I wanted to tell him that I had found a copy of my birth certificate in my mother's nightstand drawer when I was eight, but that my father's name had been blackened out. I was going to tell him that it didn't matter anyway and that he was an idiot if he thought that the answer to all of this would be contained in a three-minute phone call to Leah or that there was anything my father could do to fix things. More than anything, I wanted to wipe that smug look off of his face.

I opened my mouth to speak, but stopped when I saw the corner of his blue shirt hanging out beneath the hem of his jacket.

Like a cape.

Franny

Besides Evelyn, kids didn't invite me to sit with them at lunch or to go to parties or to play after school. They'd smile at me or say hi but that's about all. Some of the time, I wished I could disappear even more, and other times I wondered what it felt like to be normal. So when Leah offered to take Evelyn and me to a movie, I thought about courage. Evelyn was so excited and I didn't want to tell her that I had never been to the movies. My mother sometimes took Matilda, but the thought of my going with them had never crossed anyone's mind, including my own.

We picked a movie about a princess who falls in love with a monster and after we got the tickets, we stood in line at the concession stand. Leah bought us each a bag of popcorn. I didn't tell her that I was scared of popcorn. That it was crunchy and loud was troubling enough, but the fact that it needed to explode before you could eat it terrified me even more. While Leah paid, I threw half of it into the trashcan. I folded down the top of the bag and when Evelyn asked if I was going to have some, I told her I was waiting until we got inside and then I stuffed the rest into my coat pocket.

The theater was dark, which I liked because then no one could see the letters slipping past my lips. I sat between Leah and Evelyn. Leah eased down into her chair so that her knees pressed into the seat in front and her head was level with mine. The lights went down and then it got darker, like a blanket I could hide under. Suddenly the curtain went up and the screen was filled with light and I felt like I was in the middle of a snowstorm being pelted by hail. I felt my stomach squeeze like it did sometimes when we drove in the car for too long. My grandmother always told me to find something steady to fix my eyes on. It was dark enough in the theater that I could turn my head and focus on Leah without anyone really noticing. The brightness from the screen made her face glow like she had swallowed a candle, flame and all.

The sound was as much of a problem as the lights. It pounded at my ears and made the room feel like it was shaking, so I held on tightly to the armrests. Leah leaned her head into mine and I breathed in the smell of flowers and butter. One time she caught me staring and gave my hand a squeeze and then laid her head back next to mine and I breathed her in some more. I hated that I could still feel the flutters in my stomach, like I had swallowed a nest full of baby birds.

When the movie ended and the lights turned on, I felt shaky and disoriented. All I could think about was getting to the bathroom. We stood in line and everyone around me looked disheveled, like we had all taken a long nap together. Leah and Evelyn talked about the movie, but because I had spent most of my time staring at Leah, I didn't have much to say so I just nodded my head.

The line moved slowly and it was hard for me to focus because I felt like I was going to pee in my pants. When I finally got into a stall, I squatted like my mother had taught me and tried not to let the sound of all the flushing toilets make my heart pound faster. I covered my ears, but all I could hear were the toilets flushing, one after the next, until the fluttering in my stomach leaped through my throat and into my head and bounced between my ears like a big hollow ping pong ball. I wrapped my arms around myself and rocked back and forth, trying to make it stop. Leah knocked on the door quietly and then more loudly. She called my name over and over, but I couldn't answer.

I tried to remember how wonderful she smelled and how good I felt when I was with her. I wanted so much to make it stop, but I couldn't move. I took some deep breaths, but that didn't work either. So I started spelling, first the letters floating randomly in my head, then the graffiti written on the door of the stall. Leah was still calling out my name, her voice shaky, like it might break. I forced myself to bite down on my lip and make it stop long enough so that I could open the door.

When I came out, I saw that her face was white and she hugged me. We went outside where it was cool and it made the hotness on my face feel better. We waited for Evelyn's mother to pick her up and Evelyn and Leah talked more about the movie, but their sentences were short and choppy and when they talked they looked down at the ground. I tucked myself into Leah and she rubbed my arms up and down like it was freezing outside, even though it wasn't, and we waited until Evelyn's mother came and she got in and they drove off.

When we got into the car, Leah helped me with my seat belt. I was shaking and she turned the heat on high until it got very warm. Finally, it was quiet and all I heard was the sound of our tires rolling over the pavement and Leah crying. She made a funny noise and said, "Franny, when I am with you, I remember the person that I was before. The person I am supposed to be."

I didn't know what to say because I didn't know what she meant. I went into my pocket and uncurled the top of the popcorn bag and stuck my hand inside. It was cold and greasy, but I managed to get one out. It felt stiff in my fingers, like a piece of Styrofoam and I couldn't imagine eating it. But then I thought about Leah and how I had made her cry and before the flapping in my stomach could start again, I shoved one into my mouth. I only bit it once before I heard a loud crunch that rumbled in my ear and sent slivers of pain into my forehead. It scratched the roof of my mouth and before I could swallow, a little piece got stuck in my tooth. It was hard as stone and after I pried it loose, I swallowed it.

My eyes filled with tears and I didn't know if I was crying because of the popcorn or just because. The traffic light turned red and, when I looked outside, I saw that we were stopped in front of a park. I wiped my nose with the back of my sleeve and watched perfect little girls with perfectly bouncing ponytails circle the baseball field in their perfect pink bicycles. I couldn't take my eyes off them, but then the light turned green and Leah sped off, the sound of bicycle bells ringing in my ears.

The next day at school, Evelyn and I were standing beside the pencil sharpener, which was bolted to the window ledge. I turned the handle hard and listened to the sound it made as it chewed the outer edge of my pencil. When I looked up, I saw a woman talking to Mrs. Ficsh. I couldn't hear what she was saying, but she was pointing at me and then Mrs. Ficsh called me to her desk.

"Franny, this is Mrs. Skoll. She wants to speak with you."

S-K-O-L-L. Like skull. She moved so quickly down the hallway that I had to skip to keep up with her. She brought me into her office, which was small and cluttered with papers. Hanging from the only exposed wall was a poster of a little boy holding a baseball glove that read, "Smiles are Catchy." The tape had come off one of the corners, which curled over the word "catchy."

"Please sit." She moved a stack of papers piled on a chair. It was warm in her office, but I crossed my arms across my chest and cupped my elbows like I was cold.

"How are you, Frances?"

"It's Franny," I whispered.

She was flipping through papers, but then she stopped. "I understand that you are living with a family friend? Leah Dugan?"

I nodded.

"Things going okay?" When she spoke, she looked down at my shoes so I looked down, too.

I nodded again.

"That's good." She scribbled something on a piece of paper and when I squinted I could see that her writing was curly and big. "Is there anything you would like to talk to me about?"

I rubbed the rounds of my elbows.

"I know this has been a difficult transition for you. I just want to make sure you are doing okay and see if there is anything we can do to support you." Her skin was pockmarked and when she smiled, her face reminded me of a walnut shell.

I shook my head.

"Change can be hard and Ms. Dugan doesn't know you the way your mother did."

I brought my hands down from my elbows and put them in my lap. The movies. The bathroom. The car ride home. Leah was why I was here. Skull was staring at me, waiting for a response, but I didn't know what to say. She clicked the top of her pen on and off like she was sending me a message in Morse code. I looked up at the poster, at the boy with his catcher's mitt, and I swallowed hard to get rid of the lump that was forming in my throat. My face turned red and then my eyes filled with the kind of tears that feel hot when they touch your skin.

"It's okay, dear." She pulled open her desk drawer and handed me a tissue.

I took it from her and then wedged it into the corner of my eye like I was filling up a hole in a sinking ship.

"We are just trying to figure out how to make things easier for you, Frances." She shuffled through some more papers.

The tears distorted my vision and made her look like a big brown smudge. She said something else, but because my heart was pounding so loudly in my ears, I didn't hear.

"We will come up with a solution that is good for everyone."

I nodded, not sure what she was talking about. She stood up and motioned for me to follow. She walked a little slower this time so I didn't have to skip. The hallways were covered in artwork, which I usually liked looking at, but this time I walked with my head down, counting the tiles on the ground. I counted seventy-three before we got back to the classroom. Mrs. Ficsh nodded at me when I walked in and again she and Mrs. Skoll whispered to each other.

Evelyn poked me in the arm. "What did she want?"

"To find out how I am doing."

"Be careful around her. Last year she talked to Bobby McCarthy and the next day they took him away."

I picked up my sharpened pencil and pressed the pad of my thumb into its tip. It left little dots where it pushed up against my skin. Mrs. Ficsh went to the board and filled it with numbers and I tried to focus but it made no sense.

None of it made any sense.

I felt like someone had forced me to swallow a bowling ball, which now sat at the bottom of my chest. Every time I took a breath, I could feel it pinning me down. I couldn't get Evelyn's words out of my head. They got louder and louder until they were all I could hear. I thought about Leah's face when I came out of that bathroom stall. I thought about my mother and the last time I had seen her and about popcorn and pink bicycles.

Evelyn squeezed my hand on the drive home. "It will be okay. I won't let anyone take you away."

My fingers were starting to pinch under her grip, but I didn't pull away. She was so determined that for a minute I believed her. Leah loved me. She wasn't going to get rid of me. She wasn't going to give me away. I took a deep breath and closed my eyes.

When I opened them, Evelyn's mother had almost reached Leah's house. The street was usually empty but this time there was a car parked in front. She pulled up beside a white Ford that I recognized instantly.

Because it belonged to my grandmother.

When I got to the front door, Evelyn and her mother waved and I watched as their car turned the corner, shooting streams of exhaust into the air. I held the doorknob in my hand and rubbed the key hanging around my neck.

Then I walked away.

At first I walked fast, thinking someone might be following me, but when no one came I slowed down. The thought of being left again, of Leah sending me off, was just something I could not bear, so I pushed it out of my head and started numbering each cement square on the sidewalk, counting twice every time the root of a tree buckled one in half. Once I finished, I realized I was lost. I started to feel something puffing in my belly, so I squeezed my fists tight and squinted my eyes and after a few minutes it went away. I told myself that I wasn't lost because you could only be lost if you had somewhere to go.

I stepped over tricycles and walked past driveways with happy faces drawn in chalk. Women smiled at me as they pushed baby strollers down the street. It was getting close to dinnertime and I watched fathers get out of their cars, trading briefcases for small children. I had never been on my own before and something inside of me tingled. At the corner, I decided to follow a yellow butterfly fluttering along a line of pink flowers. I had to walk quickly to keep up, but then suddenly it disappeared and I felt more alone than I did before.

My stomach started to rumble, so I unzipped my backpack and searched inside but all I could find was a half-eaten banana, now much darker than the yellow it had been that morning. I ate it anyway. It was soft and ripe and tasted brown and made me think of Leah.

I walked faster and my legs were getting tired and my stomach was grumbling more. I reached the end of the houses and then I saw a street with a Laundromat and a convenience store. Ignoring the buzz vibrating through my ears, I found a bench and sat down and told myself that the swelling growing in my belly was only happening because I was hungry.

Four bicycles leaning against the front of the store caught my eye. They each had red ribbons woven into the wheels and I tried to trace the pattern with my eyes, but I couldn't drown out the throbbing in my head so I took some long deep breaths. Then I pretended I was underwater, in the pool in the art building, with Leah up in the stands watching over me. I was so lost in dreams of blue that I didn't notice the girls who came out of the store to reclaim their bikes.

"Library Girl!" one of them shouted.

"Wanna play, retard?" the second one said as she moved in behind the first. They were the girls who snickered at Evelyn and me when we left the cafeteria after lunch to go to the library.

The third one lifted the top off her can of Pepsi and it popped open like a gun. She edged in behind the second so that I was surrounded. I did what I usually do when I don't know what else to do.

P-E-P-S-I.

"Did you say something, Library Girl?" Number one got close to my face. She was sucking hard on a candy that made her lips purple. I turned my head and she laughed.

"I think Library Girl likes my soda." Number three smiled. She lifted the can high into the air and then tipped it so that it splashed onto the cement, spraying my shoes and legs, but I didn't move. She put her face close to mine. "What do you think of that?"

I stared down at the foam, which was now sizzling on the ground. The sound of fizz filled my ears until that was all I could hear, so when the fourth girl came out and spoke, I couldn't make out what she said, but the other three moved away.

The girl was taller than the others and she wore a dark gray shirt with its sleeves cut off. The material around the holes looked frayed and I wondered if it was itchy. The other three got on their bikes, but she came closer. She was chewing gum and blew a big bubble that popped near my nose. It made me jump, which made her laugh. When she spoke, her words were heavy with sugary spit and they didn't make any sense—maybe because the sound of the fizzing soda was still in my ears. Finally, I had to look away because her face was too close.

When I looked up again, she was getting on her bike and a man was waving his arms and yelling. I rocked back and forth with my hands wrapped around my elbows. I didn't look up at him and after a while he walked away, too.

It was getting cold and I was tired and hungry and the bench had a stray nail that I kept forgetting to avoid. It had already poked a hole into my tights, so when I moved I could feel the wood pressing up against my bare skin. It felt rough and dry and I wondered if I would get a splinter and if it would hurt and then I thought about how tired I was of being scared of everything all the time. I rocked harder and faster, ignoring the dark and the cold, so that all I could feel was the rhythm running through my body and then I started thinking about flying.

Specifically into space.

We were studying the planets in science. I memorized their order, loving mostly how they each seemed to know exactly where they belonged. When I finally stopped rocking, I went inside the Laundromat and took a seat in front of a row of dryers, watching the clothes whirl and turn. I pretended that I was an astronaut. I imagined what it would feel like to spin around on Saturn's rings, riding faster and faster through the black air. A voice that took me a few minutes to recognize broke me out of my dream: the man who had chased away the girls in front of the convenience store.

"Want some?" He opened his hand, exposing a fist full of M&Ms, but I shook my head. He dropped them into his mouth and they crackled as they mashed against his teeth. When he finished, he wiped his hand down the length of his thigh. "Is your mother here?"

Again, I shook my head. My stomach started to growl and I wondered if I should have taken him up on his candy offer. I looked at the vending machine and tried to remember how much change was floating around the inside of my backpack.

"You do the laundry to help her out."

I wasn't sure if it was a statement or a question so I just shrugged. He handed me the bag of candy and this time I took some. I ate two at a time, sucking them slowly so that I didn't have to bite into the crunchy coating covering the chocolate.

"I used to help my dad out." The man's arms were brown and skinny and covered with silver fuzz that looked like dust balls. "One time he was doing some work on the roof. I told him not to. I told him it was dangerous. But he didn't listen to me."

He dropped the last few candies into his hand and then folded the empty bag into a long skinny rectangle. I waited for him to finish the story. To tell me what happened. But he didn't. He popped the chocolates into his mouth and picked up the newspaper and started to read.

I unzipped the pocket in my backpack, took out some change, and walked over to the vending machine. Uncertain as to what a real astronaut would choose, I decided on a bag of pretzels and slowly punched in the code, holding my breath as a big metal ring turned and dropped the bag down. Back at my seat, I sucked the pretzels until they turned to mush in my mouth. The man was gone. He left his newspaper on the seat next to me.

I wasn't sure what to do next. My stomach started to tighten, squeezing the M&Ms and pretzels inside of me. I pressed the palms of my hands together and stared at the spinning clothes, but now all it did was make me feel dizzy. I dug around inside my backpack and found a book I had taken out from the library about a pig and a spider. The farmer wanted to kill the pig because he was a runt. After a few pages, I put the book away.

A woman came in, dragging a big bag of laundry behind her, and two little boys followed. They looked the same, one bigger than the other, with short buzz haircuts that made me want to rub the tops of their heads. The older one kept pinching the younger one, but every time the mother looked over he would stop. She didn't look over very often because she was too busy trying to stuff all of their dirty clothes into one machine. The older one was drinking milk out of a carton. When he saw me looking, he stuck his tongue out and his spit spilled out in white stretchy strings. His mother walked over to the change machine and he got out of his chair and came closer to me. He still had the milk in his hand and I could make out the picture of a missing child on the side. I wondered if Leah would put a picture of me on a milk carton. I wondered if I was missing.

I took a deep breath, but all I could smell was electric heat and detergent. I put the half-empty bag of pretzels into my backpack and went outside. Walking in the dark made me feel clean and I wondered if that's how the astronauts felt when they were floating in space. I started thinking about planets again and how easily they understood where they fit in and before I knew it I found my way back to Leah's house.

It looked different in the dark. All the lights were on and I could make out the white and blue flash of the television. I started to walk up the path, but then I stopped and instead, I turned and walked to the back of the house. I lay down on the grass and propped my backpack underneath my head and stared up, breathing in so deeply I worried I might loosen one of the stars from its spot in the sky. It was black outside and I felt like I was invisible. I pulled my jacket up close around my ears and turned on my side. Soon the letters in my head quieted and Leah's garden wrapped itself around me. Fireflies danced near my head and the air smelled sweet, like candy. I looked back up at the sky and wondered if one day I would finally be able to figure it out.

Exactly where I fit.

When I woke, she was lying beside me. The sun was starting to rise and I wasn't sure if I was dreaming. She looked still, like a house after everyone had gone to bed, but then she opened her eyes and reached across to touch my face.

"Where did you go?" she asked, still cupping my cheek. I put my hand on top of hers because I wasn't sure if she was real or if I was lost in a dream.

"Nowhere."

The pink in her cheeks started to fade.

"I won't do it again."

Her eyes got glassy and I felt sadness begin in the roof of my mouth. I squeezed tight and it formed a lump in the back of my throat. I promised myself that this time I would be good and that no matter what, I would not give her another reason to give me away. I promised myself that I would be the person I was supposed to be. The person she wanted me to be.

"Nowhere isn't a very nice place to be." She traced her finger down my cheek and under my chin. "There's something I want to talk to you about."

Her breaths were long and heavy and their heat spent a second at the tip of my nose before disappearing. The thought of losing her was too much and I didn't want to watch her say the words, so I closed my eyes. But then I was alone and I felt the letters peeking through the darkness, so I opened them.

"When I was a little girl, I spent a lot of time nowhere."

I didn't speak and she was quiet for a few minutes.

"Franny, when I was a little girl, terrible things happened to me. The only place I had to go was nowhere."

I started to pull at the grass. "What kinds of things?" I wanted her to tell me, but then when she opened her mouth to speak, I was afraid that she would.

"Ugly, terrible things. And until I figured out that I could draw, I thought I was all alone. I was nowhere most of the time. But you don't need to be nowhere. You will always have me. Always."

More than anything, I wanted to believe, but then I thought about my grandmother's car parked in front of Leah's house and I remembered the look on Mrs. Skoll's face when she led me to her office. I tucked my chin down and she brought my head close to her chest. I heard the pounding of her heart and I wondered if it was the little girl that bad things happened to trying to get out. She kissed the top of my head and wrapped me more closely into her. I felt warm and, as the smell of wet grass seeped into my nose, I wanted to believe what she was saying because I could not imagine losing her.

We separated for a minute and she stared at my face. "You belong with me."

She licked her finger and used it to wipe a line of drool that had drizzled out during sleep and then helped me stand up. The moment we walked through the front door of the house, the telephone rang and Leah ran off to answer. She was in the kitchen speaking in hushed tones so I couldn't hear what she was saying.

The television was on with the volume turned down and my grandmother was lying on the couch. I watched the people on the screen move in silence and then I sat on the floor beneath her, leaning back, the vibration of her snores skimming the top of my head. We sat that way for a few minutes and then the pattern of her breathing changed and I knew she was awake. She reached out, touched my shoulders, and then pulled me close to her.

"The first time I saw you, I knew you were special."

I cringed, but my grandmother didn't seem to notice. "Is that why she left?"

Her face shifted for a second before she spoke. "Your mother left you here with Leah because she thought that was best."

Leah walked back into the room. Her face looked gray, like a storm cloud had rubbed itself across her cheeks.

"Anything important?" my grandmother asked.

Leah just shook her head. "No, nothing important. Are you hungry? Why don't I go make some breakfast."

I found a pillow and hugged it close to me, rocking back and forth as Leah quickly left the room.

"Do you think a lot about being left?" my grandmother asked.

I shrugged, folding myself more tightly into the pillow.

She clasped her arms around me, squeezing so hard that it hurt. She was quiet then and sunk her face into my hair. We rocked together. "Would you like to come home with me?"

I didn't want to always be the one that everyone worried about. I was tired of causing trouble for all the people around me. I shook my head.

"I will always love you, Franny."

I know she meant to make me feel safe and I wanted to feel that way. I could hear Leah humming small little pieces of songs that I did not recognize. I felt my grandmother's arms around me and I thought about her words. I wanted to feel protected, like everything was going to be okay. But all I felt was tired of being scared. Tired of being the one that people always thought they had to take care of.

Therese

It was Therese's job to spot the red ones.

Then Tim would slow the car down so that by the time they reached the traffic light, it would have already changed from red to green, without them ever having had to come to a full stop. There were no cars on the road at that hour of night and they coasted along the black streets like pirates.

Matilda craved motion. She needed to be rocked, pushed, moved, and driven. The few times they were forced to stop, she would hold her breath and let out a scream that made Therese's eardrums vibrate so violently that afterward she would need to lie down with a cold compress across her forehead. Tim took Matilda driving at night because that was the only way to get her to sleep. Therese came along because she liked looking into other people's houses.

"We need to start thinking about a place of our own," she said, trying to peek inside a house whose lights were on.

"No."

As they slowed down at a stop sign, Matilda started puffing air through her lips.

"What's your problem?" Therese asked, turning away from him and tilting her head to get a better angle of the house they were passing.

"She's going to lose it any minute."

"I didn't mean about the baby. I meant about your mother. Why can't we leave her and find a place of our own?"

"No."

He pumped the gas and the car lurched forward. Therese looked up, realizing she had forgotten to warn him about the red light. He came to a full stop even though they were the only ones on the road. The sputters coming from the backseat sounded like the first few drops of a rainstorm getting bigger and meaner until they all ran into each other and formed one long continuous wail.

"Just run it," Therese said, reaching back to jiggle Matilda, which only made her angrier.

"No," Tim said as the shrieks got louder and bounced off the windshield, making the air around them shake. Therese pursed her lips and squinted her eyes, but he just gripped the steering wheel tighter and waited for the light to turn green.

"Are you trying to punish me?" she asked.

"The light will change in a second."

"I don't mean about the light, I mean about your mother."

Tim hit the gas hard and the tires squealed as they spun on the asphalt. Once they were moving, Matilda quieted.

"If we have to stay in that house then I am going back to work and your mother can take care of the baby during the day."

"No." He was doing laps around a series of blocks with no traffic signals.

The third time they passed the same street sign, she turned back to look at Matilda, who was snoring peacefully. "She's asleep."

They drove up to a stop sign and he put his head back and closed his eyes. Therese reached over and stroked his knee. As he arched his back, she slid her hand beneath his shirt and drew circles on the skin above his belt buckle. She lifted herself and started to move towards him, but Matilda stirred and he pushed her hand away.

"There's no one here. It's the middle of the night."

"No." He straightened and flipped on the turn signal. The loud automated click made her feel like she was trapped inside a clock. She turned her head and stared out the window.

They drove home in quiet. It was late and none of the homes they passed had lights on anymore. The whole world was asleep and she felt like an intruder. "Your mother can at least watch the baby for a few hours."

"We will find someone else to take care of her. Not my mother."

They drove past a park that during the day was filled with children but was now empty and quiet. Suddenly she wished she could run out of the car and find the swing set. She wanted Tim to push her as high as he could and she wanted to feel the cold night air wrap around her as she went up higher and higher. She opened her mouth to speak, but he spoke first.

"I'm serious about this, Therese. I will kill you if I find out you involved my mother in any of this."

She didn't respond, just closed her eyes and tilted her head back. For a minute, she thought about telling him.

That she was suffocating.

It was a heavy feeling that interrupted her sleep and caused her to catch her breath so that all she could think about was getting out of the little red house she had worked so hard to get inside of. Now that the secret of Barbara's rape had been told, there was no reason to stay. She could not bear to watch Tim cook and clean and plump the pillows behind Barbara's head. She turned away when he brought her snacks and sat with her to watch her favorite television programs, like he was paying back a debt he thought he owed.

She left newspapers on his nightstand with apartments for rent circled in Matilda's red crayons. She tried talking to him about it at night, but he got into the habit of sleeping so deeply underneath his pillows that when she turned to him, all she could see was a mound of bed linens. In the mornings, when he kissed her goodbye, she nuzzled his neck and whispered how wonderful it would be to have a place of their own. He punished her by ignoring her for the rest of the day and eating his dinner on a tray next to his mother. When she woke, gasping in the middle of the night, she would reach toward his side of the bed, but he was always gone. She didn't need to look for him because she already knew that he was outside in the shed in the backyard.

Turning her focus on Barbara, she encouraged Matilda to play in front of the television, blocking Barbara's view but all it did was make Barbara holler louder at the screen, which made Matilda cry and run out of the room. She poured milk down the drain at night so that there was none left for Barbara's coffee in the morning and opened magic markers and tossed them into the wash. None of it worked because Tim replaced the milk and rewashed the stained laundry.

To try to make amends, Tim allowed her to return to work after he arranged for a neighbor they both trusted to watch Matilda. It infuriated Therese that all her hard-earned money was going to a babysitter when Barbara was perfectly capable of watching Matilda for free. Weeks passed, and, although she tried to put it out of her mind, she was consumed. Regardless of how creatively she plotted, the large lump bolted to the couch blocked their escape. There were two options—distract or eliminate. So Therese started buying her extra cartons of cigarettes.

It started innocently enough, but before long, Barbara began expecting the offering, stretching out her hand every afternoon. Therese delightedly emptied ashtrays that were filling at a much faster rate than before. Tim began to notice, too, and asked Barbara if she was smoking more than usual. She barked at him to keep quiet and Therese reminded him that his mother was under a great deal of stress because she wasn't used to having a toddler underfoot all the time. Maybe, she said again, it would be better for all of them if they moved out. He lifted the newspaper he was reading until it covered his head and she smiled, satisfied.

Weeks passed and cartons of cigarettes came and went, but all that changed was the darkening of the stains covering the walls. Whatever needed to happen was not happening fast enough and the little money

Therese had managed to save for their new home was slowly dwindling to nothing. Therese decided she needed a new plan, and it came to her early one morning when she woke, gagging. It was what everyone needed to feel complete.

To be part of a set.

They had not seen each other in months, so Joan seemed surprised when Therese called and suggested lunch. She was tired of standing outside of movie theaters, lingering around park benches, and sitting through poetry readings at the library in search of a companion for Barbara. Lunch with Joan at the hospital cafeteria was her last resort, and she looked around to see if there was anyone she might have missed since sitting down.

"Things have been kind of rough for me." Joan took a bite out of the sandwich she had cut into four triangles.

"What's going on?" Therese eyed an elderly woman sitting three tables away.

"What are you looking at?"

"Who is that woman?" Therese asked, tossing her head to the right.

"Bessie? She comes here all the time. I think she's a widow."

"Really?" Therese slapped a packet of sugar against the edge of the table.

"Why are you so interested?"

Therese shrugged. "No reason. Just curious."

"Not sure you two would have much in common."

"Why's that?" She ripped open the packet and poured it into her tea.

"Because she had a stroke six months ago and can't talk."

Therese muttered something under her breath.

"What was that?" Joan asked, breaking a large chocolate chip cookie in half.

"Nothing. Never mind. So how are you?"

"I'm great." She pursed her lips like she was sucking something sour. "It's one thing living with my mother, but now that she's invited my aunt to live with us, it's just too much. I can't stand it."

Therese felt heat creep into her face. It started in the back of her neck and quickly moved in around her ears, and she recognized the sensation immediately.

Shame.

For allowing herself even a lingering moment of doubt when what she should have done was trust her instincts. She folded a napkin and used it to fan herself. "What's she like?"

"Awful. I can't take much more of her."

Therese took a deep breath and despite the plastic wrap smell of the cafeteria, felt invigorated.

"Why don't you tell me more about your aunt?" She reached over and took the other half of the chocolate chip cookie from Joan's hand.

Aunt Olive made her appearances at the little red house in the mornings when Joan dropped her off on her way to work. At first, Barbara was furious at having someone invade her home, but Therese explained that Aunt Olive had nowhere else to go and that it would only be temporary. It was a favor she could not deny a dear friend. Slowly, Barbara's objections began to fade and Therese watched confidently as her plan fell into place.

Aunt Olive was so tiny, she easily fit onto the couch beside Barbara. She made herself useful by offering to hold whatever snack Barbara was consuming in a bowl on her lap. She didn't talk or eat much, but Therese quickly discovered what it was about her that Joan found so displeasing. Her laugh started up high in her nose and then continued like a siren wailing throughout every corner of the house. She started packing wads of cotton into her pockets so she could stuff them into her ears whenever Aunt Olive was around.

Even more annoying than the laugh was her unmitigated talent at leaving drinking glasses wherever she went. Therese would find them on the sink top in the bathroom or displayed in an odd artistic arrangement on the windowsill. Each would have three sips left of whatever it was that struck Aunt Olive's fancy at the moment, and they propagated around the house like rabbits. Therese started buying red plastic cups because she got tired of watching Tim wash dishes. They were everywhere and reminded her of overturned Santa's hats. At the end of the day, she swept them into a bag that she took out to the trash. She pressed the bag down hard, listening to the crunch of the plastic, reminding herself that each filled garbage can brought her that much closer to her goal. She stuffed cotton into her ears and plastic cups into the trashcan and then she waited for the moment to present itself.

Her patience was wearing thin and soon she wondered if the time would ever come when she could make her move. In the meantime, it was Matilda who was enjoying herself the most. She loved playing with Aunt Olive's plastic cups. She stacked them into tall towers, which she then kicked down with her foot. Each time they toppled onto the floor, the sound would echo throughout the house. One day Therese became so angry, she could no longer contain her irritation. Her words shot out in small, perfectly timed explosions.

"Stop it right now. Just stop. Do you hear me?"

Matilda's lower lip dropped and began to tremble. Her eyes got round and watery, and before Therese could say another word, she opened her mouth and let out a scream that splattered against the walls and made Tim come running out of the kitchen to see what had happened. Matilda ran to him and wrapped herself around his leg, but he stood straight and stiff, as though he didn't know what to do with his arms.

"What's going on?" Tim asked looking at Therese and then at Matilda, who was howling even louder. He tried to stroke the top of her head but his hand moved like it was made of clay, and the gesture was heavy and awkward. They both looked at Therese, waiting for her to fix things. Matilda's face was pink and swollen, and Tim's hand was firmly clamped down on her scalp.

They were lost with no idea how to find their way. Something within her cracked. She let out a deep throaty laugh that sounded like a howl and was so ear piercing that even Barbara got up from the couch to come see what was happening.

"What's going on in here?" she asked, her voice graveled from an afternoon's worth of cigarettes.

"Nothing, Ma, I'll take care of it." Tim peeled Matilda's hands off his knee and stood in the middle of the three of them.

"We need to get out of here, Tim. You need to tell her we are leaving."

"Timmy you can't let her act this way. Tell her to shut her mouth." Barbara pointed at Therese and then crossed her arms in front of her chest.

But Tim didn't move.

She wasn't sure how long they stood that way, trapped in some oddly perverse triangle. Most of the time she could keep it at bay, but at this moment the image of the father she had never known poked so hard at her, it became difficult to breathe. She shook her head and closed her eyes, desperately willing Tim to stand by her side, but still he did nothing.

She wanted to scream, to yell at the top of her lungs that she needed him to choose her because the thought of not being important enough was too much for her to bear. He stood motionless, frozen in indecision. She turned away and told herself it was because she felt pity for him, but she knew it was more. She couldn't bear to see whom he would have chosen if just one more minute of time had been permitted to pass.

She walked toward the pile of scattered cups and got down on the floor to collect them. Soon Matilda was beside her, matching her movements, and when she looked up, Tim and Barbara were gone. They didn't speak about it, and even if they had, she would not have known how to explain herself; she didn't completely understand the feeling of betrayal that had tucked itself inside of her. They made dinner and ate and carried on as if nothing had happened, but when Therese woke in the early hours of the morning, Tim was gone. She knew he was in the shed, and when he came back to bed she pretended she was asleep. He tiptoed around in the dark, pretending not to wake her.

The next morning at work, she tried to distract herself. She ended up in the storage closet, searching for pens. The dust in the room clung to her skin, making everything she touched feel dry and brittle. She sneezed and continued rummaging through boxes looking for supplies. Her search proved mind-numbing, and once again she was thinking about Tim. They didn't say much to each other after what had happened, and she replayed the events of the day in her head, but mostly, she thought about triangles.

A box slipped off the shelf and she kicked it hard, leaving a satisfying dent in the corner. Dusting herself off, she remembered she forgot to pack lunch, so she gave up on her pen search and went to look for something to eat in her desk drawer.

He was standing in the office when she came in, looking like he had just pulled over for directions. She walked toward him, covering her surprise with a cough and trying to ignore the obvious amusement the situation provided for Maryann, the secretary who sat behind her.

"You left your sandwich on the counter at home. I thought you might like this better." The plastic grocery bag he opened made a crinkling sound like wrapping paper on Christmas morning. Tim pushed a container of food toward her. "Here."

She didn't need to open it to know what was inside. Baked ziti, still warm from the oven. Her favorite—a peace offering. "Thanks."

"Sure." He crumpled the bag into a ball and stuffed it into his pocket and stood with his hands at his side.

It suddenly occurred to her that other than dropping her off, he had never come inside. "This is where I work."

He nodded and looked around. Maryann stopped typing. Her expression sent the tiniest little sparkle down Therese's arm. "This is Tim."

It took a few moments for Maryann to reset her lips, but once she did, she smiled. "Hello, Tim."

"Tim was just bringing me some lunch," Therese said.

"Isn't that sweet." Her pretty manicured fingers perched over the typewriter keys, calculating when next to strike.

"I have to get to work," Tim said, nudging the container of food closer to Therese. "Bye." He nodded in Maryann's direction.

Therese went to the window, watching as he walked to his car. Before he got in, he looked up and waved. She waved back quickly, and then walked back to her desk. She eyed the container of food, trying to ignore the pangs of hunger that poked at her like an angry mosquito. There was something more pressing to which she needed to attend. She swiveled her chair so that she was facing Maryann, whose smile now stretched expansively across her face.

"That's your Tim then, is it?"

"Yes," Therese said. She tilted her head to the right, softened the arch of her eyebrows, and parted her lips just like she had practiced all her life.

Then she waited.

The air moved differently.

Therese noticed it the moment she walked up the path, but all she could think about was getting inside. About seeing Leah and emptying herself of what she was carrying. She thought about ringing the doorbell, but she still had Leah's key on her keychain, so she used it. Something big and unformed and angry vibrated inside of her and she tried to ignore the buzzing sound it made inside her ears.

"Back already?" Leah called from the hallway. She rushed toward the door, wearing a man's shirt splattered with paint, and as much as Therese tried to push it out of her mind, she knew.

Something had changed.

For a minute, Leah hesitated, and her smile disappeared. Then she wiped her hands along the shirt's length, leaving behind a trail of green smudge. "It's you."

"Sorry I didn't call first. . . . I know it's been a while."

"It's been two years," Leah said, and she turned and walked back down the hallway.

"I can explain." Therese said. But she knew she couldn't.

She thought about what to say, but little bits of spit sat on her lips instead of words. She could talk about needing to be with Tim and about the nights she spent terrified that Leah's suspicions about him would be confirmed. She could explain how many times she had reached for the telephone, especially when Matilda learned to walk and then talk. Or how she used to play a silly game called "What Would Leah Do?" when she had no idea what to do herself . . . and how she had to stop playing because sometimes Leah's warnings would curl themselves up inside her ear and whisper to her throughout the night.

Giving up their friendship was the only way she knew how to forget, and it became even easier to do when Leah took time away from the college to work on her art. Or at least, that's what the gossip was, but Therese knew it was probably more because she had broken her heart. She didn't say any of this to Leah because she knew that no matter what explanation she gave, no matter how she arranged the words, they would ultimately lead Leah to the conclusion that she had been betrayed. And as difficult as it was for Therese to admit, she was probably right.

Two and a half years had passed, and the two women, who had been closer than best friends—than sisters, even—had altogether stopped talking.

But then, Therese learned Barbara's secret. And she had to tell Leah because she was the only one who would understand.

She passed through the archway into the kitchen and saw that drop cloths lined the floor and small containers of paint covered the counter tops. She felt overwhelmed, as though her name was being called from various corners of the room. When she looked around, she realized that every surface in Leah's kitchen was painted a different color. There was no pattern, no symmetry, just random splashes of paint launched arbitrarily throughout the room.

They moved to the living room, where Therese noticed a pitcher of water and a few glasses on the coffee table. Leah had been expecting someone.

"Sit," Therese said, taking a seat and leaning forward to pour them both some water.

Leah stood.

"Please." Therese handed her the water, and Leah took it and sat at the other end of the couch.

Leah shook her head. "What do you want?"

"I had to see you, Leah. I'm sorry. There's something I need to tell you."

Leah breathed in heavily, and suddenly Therese wondered if she had made a mistake. If whatever had been between them was now irreparably broken.

"Okay," Leah said, though she hesitated, and, in those few seconds, Therese almost began to cry.

She took a sip of water, and the coldness numbed her tongue. "I found out something today. Something I didn't know. Something that will change your mind. About Tim." At that moment, she realized how important it had suddenly become for Leah to understand, but Leah just stared back at her, emotionless.

"Well, not exactly about Tim. Really more about his father."

No response.

"Turns out his father wasn't a rapist after all."

There. Now it was out. The words burning inside of her released into the air. Leah looked down at the table and traced the circle of condensation left behind by her glass.

"Did you hear me? He isn't the son of a rapist."

"Yes, I heard."

"Maryann told me. She went to high school with Barbara. Told me about the boy and how he ran out on her and how she made up the whole story about being raped. Said that Tim looks exactly like him."

Leah put her glass back down on the table, positioning it perfectly inside the circle.

"So what do you think?"

Leah took a breath and then opened her mouth to speak, but Therese never heard what she said because just then the front door opened, and a young man with hair as wild as a lion walked inside.

Sparking was rarely violent, but this time it shook her so hard, the glass she was holding flew out of her hand and crashed down to the floor. The shards twinkled like diamonds. Leah ran into the kitchen to get a dustpan and was soon on her knees, sweeping up the remains.

He stood silently in the hallway.

Smiling.

Therese's arms tingled as she turned toward Leah, whose head was bowed over the broken pieces. She wanted to move, but she couldn't, so instead she stared at the back of Leah's head.

"Here, let me help you." He dropped the paper bag he was holding and took the dustpan from her hand.

Therese blinked, took in a breath, tipped back her head to scream, but then stopped. The tingling up and down her arms turned into deep, penetrating stabs.

"It's not a big deal. Just a glass," Leah said as she turned around.

Therese's throat felt dry, and she couldn't speak. She stared into Leah's eyes and willed her to see.

"Why don't I get you another glass of water?" She went back into the kitchen, and the disconnection was so abrupt, it caused Therese pain. Leah was gone, and now she was alone with him. She rubbed her arms up and down, trying to make the piercing jabs she was experiencing stop.

"You must be Therese," he said, without looking up. There was a hint of arrogance in his voice, as if he had just calculated the answer to a difficult math problem. "Leah talks about you."

The water running in the kitchen made the pipes hum. She felt a faint throb above both ears. She wanted to sit down, to rest, but she refused to take her eyes off him.

"Here." Leah walked back into the room and handed her the glass. She drank, feeling her throat open and close around the cold water, numbing her insides and making the tingling finally stop.

"Sit," Leah said, this time pulling her by the sleeve. They sat together on the couch with him in the chair across from them.

"I guess it's my turn to tell you my news," Leah said.

Therese picked up her glass, searching for the last few drops.

"I'm Lionel." He wiped his hand on his shirt before extending it to her.

His arm hung in the air for a few seconds. Then he shrugged, and withdrew.

"I should go," he said as he stood.

"Yes." The first words Therese spoke since he had entered the house. "You should."

"Therese!" Leah put her hands on her hips. She seemed angry, but Therese didn't care.

"You two have some talking to do." He began to button up his shirt. Until that moment, Therese had not noticed it was even open.

Leah grabbed his hand. "No. You don't have to go."

He put his arm around her so that his hand rested on the small of her back. He pushed her into him, spreading her legs open with the curve of his knee. Then he nuzzled her neck and whispered something in her ear that made her laugh.

Therese turned her head. She had seen and felt it—the sparking—the moment he walked into the room. She felt overwhelmed by her situation, her emotion, and by the fact that she knew, without a doubt, that the day would come when she would watch Lionel die.

Therese tried to listen as Leah spoke. She was guarded at first, not forthcoming with many details, but the longer they sat together, the more comfortable Leah became. While Therese tried not to fold in on herself.

Leah talked about how she had never met such a talented painter and how sweet and kind he was and how his art moved her. After a while, it all blended together until finally Therese made an excuse for why she had to leave and stumbled out of the house drunkenly, though she'd consumed nothing but water.

She picked Matilda up from the babysitter, and even though she normally chattered like an angry bird, today she was quiet. All the better, because Therese needed time to think and clear her mind of what she had seen.

Anger pulsed through her fingertips, making her sweat and lose her grip on the steering wheel. She moved her head from side to side, trying to shake the intimacy of Leah's laugh out of her mind. Even though she trusted her instincts, even though she knew it would be okay, her heart still pounded so loudly in her ears, she thought it might explode. She parked in the driveway just as Joan was pulling away with Aunt Olive beside her. Joan waved. Therese waved back, afraid that if she didn't, Joan might stop to talk, and she couldn't trust herself to speak. She opened the front door to discover an array of red plastic cups artfully arranged in a circle around a stack of mail. Her breath quickened as she lifted her arm and swept them off the table, sending them toppling to the ground like bowling pins.

"What's going on in there?" Barbara yelled as she lifted herself from her spot on the couch.

"Go wash up," she told Matilda, putting her hand on the little girl's back and giving her a push. Matilda turned back once before dropping her coat on the floor and running to the bathroom.

"I said, what's going on in here?" Barbara's eyes narrowed, and her chin jutted out as she folded her arms across her chest.

"I know."

"Excuse me?" Barbara stiffened, as though she had just been told to make her own dinner.

"You heard me."

Barbara coughed a long, deep, throaty expulsion that made her chest heave up and down.

"I know. All of it. I know you are a liar."

Barbara came closer. "You better calm yourself or I will tell him and this time he will take care of you. You and your little brat will be gone." She snapped her fingers and her words bounced off little bursts of spit.

Therese wiped her cheek. "It's all your fault."

The only thing she could think about right then was how important it had been to see Leah, to tell her what she had uncovered, and in a flash she saw Lionel.

All of it because of Barbara.

Barbara walked back into the living room, her enormous mass swaying back and forth like a pendulum. For a second, Therese lost her focus, but then it came back, firing through her, catapulting her so that they were again face-to-face.

"From now on, things go the way I say," Therese said, grabbing her arm.

"Are you crazy?" Barbara asked, panting as she tried to free herself.

"Did you hear me?" she asked. "I know all of it."

Barbara's eye twitched. "What are you talking about?"

"Tim's father."

Barbara's cheeks got red and her breath came out in puffs. "You don't know anything."

The high pitch of her voice, which now sounded childlike took Therese by surprise. She released Barbara's arm. "It's time for us to go. Tim and me and Matilda. We need a home of our own."

"No." Barbara shook her head.

Therese leaned in closer. A waft of flowery perfume laced with sweat lifted from the folds of the fat woman's skin. She breathed in deeply, savoring the moment. "I will tell him. Everything."

Barbara fell onto the couch like a wounded elephant. As she covered her eyes and began to cry, the room trembled and the windowpanes shook. She rocked back and forth, hitting the edge of the table, sending a second pyramid of plastic red cups cascading down. They bounced and scattered across the wooden floor, and one rolled near Therese. She lifted her foot and smashed it. Soon, she was wiggling and dancing around the room. Matilda watched from the doorway, covering her ears. Therese twirled and stomped, cracking every cup she could find, drowning out the whine of the television, the howl of Barbara's sobs, until all she could hear was the sound of crushed, fractured plastic.

She hated herself for it, but she could not bring herself to return to Leah's after that night. She knew there was nothing she could do to make it stop. But one night, weeks later, she woke up and wished for rain. She wanted a storm to match the one she was feeling inside, but instead, it was dark and quiet and calm, and when she rolled over in bed, he was gone. Downstairs, she put a jacket on over her nightgown and got into the car. She turned on the windshield wipers, hoping for a torrential downpour, but the squeaky scratching noise annoyed her, so she turned them off. The streets flew by as she drove, and the next time she looked up, she had arrived.

Parking across the street, she stared at the house, whose lights were on even though it was two in the morning. She watched from the darkness of her car, and then the front door slowly opened.

They whispered, moving in and out of each other softly, and then he made his way to his car and drove off. She sat motionless, watching his taillights disappear into the blackness. Her hands were clammy from sweat, and she twisted them around the rim of the steering wheel. She could feel it growing inside of her, forcing her to get out and run like she was being chased. She landed on the welcome mat, pounding so hard at the door, she thought she might break through. Then without warning, it opened.

It was the state of Leah's hair that startled her. The usually perfect curls were untwisted, hanging limp and lifeless down her shoulders.

"Please, Leah. Please. You have to listen to me." She pushed her way inside, sending Leah tumbling several steps back.

"What are you doing here?" Leah asked, as she tried to pull her robe closed. The robe was clearly too small on her, though.

"You have to end it."

Leah walked into the kitchen. "Tea?"

Therese ran after her, grabbing her arm. "Leah, I'm serious. This has to end. Now."

Pouring water echoed around the room as Leah filled the kettle. "First, I don't hear from you in years. Then you come back into my life and think you can undo everything I've worked for and then you disappear *again*. Now, here you are, in the middle of the night, telling me how to live my life."

Therese stood up, the colors on the walls swirling through her. She thought it had been days, but maybe Leah was right. Maybe it had been weeks. Weeks of sleepless nights, waking with sweat plastering her hair to her forehead, feeling the danger that Leah was in, but not having the words to explain.

"Please, Leah." She could feel the tears waiting to fall at the next breath. "Please."

"What has gotten into you?" She opened a cabinet door, stretching her arm high to reach a cup on the top shelf. Therese spun her around so that they were facing each other. "He is bad, Leah. I get a feeling about these things. Please, listen to me."

Leah shimmied herself out from Therese's grip. "I never thought you would do this to me. I never thought you would stand in my way. Don't you think I can make my own decisions?"

Therese took in a breath, her eyes glazed over, and then the words came except that they were flat and disconnected. Like she was reading from a script. "Leah, he is going to hurt you."

Leah shook her head. "Are you jealous of him?" The words made a ripping sound as they flew from Leah's lips and almost knocked Therese to the ground. "You make this about him when it is only about you. When it's *always* about you."

Whatever emotion Therese had expelled suddenly latched itself onto Leah. She walked over to the teacups, her hand shaking, and with one swoop, knocked them all off the counter and to the floor. The crashing sound made Therese suck in her breath, but Leah did not move. She stood with her back to Therese, her arms drawn around herself.

"I am going to have a baby and I am not going to let you ruin it."

Baby.

She was going to have a baby.

Therese reached out her hand, but because Leah's back was turned, she did not see. Therese felt despair sink down inside, becoming a part of her, and she knew there was nothing left to do. She turned and walked out of the room, out of the house. She sat in the dark as thunder rumbled above, and then, even though everything inside of her screamed that she was right, she pushed it so far down that it became nothing more than a whisper, easily drowned out by the long-wished-for raindrops that now slapped angrily at her windshield.

It was worse at night, when darkness took away the reason of light. She closed her eyes and remembered the promises they had made. The risk of losing Leah was too much to bear, so she hired a babysitter for Matilda, put on her best dress, and she and Tim invited Leah and Lionel out for dinner. Tim chose the restaurant, which was surrounded by windows that overlooked a parking lot. When she closed her eyes, the sound of traffic reminded her of waves. When she opened them, Lionel was helping Leah into her seat, his hand cupping the small of her back.

"Hi." Leah's eyes were glassy, like she had just woken from a dream. Her belly looked large and round, and Therese wondered why she hadn't noticed it before. Now it protruded outwards, making itself known. Leah pushed slightly away from the table to make herself more comfortable, and Therese resisted the urge to pull her close and sit like they always had when she was pregnant with Matilda.

Before Lionel.

He reached over to shake Tim's hand and nodded at Therese. "So, what looks good?"

As usual, Tim was completely lost in the menu, which gave Therese time to stare at the happy couple. Once, when Lionel caught her looking, he winked. The waitress came and they ordered drinks, Lionel insisting that he and Leah share from the same glass, which seemed to delight Leah. During the meal, Lionel pulled Leah's chair closer to his, and when Therese bent down to pick up a spoon that had fallen to the floor, she saw that they were holding hands. When he spoke to Leah, he whispered in hushed tones, as though he was telling her a secret that no one else was worthy enough to hear. Everything seemed to be going fine, yet no matter how she tried, she could not rid herself of a foreboding sense of impending doom. It hung on to her and made it difficult to swallow.

"Where are you from, Lionel?" she asked, raking her fork against the mashed potatoes on her plate.

He looked up and smiled. "Here and there."

"Will you settle down here when the baby comes?"

He was quiet for a few minutes, or maybe it was longer, because soon she wondered if he was ever going to answer at all.

"I remember once driving through this town. Had this cute little diner in the center. Think it was called Emerald. I knew the moment I saw it that's where I was going to end up. It's the kind of place you settle down in once you know you're done running."

"It sounds like the perfect place," Therese said.

Leah reached over to rub the top of Lionel's hand, and he looked down at his lap like he was embarrassed, like he had revealed too much. Then she smiled at Therese, who stared even harder at her mashed potatoes.

It was at the end of the meal that she found herself alone with Lionel. Leah had excused herself to use the bathroom, and Tim had gone to get the car. They were standing outside the restaurant, he with his hands stuffed into his pockets and she with Tim's jacket draped over her shoulders. She was stepping back and forth, trying to stay warm.

"Cold?"

He stared at her so intently that she briefly understood what it was that Leah found so captivating. When he smiled, he looked like a boy, mischievous and fun, but there was also something masculine and strong about him. Even his smell was seductive, and although she fought against it, she could feel herself being drawn in, unable to regain her footing.

"I'm fine."

It happened in a second, maybe when she was staring down at the pavement thinking about the ocean. He grabbed her by the collar. The movement was so sudden, it squeezed the breath out of her. Then he grit his teeth, the words coming out like the snarl of an animal.

"You and me? We are the same. Only difference is that she's mine and you can't have her. The sooner you get that through your fat head, the better. Understand?"

He brought her up to his face so that she could feel his heat. His lips came close enough to kiss her, but then he laughed and pushed her away, sending her stumbling backwards. When Tim drove up, she got inside the car, feeling the rage well up inside her, pushing into her chest. She wanted to scream, but her voice seemed to have disappeared. Anger crept across her cheeks, and she admonished herself once again for questioning her instincts and not doing what needed to be done.

"Everything okay?" Tim asked, poking her playfully in the arm.

She nodded, even though she knew. Nothing was okay.

Matilda

Drawing circles.

It was something I did when I felt lost. Little ones inside of big ones, with no beginning and no end.

"Pretty," Sara said as she shifted past me, order pad in hand. "Is Lavi supposed to meet you here?" She glanced down at her watch.

I shrugged. I didn't tell her I hadn't spoken to Lavi in days. That I honestly had no idea what had drawn me inside the restaurant or what I was doing sitting at the counter. There weren't many customers and once they had their meals, the room got quiet. Sara slid behind the counter, dragging her rag over a crack in the Formica.

"Daryl and Lavi are still not speaking," she told me and pushed the rag harder, making it squeak with each pass. I drew a medium-sized purple circle in the corner of my placemat.

She cut me a slice of apple pie, then took a canister from behind the counter and sprayed a pyramid of whipped cream on top. "I can tell about you, Matilda . . . you are like me."

I drew a smaller circle inside the purple one.

"We both follow our hearts."

I plunged my fork into an especially large slice of apple.

"That's why Daryl likes you so much."

Lightness filled my insides and I instantly knew that later—after I left the restaurant and walked all the way home, after I climbed in bed and shut off the light, after I got ready and left for school the next morning—I would replay the moment over in my head. She picked up the rag and concentrated hard on a stain that looked so ingrained, nothing short of a sandblaster would make it disappear.

"That's what it's all about, Matilda. Finding the person that makes you feel special and never letting go. No matter what."

She dropped the rag and reached across to pat my hand. I smiled back at her. There was something so easy in her way of thinking and more than anything I wanted to believe what she'd said. She was different than my mother: committed to love, no matter the cost. I nodded my head in agreement, went back to eating my pie, and watched as she continued to scrub the spot, which we both knew held no hope of ever coming out.

That night, it was the taste of baked beans that woke me. It rose from my insides like a geyser, leaving behind a burning pool of acid. I took a sip of water and the coolness made its way down until it reached a point beyond which it could not pass. I closed my eyes and laid back my head. Hot dogs and beans was my favorite meal to make when my mother wasn't home. More acid came up, but this time it wasn't because of the beans.

It was the dream.

The one I remembered having since I could remember dreaming, coming both by routine and surprise. I tried to shake the image, but it clung to me like a cold, damp towel. So I sat up, pinched my skin to make the likelihood of falling back asleep impossible, and decided to go downstairs. I needed to get away from that room, that bed, those sheets.

The house was quiet and I tried to remember where she said she was going. I went into the kitchen and considered the sink, still full of dishes. The pot from the beans sat on top, crusted in dried brown goop because I forgot to fill it with water. The goal was to see how high I could stack them before my mother would relent. Before she would wash and dry and put them away so that the game could start all over again.

I opened the refrigerator and scanned the contents: yogurt, grapefruits, and cottage cheese. In the freezer, behind a box of whole-wheat waffles, I found a small, forgotten container of mocha chip ice cream. In the dark, I stabbed at the hard, frosted ice cream with my spoon and then I gave up and tossed it onto the coffee table. The spoon bounced and landed on the rug. I kicked it underneath the table and then picked up the remote control and turned on the television.

A cooking show was on and the host was excitedly demonstrating how to poach eggs. He made tiny tornadoes in the water and then slipped raw eggs into the tornadoes' eyes. I watched as the white part swirled around its yellow center like a cloud surrounding the sun. The audience's oohs and ahhs bounced around the walls of the blue-lit living room. I turned up the volume and wondered if I would be able to hear her when she came in. I turned it up louder and watched those pretty white eggs spin out of control in their hot water bath. I flipped the channel just as he sliced one open and the camera zoomed in on the bright yellow insides oozing out like blood.

I flew past a few late-night comedy shows and two infomercials. Nothing held my attention so I turned the television off and stuffed the remote control under a pillow cushion. I walked past the front door, telling myself I was only peeking through the window out of habit and not to see if she was home. It was dark and empty and the silence vibrated in my ears, so I went back upstairs.

Usually I liked escaping into my room, but tonight I felt restless and out of place. I sat at my desk, turned on the lamp, and stared at the dust particles floating through the air. Deciding it was better not to know how many ugly things were swimming around me, I flicked off the light. I got into bed and felt the sheets mold to my skin, as though they had a memory and were waiting for me to return, waiting to pick up where we had left off earlier.

Dread made its way into my chest so I grabbed a pillow and tossed it where my feet usually went and switched my body on the mattress. It felt funny lying on the wrong side of the bed, so I put my pillow back where it belonged and turned around again.

My hips sank down and my eyelids got heavy. I stared at my night-light, willing myself to stay awake, but then the brightness got smaller and dimmer and before I could stop myself, I was back in the red, in the dampness, in the cold. Someone was screaming loud, shrill empty screams that became hollow-sounding the closer I got. I wanted to wake up. I wanted it to stop, but something pulled me down further and then it was so close I had to cover my ears. The lights flashed and the floor shook and in the streak of white I saw.

The person screaming was me.

When I opened my eyes, she was sitting beside me, stroking my hair and whispering that everything was going to be okay. She was wearing a white blouse with light blue buttons that reminded me of a doll I once had.

"Where were you?"

She stood up and I leaned into my pillow. She walked over to the mirror, bringing her face so close that it was almost touching. "I told you, Matilda. I had to work and then I went out for a late dinner." She licked her finger and stroked her eyebrow into shape. "How was your evening?"

I hugged the pillow tight and mumbled into the softness. "Perfect."

"Good." She smiled, turning away from the mirror. "You were screaming when I came in."

I didn't answer.

"Are you okay now?"

"You went out for dinner?"

She pulled her fingers through the back of her hair. "Yes."

"When are we going to get Franny?"

A piece of her hair fell out of place.

"Mom?"

"Hmm?" The renegade hair was now back where it belonged.

"When?"

She reached out to touch my shoulder, but I batted her hand away and then the perfectly smoothed eyebrow arched.

"Goodnight, Matilda." She came so close I couldn't help but breathe her in. Her eyes darted back and forth across my face, like she was reading a book. Then she whispered in my ear, making the hairs on the back of my neck sting. "You have been seeing that boy."

"Leave me alone."

I turned away, but not before she reached across and slapped me. The pain radiated quickly through my skin and then settled inside my mouth. I clenched my teeth.

She stood up, walked to the door, and then turned back around.

"I don't care what you think of me," she said. Her face turned white, like it was covered in chalk dust. I tried to sink further into the bed. "I only care that you do what I say. Do not go near that boy again."

I didn't answer.

"Matilda." She spoke my name, quietly even though her fists were drawn up at her sides. "Did you hear me?"

I nodded.

"Then we understand each other." She left the room without turning around again. I heard her walk into hers and slam the door.

I got out of bed and peered into the mirror, tracing an outline around the faint red mark she had left behind. I leaned into it like she had, so that I was almost touching, and licked my finger. I swept it across my eyebrow, until it lay down in place, perfectly groomed and shiny from my spit.

After that, I tried to keep to myself and stayed away from him. I took the long way home from school and every day I passed a picture of a boy staring at me from beneath a sheet of plastic. He was smiling and happy, as if somehow he knew that photo would one day be tacked up onto the tree that his car would crash into. Someone had taped flowers underneath, which disintegrated at my touch.

"He was an asshole."

I jumped backward and fell into him. He snickered.

"His name was Joe Devaney," Daryl said.

I started to walk because I didn't want to know anything more. I just wanted him to be the smiling boy who stared at me from beneath a sheet of plastic.

"Haven't seen you around."

I didn't respond and crossed from the main road to the edge of the forest.

"Where's Lavi?"

I wasn't going to tell him I had snuck out early to avoid her.

"What's going on?" He gave up trying to walk beside me and fell behind.

"Nothing."

Dried twigs cracked underneath his feet as he kept pace. I knew he wanted to ask about my father, but he didn't. He just followed, letting me take the lead. I found a spot under a tree, swung off my backpack, and sat on the ground. We stared off into the dark green like there was something there to watch.

"My mom doesn't want me hanging out with you anymore."

"Oh, yeah?" He lay down, put his hands behind his head, then reached up and grabbed the back of my shirt, pulling me down with him. The movement startled me, but I pretended it didn't. Birds chirped, and every few minutes there was a rustling noise, and then all I heard was the sound of his breathing. Slow and steady and, even though I didn't want to, I found myself trying to match it.

"Your mother's a bitch."

The ground was wet and the coldness seeped into me.

"Bet that's why your dad left."

"She left him."

I heard a crinkling sound and saw the familiar bottle of brandy come out. He handed it to me and I pushed it aside. He took a sip, then put the bottle back into a paper bag and packed it away.

"Got anything more interesting in there?" I asked as I slipped my hand into his bag and found his notebook. This time he didn't fight—just watched as I flipped through pages of his black and white undercover superheroes. He lay back down and closed his eyes and soon he was asleep. I couldn't help but notice his features soften, erasing all signs of Mean Daryl.

I lay beside him, on my back, listening to the sound of his breaths. He made a low rattling noise every few seconds that reminded me of my sister. Before I could prevent it, my eyes filled with tears and the trees whirled around me. My heart pounded angrily inside my chest and then I felt him slip his hand into mine. I held on to him because everything was spinning around me and I couldn't help but be scared that I might suddenly disappear . . . and that no one would remember that I was ever there. I held on tightly and he squeezed back just as hard.

Maybe he was scared of the same thing.

When I woke, I felt disoriented.

"I want to go home."

I brushed a leaf out of my hair. He didn't answer. Just gathered his things and tossed them into his bag. We walked in silence and I felt unbalanced, like I had left behind part of me in the forest. When we reached the clearing, I could see the townhouses and I walked to my front door.

He followed without hesitation.

We went inside and, when I turned, his face was so close, his breath tickled my cheek. We stood seconds apart from touching, listening to the muffled voices of his mother and sister in the unit next door, but then something changed and he shook himself from me.

"Got any milk?" he asked and walked toward the refrigerator.

I reached into the dish rack and handed him a glass with a daisy painted on the side. My mother's favorite.

He opened the freezer and cracked the ice tray. Ice cubes crashed onto the kitchen floor and shattered like glass. He rummaged in the refrigerator until he found the milk and, after he poured some into his glass, lifted the carton to his mouth and took a sip. I watched as he gulped, tilting his head back and closing his eyes, hearing the backwash hit the sides of the carton when he finished. He closed the refrigerator door, leaving the carton out on the table.

"C'mon." He swirled the ice around in the glass and headed upstairs.

He walked straight into my mother's room and I didn't stop him; I just stood in the doorway and watched as he put his glass on the dresser. He switched on a light, turning the room the color of honey, and then walked over to a chair that was piled with clothes from the day before. He lifted her blouse and dropped it so that it fluttered back down as if it had fairy wings. Her bed wasn't made and he sat on it, pumping up and down as if he was testing the springs. Then he stood in the middle of the room, breathing her in and when he was finished he turned off the light and picked up his milk.

He walked into the hallway and I followed him into my room. I sat on the bed and again watched as he walked around, looking at my things, sometimes picking items up to hold in his hand. He looked at a photo of Franny and then he walked over to the window.

"When's your mother coming home?"

"Not till late."

He came over to the bed and sat at the edge of the mattress so that all I could see was the back of his head. He held the glass in his hands and stared down at the floor. The ice cubes must have all melted—there were very few clinking noises coming from the glass.

The window was open and between the chirps of the birds there was quiet. Something pushed me to fill it. Maybe I had known all along or maybe I had just decided, but either way, I told him. "I'm going back."

He turned to look at me. Milk speckled his upper lip. "I know."

He looked like there was something he wanted to say, but then he didn't. Instead, he went downstairs and the next thing I knew, he was gone and I was alone.

I went into the kitchen and wiped the melted ice cubes from the floor. I washed the glass and put it back in the dish rack. I scrubbed the kitchen counter, trying hard to focus so that I didn't have to hear his muffled voice coming from next door, and then I poured the rest of the milk down the sink, watching as it coated the basin, leaving behind a thin film of white that took several seconds to clear.

As the days passed, I thought a lot about Daryl and Franny and how it was all coming apart and how I had no idea how to put it back together. One afternoon, I found myself standing in front of their door, pretending that I didn't care if my mother caught me. It was unlocked and opened at my touch.

Her lipstick was smeared and it looked like she had lost her balance. Sara grabbed me by the arm and pulled me inside. "Come in."

She took a few sips from the paper cup she was holding and then licked her lips.

"What do you think?" The bottom of her dress flared as she twirled. She held out her hands and cocked her head to one side and let out a squeal that sent shivers up my spine.

"You like it?" She spun again.

"It's pretty."

It wasn't. It was tight in the wrong places and looked like it was borrowed. Maybe it was. The dress flew over her head and landed on the floor. She stood in front of me in her bra and panties and I couldn't help but notice the pouch around her belly.

"Maybe this one's better?" She grabbed a black one from a pile she had on the couch and pulled it over her head. "Can you help?"

She turned her back to me and I struggled with the zipper, but before I could finish, she pulled away and ran her hands down the front as if she was ironing out the wrinkles.

"Better?"

Her bra strap hung over her shoulder but, again, I just nodded. She walked to the counter and poured more of whatever she was drinking. "It needs to be perfect."

I leaned against the wall. The dress kept falling and she clutched it to her chest but then gave up and just let it hang. She found her purse and dug into its depths like she was searching for treasure. Out came a small perfume sample into which she dipped her pinky. She ran it across her wrist and then pushed her hand toward my face. The assault took me off-guard and I must have cringed because, suddenly, she was back rummaging inside her bag.

"Better?"

She stroked more onto her wrist, but before she could get any closer, I nodded my approval.

She smiled and took another sip. "I want it all to look right."

She picked up a shoe, licked her finger, and cleaned a scuff mark off the toe. I started to back out down the hallway, but she caught me.

"Daryl will be home soon." She winked.

I imagined Daryl walking in, watching me watching her. She moved over to the mirror, the contents of her paper cup splashing out in an almost perfectly shaped circle. It seeped into the rug, disappearing as if it had never been there. I started to feel dizzy; all I could think about was getting out. I leaned against the wall, backing my way down the hall again, hoping I could make it out without her stopping me.

"Where are you going?"

More than anything, I wanted to run, but instead I came back inside. She walked toward me, still unsteady on her feet. She put her hand on my face and looked at me, but her eyes were wildly unfocused. Her touch sent fiery stabs down my back.

"I told you, Matilda. You are just like me."

I don't know why, but suddenly I felt like I couldn't breathe, so I pushed past her and ran out of the room, out of the unit, and back next door to my home. Even though I closed the door behind me, I could still hear her laughter coming through the walls. I wiped the cold sweat that had wrapped itself around my neck and then I went to the bathroom and opened the medicine cabinet.

Small red pills.

Wedged between a box of Band-Aids and a bottle of purple cough syrup in the medicine cabinet. I shook the bottle, listened to the rattling noise they made, and then swallowed three. I waited for the alarms to go off, the sirens to blare, something warning the world that I was about to cross the line. Nothing. So I shook a few more into my hand and that's when I noticed him.

Leaning in the doorway.

The bottle slipped onto the ground and the little pills scattered across the tile floor like candies.

"Headache," I whispered.

The word bounced off the mirror because I didn't want to turn and see his face. I didn't ask what he was doing there, why he was in my house, watching me swallow too many Extra Strength Tylenols, because then I would need to explain and I figured if I didn't ask him, he wouldn't ask me.

"Let's get out of here."

I wasn't sure which one of us said it first.

I followed him outside and, even though the weather was warmer than it had been in months, he zipped his jacket. We walked into town and then towards the building he had taken me to months ago. We climbed onto the roof and I could hear the traffic below, cars honking, people talking. He took out his sketchbook and started to draw and I waited patiently.

A little while later, he walked to a corner of the rooftop and turned away from me to pee. It pooled and then trickled down and reminded me of a misshapen cloud.

"You saw my mom."

Everything inside screamed at me to lie. "Yeah."

He dug inside his pocket and stuck a piece of gum in his mouth, throwing the crumpled wrapper onto the ground. He chewed, making it crack like gunshots, and then he was next to me. Before I could stop him, his hand was behind my neck and he was pushing his face into mine, his lips into mine, and then finally, slipped his gum into my mouth. Cinnamon saliva dripped down my chin and I wiped it with the back of my sleeve.

"Here." He shoved an envelope into my hand.

"What's this?"

"Take it."

I didn't have anywhere to put it so I held it in my hand.

"Look at it after you're gone."

Franny

The ball inside me was bouncing.

I did two crossword puzzles and one word search and then turned on the television and matched my breathing to the click of the channels, but nothing made it better. The next thing I knew, Leah handed me my bathing suit and I put it on underneath my clothes.

When we got to the pool, there was a man swimming laps. I sat on the bleachers, counting each time his arm sliced into the water. When I looked back up, Leah had taken off her shirt and was standing beside me in a shiny black bathing suit.

"Let's go in together."

I nodded, not really sure how I felt about the change in routine. Leah always sat and watched me. The ball inside me bounced harder, but I vowed not to disappoint her again, so I stripped off my clothes and stuffed them inside my bag.

She tiptoed around the puddles, reminding me of a ballet dancer.

"C'mon." She took my hand and led me to the edge of the water. We sat together, the skin of our thighs touching, holding hands like little kids.

We slid in above our waists. She braced herself on my arms and arched her back so that the water lapped around her face. The tip of her nose disappeared every few seconds and then popped back up. When she straightened, wisps of hair streamed around her shoulders like yellow ribbons.

"Your turn," she said, reaching out her forearms for me to hold.

I shook my head.

"Yes, Franny. Just try."

So I gripped myself tightly to her and arched my head back, feeling the pulse of the water vibrate through me. I was floating, but grounded at the same time. When I came back up, she started to swim and I followed her, synchronizing myself so that I rose when she fell. I liked looking at her when she didn't know that I was.

I'm not sure how long we swam like that, side by side, like twins.

Finally, she stopped. We bobbed up and down in the water, spreading out our arms and legs to keep afloat.

"Why didn't you tell me how much fun I was missing?" she asked.

For a second, I thought she was angry with me for keeping something else from her, but she was smiling, so I smiled back. She shimmied her fingertips back and forth, making tiny little bubbles in the water, and then sunk down to her ears, blowing them in my direction. It felt funny seeing her wet. The only other person I had ever seen that way was Matilda when we were little and took baths together. Leah lifted herself up and floated on her back. Her body, at the mercy of each rippled wave, lay limp. I briefly worried that she had stopped breathing, but then her eyes opened and she was back with me, smiling.

The buzzing inside got louder, so I turned away from her to swim on my own—back and forth across the pool, hoping that each time I sank underneath, I would reemerge cleansed. I went deeper until I felt the rough bottom scrape my chin. When I came up for air, I saw that she had gotten out and was sitting on the bleacher next to the man I had watched swimming laps. She smiled at me and waved and I saw him turn and look at her. I dove down again, wanting to make the whirling inside my head stop.

But it didn't.

Instead, it got sharper. Clearer. Pushing me down farther. When I closed my eyes, I saw the pretty little girls riding pretty pink bicycles from the park and then my chin started to throb and somewhere in the swirl and crash of the water, I understood that I could fight and protest as much as I wanted. I could hold my breath, stay underwater, and pretend that it wasn't there, but none of it would make a bit of difference. Because, in the end, I never had any other choice.

I felt like a werewolf during the full moon. The pool didn't help, so when we got home, Leah set up the Scrabble board. The fact that the letters wouldn't sit straight on the board provoked me. I tried to nudge them into place, but my fingers felt big and puffy and after a while I just gave up.

I didn't want to be like this.

"It's the letters," I whispered, but even the sound of my own voice felt loud and sharp inside my head.

"Hmm?" she asked in a sweet, absentminded way that on a normal day would have made me smile. But not today, because something was inside that left no room for anything else. Something big and bouncy and wild.

"It's the letters. You need to make them line up the right way."

She looked down at the board and then back up at me. I don't think she understood how important her task was.

"Please!" I yelled. "Please, Leah."

"Okay, Franny, I will." She bent over the board, lining them up the best she could.

"No! Not like that. Not that way!" I covered my eyes as if the sight was too much to bear. "You're doing it all wrong." I could feel it growing inside of me, getting bigger, bouncing harder.

"This way?" She arranged the letters so that they ran across the board diagonally.

"No!" I shouted, because at that moment, all I wanted was for it to be right. For all of it to be right. "No. That's not what I mean!"

And then it came, like those rainstorms that happen on sunny days, with no warning and no explanation. I covered my mouth with my hands as sounds I didn't recognize slipped from between my fingers. The thing inside me bounced harder and all I could do was rock myself on the couch and hope that soon it would end.

I knew Leah was still in the room, but she didn't come close and I was grateful because I didn't want to be touched. I wanted to crawl deep inside myself and close my eyes until it passed. More rocking, more yelling, more tears . . . and then just rocking. Slowly, back and forth, until I felt her arms around me, moving with me.

I fell into her and, as she hummed in my ear, I knew it was almost over. I clung to her as though she had suddenly announced she was leaving. I buried my face in her hair, and she held me in her arms, the rocking slowing to the pace of our beating hearts.

After a few minutes she shifted, kissed the top of my head, and whispered, "It's okay, Franny."

The clock chimed, reminding us that something had passed. I laid my head in her lap and curled my body, because even in the quiet, in the calm, I could still feel it. Not as big as before, but small like a pebble in my shoe.

"What is it, Franny?"

I couldn't give it words.

"You are so brave." She held me tightly, like if she didn't, I might disappear, and I shook my head. She pushed me away so that she could see my face. "I know how hard things are for you. And still you never give up. I wish I was as strong as you."

"No."

"The thing inside that makes things hard is also the thing that gives you gifts. Helps you see things that no one else can see. Makes you special."

"I don't want to be. . . . Special."

"But you are."

"You mean because of the spelling?"

"No, not because of the spelling. Your letters form words and that gives you comfort, but someday you won't need the letters. Someday all you will need is your voice."

I wanted to understand what she was telling me. I closed my eyes and tried to listen, but all I heard was a rumble that became steady like a heartbeat, rhythmic and loud and present.

A few days later, Evelyn and I had resumed our habit of meeting at the library. I tried to focus on the page I was reading. Evelyn grabbed a handful of hair and twirled it around her finger. For a second I forgot that she was waiting and then I remembered.

She was waiting for me.

We hadn't talked very much after the day I ran away. Something about me had changed, but I couldn't find the words to explain so instead I said nothing.

Miss Betty wasn't there today. In her seat sat a skinny blonde woman who kept shushing a pair of teenagers at the table next to us. Each time she hissed, I jumped.

"What's wrong?" Evelyn repeated.

"Nothing," I said.

"Looking at the lovebirds?"

"What?"

"Their feet have been touching since they sat down and the girl keeps giggling."

The skinny librarian let out another hiss, which startled me so much that the book I was holding flew out of my hand and onto the floor.

As everyone turned to look, I felt myself getting hot and Evelyn leaned over to pick it up. "Here."

"Thanks." I stared down into my lap.

"Do you think everyone sees colors the same?" she asked.

"What?"

"Take red, for example. Do you think that what your brain tells you is red is the same as what I see?

"I don't know." Not once had it occurred to me that the color red might look different to someone else.

She dug through her bag until she found her pencil case. She took out a red magic marker and drew a square. "What do you see?"

"A red square."

"I know that, Franny." She sighed, sounding frighteningly like the hissing librarian. "I mean describe red so that I can know if it's the same thing I see."

"I don't know how to describe red."

"Is it bright?"

I nodded.

"Is it hot, loud, mad? Does it make you feel like jumping?"

"I guess."

"Then it must be the same thing I see." She opened her book and went back to twirling her hair. The girl behind us was talking to the boy in hushed tones. I felt warm, electric sparkles and then fiery tingles up and down my back.

Red.

I took her notepad and drew a dark black line inside the red square she had made. I filled it in; it took a long time because I forced myself to stay within the lines. Then, even though I was finished, I didn't put down the pen.

Instead, I drew thick black lines that covered up her red, turning the sides a dark sticky brown and making it look ugly and misshapen. I colored even harder, taking the lines outside the confines of her square, wild random crazy lines that suddenly took on a life of their own, moving across the page with a confident strength that startled me so much that I stopped and pushed myself away from the table. Afterward, I sat quietly with my hands in my lap because I was not sure what they might do next.

I was relieved when Evelyn finally announced she needed to use the bathroom. We wound our way to a door with a big W painted on the outside.

Once inside, we were alone.

My last visit to a public bathroom was at the movie theater. I tried to block the memory by squinting my eyes and Evelyn looked at me funny but I didn't care. All I wanted was to be quiet inside.

Evelyn hoisted herself up onto the counter, which was made of shiny stainless steel. "These sinks remind me of being on an airplane. Have you ever been in one?"

I shook my head.

"It's pretty cool. My favorite is the takeoff. Maybe we could go together someday."

The door swung open and a woman walked inside. She eyed the two of us and then chose the stall furthest away.

"Imagine if we could fly anyplace we wanted." Her nose started to twitch.

"Like Saturn."

"Why Saturn?" she asked.

The woman finished and I braced myself for the flush, covering my ears. She washed her hands in the sink, but the drain was clogged and the metal basin filled with gray soapy water. She used the last paper towel to wipe her hands and, when she walked out, the door whined behind her.

"Why Saturn?" she repeated.

I shrugged, watching the water line in the sink descend. "I like the rings."

She nodded as if what I said made sense.

"I have to go." She hopped off the counter and headed towards a stall.

I walked into the stall next to hers because I didn't want to be alone. I crossed my arms over my chest and waited. I heard the angry splashing sound her pee made when it hit the water and then I heard the flush, but this time I didn't cover my ears. I opened my door seconds after she opened hers and picked the sink with the clogged drain because there was something calming about the way the water collected. The paper towel dispenser was empty, so we used the hand blower on the wall. Evelyn tapped it with her elbow and the room filled with a loud, steady humming noise. We both put our hands underneath, rubbing them softly in the warm, dry air. The room vibrated with sound, but this time it didn't frighten me.

As my hands, still tingling with their newfound courage, sat beneath hers, I closed my eyes and for the longest second in my life, I pretended I was brave.

That evening, I decided to push my courage even further. "I want to know."

Leah sat up on the couch. She put her hand over her knuckle and rubbed the rough, callused skin. "What is it that you want to know?"

"I want to know about him. The one that hurt you."

She was quiet. She looked down at the floor, her eyes blinking quickly, almost as if she was looking through her memories, trying to pick which ones to share. "What is it that you want to know?"

"Why did you love him?"

She pushed herself farther back into the cushion and she smiled as she spoke. "He was young and funny and the art he made was nothing like I had ever seen."

I could feel the letters poking at me, so I pursed my lips. "Is that why you loved him?"

"I loved him because I could run away into his paintings. I could disappear inside of them."

My heart was pounding in my head, making my thoughts jumble together. I needed to know why she loved him, because I needed to know why she loved me. And I needed to know what he did to break her.

"I should have listened to Therese."

Lately she had gotten into the habit of referring to my mother by name.

"Did she know him? My mother?"

Leah nodded. "Therese knows things about people. I don't know how, but she does."

"You wish you had never met him."

"No, Franny, I am grateful I met him. He gave me something that I will never be able to repay him for." She brought her teacup to her lips, softly blowing across the surface.

I laid my head down in her lap because I wanted to feel her hand on me. Like we were connected. I wrapped my arms around her waist, pulling myself in even more.

"One day I will tell you about the people who teach you to find your courage and the ones who help you become the person you were always supposed to be."

I nodded, but it didn't really matter because all I knew was that she was going to tell me these things someday, which meant that there were more days to come.

Therese

She liked sleeping with the window open. The breeze blew in across a box of tissues, making the one on top wave like a white flag. The cool air was not enough to soothe her, so she got up and walked to the bathroom. She wrapped her arms around her waist, remembering what it felt like when Matilda was growing inside and how excited it made Leah to feel her kick. She thought about how much Leah wanted a child, yet how clearly frightened she was to care for one. It was as though she didn't trust herself. Therese's thoughts always led to Leah, like a stray thread unraveling in her mind.

She turned off the light and sat at the edge of the bed. Tim was snoring just enough to remind her that he was there. Kicking her foot through a heap of his clothes, she watched a shoe fly through the air. She circled her toe in the sheets and then pushed herself up against his back. Hoping he would wake, she nudged him a few times, and when he didn't, she pinched the skin on the back of his arm. He swatted at her so she pinched harder.

"What?" he muttered.

"Wake up."

"Why?"

"Because." Because the images in her mind were spinning so furiously she thought her head may explode.

He rolled over so that he was facing her, but then fell back to sleep. Each time air whistled past, his nostrils flared. She covered one up and listened as he sputtered, sending little balls of spit onto her cheek. She poked him in his chest, and when he didn't respond she poked again. It was like knocking at an abandoned house.

"Seriously, Therese, what the hell do you want?"

"Wake up."

"Why?"

She didn't know how to explain that at that moment, being alone was the most terrifying thing she could imagine. A few minutes passed and she could tell from his breathing that he was almost asleep again. She came close to his face and kissed his upper lip, but the contact startled him, and he jumped and hit her in the nose.

"Damn it." Tears formed in her eyes as a response to the sting of the hit.

"Sorry. But I don't know what you want, and I need to get some sleep."

She lay back down and he was quiet. He reached over and touched the side of her face. And then he was on top of her, and she closed her eyes and tried to lose herself in what he was doing.

But it was wrong.

It was suffocating and crushing and confusing and no matter how hard she tried to match herself to him, it made her feel like she was gasping. She wanted to push him off, but she was so tired and he was so determined. And then it was over and she could feel the dampness on the pillow and she knew it was from her tears. His breaths grew deeper and more peaceful as the minutes on the clock ticked away. It didn't matter anymore whether he was awake or asleep.

She was alone either way.

Even though it was Saturday, she was up early the next morning, but not before Tim. On weekends, she would lay in bed, listening as he walked down the hall to get Matilda. When he passed by her room, the one he himself had slept in as a child, Matilda would call out to him, and she could hear him pretend that lifting her out of bed was a chore and then complain about how he never had a moment to himself. Matilda would giggle and slip her hand into his. Therese would sit on the top step, listening to their morning ritual. Matilda twittered like a bird. When Therese heard the word "daddy," she wished that it didn't make her hurt inside.

Sometimes she would come and sit in the kitchen and watch them. She was welcome as long as she promised not to speak, and eventually they would forget that she was even there. When he made muffins, Matilda would help stir the batter, laughing as she stuck her fingers inside the bowl. When he made bread, he let her play with the dough and watched as she divided the pieces into a family, naming each rolled up ball. When they were together cooking in the kitchen, he never seemed to tire of being with her.

One morning, when he let her grease the muffin tin, she ended up licking the butter off her fingers and left shiny grease smears across the pinks of her cheeks. He dabbed at her with a wet napkin and she squealed and said, "Come here with your face!" She made a loud puckering sound against the side of his chin. Therese watched as he breathed her in. Sometimes, it looked to her as though he lingered too long, like somehow he knew there might not be enough.

One particular Saturday, Therese came downstairs to find Tim and Matilda cooking and Barbara already up, sitting at the kitchen table with a half-filled ashtray beside her. Matilda was sitting on a stool near the kitchen counter. Therese couldn't tell if it was just her imagination, but Matilda always seemed smaller when Barbara was around.

"I couldn't sleep last night." As Barbara coughed, her chest heaved up and down. She lit a cigarette and inhaled deeply.

"Sorry, Ma."

Therese could see that he was making Matilda pancakes in the shape of hearts.

"Do you want to help me mix?" he asked Matilda.

She slowly nodded her head.

"You let her get away with too much. Don't let the girl make a mess."

Therese hated that she called her "the girl," like she was some stranger's child on a bus. She got a coffee mug, clattering dishes loudly in response.

"It's fine, Ma." He looked up at Therese, which made her clatter even louder.

He went to the refrigerator and pulled out a carton of eggs and helped Matilda crack one against the side of the bowl. Therese sensed her delight as it slid effortlessly in, the yellow yolk perfect and unbroken.

"Again," she whispered.

"You spoil her rotten."

He ignored Barbara and held Matilda's little hand inside his as they both cupped the fragile egg. Therese held her empty coffee mug to her chest. They were both so focused on getting it right, on delivering a second perfect yolk, that neither noticed the second crack, which started quietly and got louder and finally ended with an incredible boom. When she turned to look, Barbara was on her back, arms flailing. The chair had collapsed beneath her.

"What happened?" Tim shouted as he ran to her.

"Don't touch me," she cried.

He knelt down and held her hand.

"Please don't leave me." The gravel that usually tinged her words was gone. Now there was just clean and pure fear. It danced across her face and made her lower lip tremble.

"Can you try and stand up?"

"I can't. I need my medicine. Bring me my medicine." But she gripped him even tighter and then pulled him close. "Thank you." She whispered fiercely, so that even Therese could hear, the tremors from her lip now extending across her entire face. "Thank you." She repeated more quietly and then she let him go.

He ran to the bathroom, and when he walked back in, they all turned to him. Therese clutched her empty mug to herself; Matilda continued to swirl her fingers inside the bowl; and Barbara, still on the floor, reached for him.

He stopped for just a second, or maybe it was longer. He stopped and looked around the kitchen, his eyes finally resting on his mother. And at that very minute, Therese knew without a doubt.

He would always take care of her and that there never had been any other choice.

Franny

The paper ripped.

I was scribbling too hard. And I didn't care. And it made me feel better.

"Why did you change your mind?" Evelyn asked.

We were sitting in her bedroom, making a get-well card for Mrs. Ficsh, who had been out sick for three days.

"About what?" I crumpled the paper and threw it into the trashcan. I took another sheet but, again, the same angry scribbles emerged so I decided just to write a message.

"About figuring out why your mother left?"

If I extended the bottom of the T in "get," I could turn it into a W for "well."

"Because it doesn't matter anymore."

Evelyn was decorating hers with pink and red hearts, which she was outlining in glue. She took a bottle of glitter and sprinkled it over the card. "Why not?"

I didn't answer; I just kept coloring in my letters. I drew them in blue, layering them like fat clouds in the sky.

"I promised I would help." Evelyn looked up, pink glitter sprinkled in her hair.

"I'm okay now." My picture looked empty, so I drew a big yellow sun in the corner with rays that intersected into the letters.

She stopped coloring. "You are?"

I made the rays pierce through the clouds, like golden arrows. Evelyn went back to her drawing, tired of waiting for me to answer. I didn't know how to tell her that I was doing everything I could to fix what was broken and that sometimes, at night, I would lie perfectly still, frightened that if I moved too fast, I would wreck it all. That I was certain that discovering why my mother left would also reveal Leah's secret, the pain of which I could not again be responsible for. I didn't want to tell her how much I wanted Leah to love me and that I could never see her sad again. I didn't tell her that sometimes when I closed my eyes, I could feel my sister and mother calling out to me, distracting me from becoming the person Leah wanted me to be. I couldn't tell her any of it.

"I don't care anymore."

I said it so softly that she didn't hear, but instead of saying it again, I ripped my card into hundreds of yellow and blue shreds and stuffed them into the trashcan, which was already overflowing with my mistakes.

That night when I went to bed, I barely slept. And when I finally woke, I could tell by the color of the light that it was too early. I didn't have an alarm clock; I woke at the same time every morning. But this morning I was early and it was hard getting up because my lips were stuck to the pages of my journal.

It's fast and round and bouncy and happens for no reason and I think maybe this time it won't but then it does and I can't make it stop and the letters come and I can't see anything else and when I open my eyes she is there whispering words that don't make sense but sound soft like feathers. Her teeth are white and sparkly and I like the quiet bird sounds she makes but then it feels tight and the rocking starts and I close my eyes. When I open them she gives me a book and a pen with red ink. She is next to me, humming, and I am circling letters and thinking that I can never leave this place and then like a wave in the ocean, the rocking starts again and I close my eyes but now the only thing I see is you.

Matilda.

Haunting my thoughts, my dreams. The journal had become my burden, filled with my sister's promises, reminding me that I had been left behind, that things were unfinished and unanswered. I wanted it to disappear along with the dreams that haunted me at night. I slipped the journal under my mattress, but that only reminded me of Leah's secret hiding place, so I pulled it back out.

In the bathroom, I stuffed it into the wastebasket where it sat on a bed of used tissues, the corner poking awkwardly from the top. That didn't seem right either, so I brought it downstairs. Leah was in her art studio. She spent a lot of time there lately, drinking tea and listening to music so softly that sometimes I didn't even know she was there. She was working on a drawing of a walnut so intricately blown up that it looked more like the surface of Mars than something you might eat.

She put a cup of tea down beside me and I watched the steam move across the surface and disappear into the air. Leaning over, she took my journal in her hand and walked into her studio. I heard a drawer open and then close and when she came back, she was empty-handed. She rubbed the back of my head softly, telling me without words that she knew exactly where it belonged.

Therese

Undertow.

Emerging from nowhere, leaving her disoriented and unsure of her footing.

She woke that morning, determined to put their friendship back together. Resigned to the fact that today, nothing would stop her from reconnecting with her friend and doing whatever it took to save Leah from the hurt she knew was coming. Leah was the only person she could truly trust, and she was not going to let her down.

Everything began as she pictured. Leah hesitated at first but then hugged her so tightly she could smell the shampoo in her hair. They sat on the couch holding onto one another just like they did in the beginning, and she quietly fell back into their rhythm, losing herself in Leah's presence. She put her hand on Leah's belly, smiling as each kick made Leah jump. It was so warm and perfect that she never even heard the doorbell ring and only mildly noticed when Leah left to answer it.

Something in the air made her breath quicken, and soon she realized that Leah was gone for too long. In the hallway, she found her with her arms crossed at her chest, precariously rocking back and forth as though at any moment she might lose her balance. There was a woman at the door. Behind her stood a young boy, and clinging to her leg was a little girl. The moment Therese laid eyes on them, she sensed it—prickling so sharp, she could feel it in her throat.

Desperation.

The woman and the little girl walked inside, but the boy leaned against the doorframe.

"So this is where you live." The woman looked around, sliding her hands across the top of a wooden console as if she was checking for dust.

"You said you needed to tell me something? Something about Lionel?" Leah's sway lessened until she wasn't moving at all.

The woman was younger than Leah. Her eyes were pretty, but only from far away. She sniffed loudly but just as she was about to speak, she seemed to notice Leah's large belly. She fixated on it, shaking her head back and forth, and then finally pointed at Leah awkwardly, like she had practiced in front of a mirror.

"He's mine and you can't take him away." The skin around her fingers was chewed, and her hand hung awkwardly in the air. "He loves me. He will never leave his kids or me. I am the one he always comes back to." The little girl pulled at her sleeve, and her arm came down.

Leah fell backward into Therese. She took little sips of air, seeming to have forgotten how to breathe. Therese could feel her tremors as though they were her own.

"Get out," Therese said.

The woman put her hands on the girl's shoulders and shook her head. "He will always belong to me." She walked out of the house, and the boy closed the door behind them.

Leah ran into the bathroom, and when she emerged, her hair was stuck to the sides of her head, and she was dripping from the water she had splashed onto her face. Some of it splattered onto her shirt, leaving dark uneven spots across her chest.

"Here." Therese pulled a tissue from the box on the table.

"You should go," Leah said, turning so that all Therese could see was her back.

"I am not going to leave you."

"I want you to go."

That's when she felt it. Pulling her under and making her stagger backward, like someone had punched her. "You shouldn't be alone with him."

Leah turned to face her. "You need to go. Now."

"I am not going to leave you," Therese said again, worried that it sounded like she was pleading.

"I don't want you here."

Leah began to push her, first softly but then harder. Wails of pain came up from inside, garbling the sound of her voice.

"Get out."

She continued to push until they reached the door, and then Therese had no control over what happened next. Leah shoved her outside and slammed the door closed behind her. No matter how much she wanted to stay, it was as if she was swept away, and the next thing she knew, she was out of the house, in her car, leaving Leah far behind.

As the days passed, Therese tried to clear her mind. Tried to believe that Leah was safe and that everything would be okay and that Leah knew what she was doing. A few mornings later, she was lying in bed, reciting a prayer she was too embarrassed to admit she needed, when suddenly the phone rang. Tim was in the bathroom, and when he turned on the faucet, the pipes rattled, making it sound even more like Leah was speaking under water. Her words came out slow and distorted.

"What did you say?" Therese asked into the phone.

Tim flushed the toilet, and the wall between them shook. He came back into the room to finish getting ready for work.

"I need you," Leah said.

The receiver dropped out of her hand. Acid filled her mouth, and the next thing she knew, she was kneeling over the trashcan. Matilda must have walked into the room. She could hear Tim singing to her. A song about boats and life being a dream, which made her insides churn even more. The room started to swirl, making it hard for her to dress. Tim asked if she was okay, and she mumbled something that must have sounded reasonable because he got his things together and left.

She had been lying to him, working extra days and leaving Matilda with Barbara instead of spending the money on the babysitter he had found. Meticulously saving every penny so that they could finally move out. Most days she was careful about waiting to leave until he was well on his way and returning home before he even finished his shifts.

But today was different.

She walked outside, but the cold wet grass made her realize she had forgotten her shoes. Inside, she found a pair of Tim's old slippers and put them on. They were too big, so she took them off in the car, and when she hit the gas, the pedal against her bare foot made her feel even smaller.

Even though logic told her there was nothing more she could have done, sharp pangs of guilt made her breath choppy and uneven. She drove to the house and slowly got out of the car and shuffled toward the front door. Looking down at her feet, she realized her toe was poking through a small hole in the slipper and wondered why it was that Tim never knew when to throw things away.

She stood in front of the house for a few minutes before knocking. The sky was blue and the smell of grass wafted through the air. Part of her wanted to run. To enjoy the sunshine instead of walking into the darkness she knew lay ahead, but something pushed her, and when she put her hand on the doorknob, it turned and opened easily.

Leah was sitting on the couch, wrapped in layers of blankets, with her back to the door. She didn't move when Therese walked in. She sat silently, and when she finally turned her head, Therese wished that she hadn't. One of Leah's eyes was swollen shut and a urine-colored circle ringed the other. Dried brown blood caked the corner of her mouth and her arm was wrapped in a sling. Hurt sunk so far down inside of Therese that for a minute she wasn't sure she could speak. She walked to the couch and sat beside Leah. She took Leah's uninjured hand and cupped it between her own, blowing on it as if it was cold. She remembered when Leah had done the same for her before Matilda was born.

"I am sorry," Therese said.

Leah started to speak, the words sputtering up like broken glass through her brown, cracked lips. "It's my fault."

"No."

"I should have known." She took her hand away and wrapped it around her bandaged one like a broken wing.

"Brutality disguised as kindness. You can thank your father."

Leah closed her eyes and seemed to deflate. "It's done. He's never coming back."

Suddenly everything felt like it was moving too fast and Therese felt feverish. "I should have done more. I should have protected you."

Leah lifted her head, her swollen eyes filling with tears, and slipped her hand back inside Therese's. They stared at the television screen, which was on but muted.

"There is something I need you to do for me." Leah's voice was so raw, Therese wondered if it hurt to speak.

"Anything."

Leah stood, her shoulders curved slightly, and walked toward the kitchen, the blankets dragging behind her. She returned carrying a basket and motioned for Therese to look inside. When she did, Therese stumbled back, the air escaping her lungs. She made a pitiful coughing sound.

"This is Frances. I named her that because it means free."

"She's beautiful." The baby's eyes moved back and forth between them, but other than that she was silent.

"And I want you to take her."

Therese looked closer into the basket. She could tell by the smell that her diaper needed to be changed. The baby turned her head toward Therese's touch in a reflex she immediately recognized. Hunger.

"I will look after her until you feel better."

"No," Leah shook her head. "I want you to take her. For good."

It was the strangest moment of silence Therese had ever experienced. As the people on the television moved quickly back and forth, Leah handed her a basket with the quietest baby she had ever seen tucked away inside.

"You've been through a lot. I'll take care of her until you are ready to take her back."

"No. I cannot protect her. I cannot take care of her. Ever."

Therese shook her head partly to make sure that she wasn't dreaming but also because of the sparks that were randomly dancing up her neck. "Everyone is scared to take care of a baby. It's normal."

"Nothing about this is normal." Leah thrust the basket toward Therese. "You promised you would do anything I asked."

"She is your child. It's what you have always wanted."

"I don't know what I was thinking. I should have known that I couldn't. I should have known it. I can't take care of another person. I cannot protect her."

Leah was speaking too fast, and then she began to move her head back and forth, like she wanted to shake out the image that was stuck inside. When that didn't work, she began to twirl her hair, and Therese wondered if that was what she looked like when she was a little girl, when she was innocent and beautiful . . . before she was broken.

As though she had read Therese's mind, Leah stopped twirling and instead started pulling so intensely that tufts of curl came out, twisting around her fingers like the twigs that make a bird's nest. She made a sound, maybe it was a word, Therese wasn't sure. She fumbled for something on the table, then slipped a cigarette into her mouth, and Therese watched the lighter shake in her hand. She blew out thick streams of smoke, and soon everything in the room felt like it was covered in gray.

"Please don't break your promise." She dropped the lit cigarette into an ashtray and began to rock back and forth. Therese set the basket on the floor gently and sat down beside Leah. She reached out to her friend, who was so wrapped up in her blanket, she reminded her of a mummy.

She tried touching her, but there was no response, so she searched for the words to explain that what she was asking for was ludicrous.

Suddenly, Leah's hand made it out from inside the wrapping, and she pulled Therese in close. Her words were crackly, like they were burning her from inside. "I need some time, Therese. I'll call you when I'm ready. Please. You are the only person I trust."

Therese didn't respond because she was too busy wiping away the tears falling down her cheeks, making it hard for her to see. She wanted to shake her, to somehow make her understand what it was she was asking, but instead she said nothing. Then Leah stood and walked to the kitchen, the blankets trailing behind like the train of a dirty, shredded wedding dress.

Therese picked up the remote control and turned up the volume so loud that all she could hear was a man calling her down to the Auto Mile for a great deal on a Jeep. She hated herself, but in that moment she actually considered leaving everything behind and running. She fought the desire to simply disappear instead of trying to figure out why she felt cracked open, as though what had happened to Leah had also happened to her.

No matter what she did, she could not stop shaking. She thought about her father, the first person to walk away from her without a second thought. Was it because she wasn't worth it? Was that why he hadn't chosen her? Then there was Leah, who had always been there for her, yet never asked for anything in return. Leah, who loved her unconditionally.

She stamped out the cigarette that Leah had left smoldering in the ashtray. She could hear Leah crying in the kitchen, steady and low and so constant she knew that it would last a very long time—if it ever did end. She stood in the living room for what seemed like hours.

When Leah didn't come back, she finally walked out of the house, carrying the basket with the quiet little baby inside, the phone number for the car dealership still ringing in her ears.

She laid the baby, still in her basket, across the floor of the backseat of her car. All she could hope was that maybe Leah would come to her senses. She turned on the radio, trying to find a song to match her mood, but nothing fit, so she turned it off and instead listened to the sound of Matilda's stroller shifting in the trunk. Even though she knew it was about to happen, each time it slammed into one side, it startled her. She turned the radio back on to muffle the noise. Frances remained quiet.

Nausea began to creep its way back up her throat as she pulled into the driveway and saw Tim's car parked ahead of her in the middle of the day.

When he should have been at work.

She opened all the windows and turned off the ignition. She decided to leave the baby in the car until she could figure things out. She looked in the rearview mirror, looped her hair behind her ear, and then thought about how to explain to Tim why it was that Matilda had been left alone with Barbara.

As she unlocked the front door, a delicate tingle danced across her arm, but she ignored it, slapping the air as though she was shooing a fly. When she walked inside, she saw that he was kneeling on the ground and Matilda was sobbing, but that wasn't what caught her eye.

It was the Red. Starting from her nose and streaked down the front of her shirt.

The tingle turned into stabs that shot up through her neck, making it hard to swallow. Barbara sat on the couch, whimpering. "I'm so sorry," she cried, but Therese's focus was locked on Tim.

"What the hell happened here?" she yelled, an angry, scared quiver in her voice.

Tim turned to her and then back to Matilda and then covered his face with his hands.

He tried to hide from her but he wasn't fast enough. She recognized the look in his eyes. The one she had seen that night in the shed. The one she had tried so hard to forget.

Barbara pushed herself off the couch and shuffled to his side. Tim brought his hands down and his face was white. Suddenly, all Therese could think about were triangles, and even though she did not understand what had happened, she waited.

For Tim to make his choice.

He stood, and she thought he was walking toward her. He reached his hand to her, like he wanted her to pull him out of whatever it was that trapped him. She could feel her arm slowly lifting, too, extending in his direction, but then something happened and he flinched and whatever was between them snapped. He turned away, and then it was so quiet she wondered if she had simply imagined the whole thing. Maybe none of it was really happening.

But then he spoke. "Take her and get out and don't ever come back."

He said it quietly, with resignation and a sense of calm that made her stagger backward.

She took Matilda into her arms. Later, she wondered why her daughter never made a sound. She started to walk and then turned back, but he was facing the window, his neck arched in such an unnatural position that she wondered if it was broken. For the second time that day, she waited for the person for whom she cared to come to their senses. When he didn't, she hugged her child close to her and walked away from the little red house.

In the car, she fumbled with the keys, her fingers numbed by the need to escape and her vision blinded by the most profound betrayal she had ever experienced. Her panic mixed with images of Leah. Broken bones and blood-splattered shirts swirled through her mind, and then it became hard to breathe, the tightness so intense that her insides felt like they were falling in on themselves.

A day that was suddenly beautiful turned gray, and even though no rain fell, lightning lit up the sky. Tears came and then her body filled with such ache that she could not sit up. The clouds turned black, and she saw Matilda lean toward the basket and whisper something to the little baby inside. She turned away, and when she looked back in the rearview mirror, this time Matilda was looking at her.

Therese replayed the look—the intensity—in Tim's eyes over and over in her head, and she knew that is where he tucked away the anger he usually kept hidden in the shed. Had he finally lost control of what he'd been holding back? Had she pushed him too far? Had he allowed himself to hurt Matilda? And what was Barbara apologizing for? She wasn't sure what the truth was anymore, and it didn't really matter because, in the end, he had made his choice. Matilda was staring at her, waiting for her.

"It's going to be okay, Matilda. I will always take care of you. You and Franny."

She hadn't realized Matilda was barefoot. She watched as her daughter extended her foot into the basket and saw the little baby inside reach for her toe.

She didn't know why she did it. Maybe because she could not think of anything else to do. But she started telling Matilda about the wonderful life they were going to have. At first she stumbled, but then it became easy, like she was reading lines from a script. And once she finished, she made sure that Matilda understood that everything was going to be just fine. She drove for hours, making sure that Matilda believed.

And then, eventually, she believed herself.

Matilda

The bus pulled into a gas station. People got off to stretch their legs, but I didn't. I stared out the window, watching a woman pump gas. What if I slid into her backseat, told her I was an orphan, and had nowhere to go? The woman slipped the nozzle back into the slot, got into her car, and drove off.

I rolled my sweatshirt into a ball and tucked it into the side of the window and then dug inside my backpack and found the envelope Daryl had given me. Three twenty-dollar bills and a screwdriver wrapped neatly into one of his drawings. A superhero with dark, straight hair that looked oddly familiar.

The bus started up again and I leaned against the window, the vibrations shimmering through the glass, making my nose itch. I sunk into the hum of the engine and felt temporary relief. The bus hurtled forward and I pretended it was taking me somewhere exotic—that when I got off I would be greeted by pretty brown women placing flowered necklaces around my neck.

The bus stopped.

Stillness surrounded me. The need to move pounded inside and I dug my fingernails into the armrest.

"Go," I whispered, my breath forming a circle of vapor that almost immediately disappeared. As if on command, the wheels began to turn and again we were pushing forward. I leaned back, this time falling into a half sleep. I tried to focus, but my thoughts became muddled, so I closed my eyes, grateful to disappear inside the lull of the roar.

Therese

The truth was that she had grown to love Franny.

Maybe more than she should have allowed herself.

The day she left Tim, she drove around for hours before finally ending up at her mother's, who asked questions that Therese ignored. Partly because she was tired, but mostly because she didn't really have any answers.

That first night, she and Matilda slept together in her childhood bedroom, and they made a bed for Franny inside a dresser drawer. The days passed, and, even though it was hard, she enjoyed the simplicity of taking care of a baby, watching as her mouth opened the moment a bottle was near and the way her skin smelled after a bath. Mostly she liked how Matilda helped take care of Franny and how effortlessly they settled into their new lives.

She called Leah once a week, but Leah never answered. She sent letters that always came back unopened. Soon weeks and then months passed, and she stopped reaching out to Leah. She didn't want to admit it, but she felt relieved. The way that Matilda cared for and protected Franny made Therese feel as though she had delivered on her promise that night in the car.

There was just one nagging fear that crept up on her, mostly at night.

She kept expecting him to show up or to call. She spent hours devising her plan, rehearsing her words, and sometimes she would stare out the window, convinced someone was out there watching, but she was never sure. The more time passed, the more relaxed things became. And then one day, without realizing the moment when it happened, they became a family.

Her mother finally stopped asking questions and just enjoyed having the house full of children that she had always wanted. Matilda and Franny were inseparable, and except for when Franny's hair curled like Leah's or when she would draw in her sketchbook, Therese forgot the real reason they had all ended up together. There was no question that she had grown to love the little girl, but she should have been more careful. Maybe if she had listened to her instincts and not gotten so comfortable, she would have been able to anticipate the moment when everything would change.

It was Franny's ninth birthday, and Therese had just finished wrapping presents and was sitting at the kitchen table, reading the newspaper, and there it was.

Barking at her. Taunting her.

The obituary she never expected to see sent her into a tailspin. There was a photo, too, but it was dark and blurry and the size of a dime. She wanted to lick her finger and rub it out like a spot of dirt, but she couldn't and she didn't and now Barbara was dead and Tim was free.

Free to come and find them.

Despite the nightmares that tormented her, Matilda never spoke about what went on in that little red house. So many years had passed that Therese herself wondered what had really transpired when she found Tim standing over her silent and bloodied child. She made sure that Tim was a topic never to be discussed, deciding quickly that she could provide just as adequately as any father could, reminding herself that she had turned out just fine without one. She told herself that it was her job to protect her children and that she could not risk another encounter. She grabbed a pad of paper and began scribbling down her plans when the phone rang, shaking pictures of escape out of her head.

"Therese?"

The voice was familiar, but it sounded like it was coming from somewhere very far away.

"I am calling because today is her birthday," Leah said.

Therese didn't respond, mostly because the blood pounding so loudly in her ears made it so she could barely hear.

"How is she?"

Therese thought about Jeeps. "She's beautiful."

There was silence on the other end, but Therese could hear Leah breathing. Slow, steady breaths designed to contain something she wasn't ready to let go.

"He started doing it to me you know. When I turned nine."

"I know."

"How is Tim?"

Therese coughed, the morning's coffee rising in her throat. "Gone."

"I'm ready now."

Therese shook her head, wishing Leah could see her through the phone.

"Therese, I want her back. Please. I want to protect her. I need to."

Whatever Therese had managed to keep at bay all those years suddenly came crashing down around her, and she felt her lungs flood. She coughed again, gagging on her insides, willing herself not to break in half. She thought about fighting, about calling a lawyer, but she knew she could never win.

"Therese, I will never forget what you did for me. How you saved me. How you saved her. Please, can I have her back?"

Because it wasn't a real question, there was no need for an answer. She wanted to shout, to cry, to hang up the phone and pretend none of this had happened, but then the swirling around her head stopped long enough for her to notice that Matilda had just walked into the room. She looked up at her for a second and smiled. Then she watched as her daughter picked up the newspaper and folded over the obituary section so she could read the comics.

"Okay," Therese whispered.

And that was that. As easily as Franny had slipped into her life, she slipped right out. She didn't anticipate how hard it would be to give her up. Even though she never really forgot to whom she belonged, she couldn't help but love the quiet baby from the basket who grew into a little girl that experienced life more intensely than anyone she had ever met. She loved her even more because of what she had done for Matilda, and she knew that part of Franny belonged to her, as well.

It was hard driving to Leah's. So much time had passed, and she felt frozen and stiff inside. But when the door opened and she saw Leah's face and they touched each other, everything that had grown hard and rough suddenly softened. Leah took her up to the bedroom, which was painted a beautiful green and dotted with fairies.

"This will be her room." Leah looked older, and instead of the innocence Therese remembered, her beauty felt chiseled. They sat together holding hands and sometimes crying like they had so often before.

"I'm different now," Leah said.

Therese nodded as she sat in the living room, stirring her tea and watching the sugar collect at the bottom. She remembered how dark this room had been the last time she was there, but now it felt filled with light.

Leah looked out the window before she spoke again. "Do you think she will ever forgive me?"

Therese put her hands in her lap and looked down. "It won't matter."

Leah was still looking out the window, but when she turned back to Therese, her eyes were closed.

"She will love you too much to care."

They talked about how to reveal their secret, and it was Therese who finally hatched the plan to just, simply, disappear. She wanted to vanish—maybe she had always wanted to vanish. Secretly, she wondered if she envied the choice of the father she never knew, but she told herself it was mostly because she could not imagine saying goodbye. Leah did not argue. Perhaps she thought it was best, as well.

Even though it was hard leaving Franny behind, things had all gone according to plan. She and Matilda settled into the townhouse and slipped into the routine of their lives. She was sure that no one watching from the outside would ever be able to tell that what she was really doing was waiting, for the knock or the phone call. She planned and plotted, watching the scene play out like a movie in her head.

Days and then weeks passed, and when he didn't come, the idea of him quieted inside of her, until it was almost like a whisper. Suddenly, there were real things in her life to contend with, and she turned her entire focus upon Matilda. She understood how much her daughter hated her, but what concerned her more was the boy she had fallen for. Even though she did not understand why, he made her more uncomfortable than she could bear. Even worse was that Matilda refused to listen, sneaking around as if Therese did not know what she was doing.

It all infuriated her, but right at that moment, it was mostly about the socks. Since they had moved into the townhouse, Matilda had developed an annoying habit of randomly tossing them into the first room she could find. They taunted her from the hallway floor, misshapen and stiff from dried sweat. She yelled for Matilda, but her voice cracked, making the sound disappear inside her throat. Anger coursed through her, and she whipped the ones she could find into the trashcan.

Outside, the wind roared, slapping twigs into the side of the house. So rarely did the weather match her mood that she closed her eyes to fully appreciate the moment. There was a tap at the door, but it took a second knock, soft yet determined, to catch her attention. She tossed the mail onto the table and went to answer it.

His hands were poked into his pant pockets, elbows awkwardly jutting out. He shifted from one foot to the other before looking up. Her heart raced into her throat, filling her insides with indefinable emotion.

"What do you want?" It came out slightly high-pitched.

Tim tilted his head and shrugged as if the answer was obvious.

"You shouldn't have come." She tried to close the door, but he easily pushed past her.

They faced each other, waiting for the other to move, and finally she walked over to the couch. Colors and sounds and lights flashed at her and she covered her eyes with her hands. The cushion shifted beneath her weight, and then he was sitting beside her, staring straight ahead, like they were taking a Sunday drive.

"Why are you here?"

He answered without looking. "I want to see her."

The sound of his voice caught her off-guard, and she hesitated for a moment. "You can't."

He shook his head. "You don't understand."

He spread his hands on his knees, the calluses on his knuckles white and cracked, his fingernails chewed to the skin, the sight of which reignited her anger.

"*You* are the one that doesn't understand."

She flew off the couch, knocking over a bowl of chocolates she put out for the guests who never visited. They dotted the carpet like little diamonds, and she watched as he kneeled over to collect them, cleaning up her mess. She wondered if now he might leave, but instead he spoke in a tone so low, it combined with the groan of the wind outside.

"I am going to see her."

More of the indistinguishable emotion swirled inside her, so intensely that she fell a few steps back.

"How did you find me?"

"I went to see your mother. She made me a cup of tea. I can't remember the last time someone has done that."

Therese crossed her arms across her chest. "She told you where we were."

"Don't be angry with her." He said it so softly that the words almost lost themselves in his breath. "She said you never told her what happened between us."

"That's because there was nothing to tell." She stumbled across another one of Matilda's socks and kicked it under a chair.

As he stood, she suddenly realized that she had forgotten how tall he was. He walked toward her. "There is a lot to tell."

"It's too late, Tim. You made your choice."

His eyes . . . she remembered them. So gray, they were almost translucent. Now, they were rimmed in red. His breath quickened, and she could feel the change in the air.

"I need you to understand."

"Why?"

"Because I've met my obligations. I don't owe anyone anything anymore. I want to see her. Please, let me see my daughter."

The plea was too familiar, and she tried to force thoughts of Leah out of her head. She had expected his rage but hadn't anticipated despair. She refocused, making herself remember her plan. She would not allow the months she had spent planning to go to waste. She was going to destroy him. To make him regret every decision that had led to this moment, to his choice.

She was about to tell him about his mother. About the lie she had perpetrated and the one he had spent his life paying for. She opened her mouth to speak, knowing exactly what was supposed to happen next.

And it would have if not for the blood-curdling scream that came from the unit next door.

Tim ran outside, and even though she could have slammed the door closed behind him, she didn't. They were standing outside her neighbor's, the sound of a woman's wail so piercing, it made her heart skip. Tim pushed the door open and walked inside. Therese guessed the woman kneeling on the floor covering her face was Daryl's mother, although they had never met.

The man standing in the center of the room had his back turned and red hair poked out like straw from his glistening scalp. He turned to look at them. For the second time that day, her chest filled with unspeakable emotion. She closed her eyes to force the memories to move quicker, but her heart was racing so fast that it all just made her dizzy.

He smiled and licked his lips. "Hello, Therese."

The woman on the floor took advantage of his distraction to rise and wipe the blood from her mouth. The two children were standing together, Daryl in front of the girl as though he was trying to protect her.

"Have you met my lovely wife and children?" He said it as if they had just run into each other at the grocery store. He extended his hand, which she had the overwhelming urge to bite.

The woman's eye was ringed in blue.

Lionel's signature work.

Her black dress was ripped at the waist. She hoisted up the edge of her skirt and used it to dab at her face, exposing a red bruise on her knee. But that was not what caused Therese to stop and stare. It was the look of desperation that she recognized.

Patiently, she waited. And then, like the seconds it takes to breathe in a deep gulp of air, it came to her. A layer of sweat started at her temples and worked itself down the side of her neck as images and sounds crashed inside her head and then suddenly none of it mattered anymore because there was only one thought left.

"Where is Matilda?"

It was Daryl who spoke. But when he did, it was so quiet she could barely hear.

"Gone."

The sweat slid cold and thin, farther down her chest. Lionel dug a flask out his pants pocket. He took a long, leisurely sip, and when he was finished, threw it down and grabbed the woman by the arm. She cried out softly, pushing him away, but he pulled harder until again she fell to the floor.

"It's time for you to get going now," Tim mumbled.

Therese had forgotten he was there.

Lionel turned to him. "You're the one who's going." He wiped his mouth with the back of his hand. "And take that bitch with you."

There was a moment of silence where no one moved or spoke. All she could hear was music in the background, maybe from the little radio on the table or maybe it was just inside her head. Then everything happened slowly, like they were all moving under water.

Lionel cocked his head back and leapt forward as if he was diving into a pool. The two men grabbed one another and began to roll on the floor. The music played and the woman screamed and Daryl and his sister huddled in a corner.

A crash a few frightened seconds later shook Therese out of the moment. She saw the girl, Matilda's friend, Lavi, standing over her father with a broken lamp in her hand. Lionel laid sprawled out on the floor, eyes closed and peaceful, with a streak of red running down the side of his face. No one spoke, and the only sound Therese heard was the woman whimpering. Lavi stood up, still holding the cracked lamp in her hand.

"We should call someone," Tim said, pushing himself off the ground and feeling his face, which already looked tender. He reached for the telephone and started to dial the police.

Therese looked around and realized they were standing in a circle, like they were playing some silly childhood game and were waiting for the one in the middle to stand up. The woman continued to whimper in a pitch that was quickly escalating. Therese tried to think about what to do, but truly all she wanted was to run. An overwhelming heaviness settled upon her, and she knew that she needed to find Matilda.

"She went to go find her dad," Daryl said.

The sound of his voice startled her, and she wondered if she was thinking aloud. Why had Matilda gone to find Tim? She had worked so hard to erase him from their lives. She had worked so hard to pretend the things that happened . . . didn't. Why couldn't Matilda just let it go? Why couldn't she simply understand that Tim had made his choice?

The image of her own father snaked its way into her mind. She needed to clear her head, but it was so hard to hear her own thoughts over Sara's cries. She closed her eyes as sheets of rain slapped against the side of the house. Then, suddenly, the whole room lit up in a bluish white light, and she wasn't sure if it was thunder that shook the house or the tree that came crashing through the roof.

Like a missile hitting its target, debris from the ceiling landed squarely on the man lying in the middle of the carpet. His hand twitched once and then stopped. She turned to Tim, just as the woman began to wail, but this time she didn't notice because at that exact moment, a second bolt of lightning hit the house.

Everyone screamed and the girl, Lavi, fell to the ground. Tim was kneeling over her, his hands cradling her head as though it were the most fragile thing he had ever held. She thought about Friendly's and apples and eggshells. When he looked up at her, she could tell he wanted to speak. She turned her head away, but it didn't matter because she could still hear his words over the moan of the storm.

"When I came home that day, I found her that way. She was locked in the basement. Just like my mother had done to me. She tried to explain, but all I wanted to do was push her down those basement stairs and run. But I couldn't. I couldn't leave her."

He pulled Lavi closer to him, whispered into her ear, and kissed the top of her head.

Therese covered her ears.

"Listen to me!" he yelled. "Do you know what it feels like to send someone you love away? I love her, Therese. Please, let me see her."

She watched as he held the girl in his lap, rocking her back and forth, his tears spilling down and disappearing inside the curves of her curls, which she realized were familiar because they reminded her of Franny's. The girl coughed and shifted in Tim's arms, and Therese let out the breath she didn't know she'd been holding. Smoke was starting to clear, and, as it did, the deep sense of his loss began to move through her like frost, making her fingers and toes go numb. She took her hands off her ears and looked at him.

He was quiet, lost somewhere in his thoughts. "Do you think she will ever forgive me?"

The familiarity of the question startled her. How could it be so different, yet the same? She closed her eyes, mostly because she wasn't ready to experience the revelations that were beginning to come. Leah and Tim and her own father's face swam through her as if she was liquid, grabbing at her insides so hard that she toppled back. She wanted to hurt him. To punish him. She took a deep breath, fully intending to tell him that he had wasted his life on a lie, but when she spoke, a different truth emerged.

"She will love you too much to care." She whispered her words—the same words she had said to Leah—and watched as they disappeared into the silky air. He looked back at her with his translucent gray eyes, except this time she could see through and into him. It made her heart skip, but before she could speak again, he had risen to his feet and run off.

Sirens blared in the distance, getting louder as the ambulance approached the development of townhomes. Therese fell to the floor next to Lavi's mother, who had crawled over to her daughter, who was now beginning to stir.

Therese knew exactly where Tim was going, and she didn't care because right now all she could think about was the question. The one that tormented her when she was alone, when it was dark and quiet and the world was asleep. The one that came to her sometimes when she dropped Matilda off at school and more often when she heard her quiet snores coming from the bedroom. The question for which she could never find a true answer and the one that she repeated almost every night before she fell asleep.

Will she ever forgive me?

Franny

I didn't notice it at first.

It was slipped underneath the door and had a shoe print stamped across the middle like a convoluted road map. I picked it up and rubbed off the dirt and then I threw it back down as if holding it too long would burn my fingers. She had been writing to me for weeks, long-winded letters with no punctuation, so that when I finished reading her words, I was breathless. But this letter was different.

This letter was hand delivered.

I sat in front of the television, eating goldfish crackers out of the bag. Silently, I counted each one before chewing. Leah would be home soon. If I could just make it until then everything would be okay.

Four.

Crunch.

Matilda's note called me from the hallway.

Two.

Crunch.

I should have thrown it in the trash or, better yet, put it in Leah's magic drawer where all things I didn't know what to do with went. Everything would be fine once Leah came home. All I needed to do was look at her and then I would know what to do.

Three.

Crunch.

But that letter kept calling. I put the goldfish crackers back in the cabinet and started talking out loud. Letters jumbled with thoughts and then I started thinking about my mother and my sister and before I could think anything else, I was in the hallway, ripping open the envelope.

"MEET ME AT THE MAILBOX AT 4—M."

Had she finally made good on her promise to come back for me? I didn't know what I would say when I saw her. I don't know why, but I put on the brass-colored key that Leah had given me. The one I wore around my neck to remind me of where I belonged. I folded the letter and slipped it into my pocket. Then I went outside.

The sky was so gray, it made the air feel dirty. The mailbox was a few feet from the edge of the sidewalk and people walked by stuffing mail into its mouth. It made an angry creaking noise that reminded me of a dungeon door every time it opened. I was thinking about all those letters buried deep at the bottom of the box so I wasn't focusing on the hand that suddenly reached out to grab me.

She pulled me hard.

Like she was trying to pull me out of the life I was living and into hers—only I didn't really think about it that way at the time. Mostly I thought about how walking beside her felt right, even though something about her was wrong. Maybe her hair, which looked longer and like it hadn't been combed for days. Little balls of fire burst inside of me and there was so much to say, but when I opened my mouth to speak, a thick ball of spit stuck in my throat. I tried to remember to be brave.

I reached out to hold her hand, which felt sticky, like a used candy wrapper. There was a quiet between us that I liked because I didn't want to have to think about words and because it gave me an opportunity to count tires. Specifically, those on parked cars that were painted blue. She led me onto a bus and I sat by the window, this time counting parking meters, but things outside were moving too quickly and the thickness in my throat got bigger. She squeezed my hand once when we reached our stop. I still didn't know where we were going, but it didn't seem to matter because she was with me and I couldn't imagine not following wherever she led.

"I will never leave you again." She said it without looking at me, her words skimming the top of my head, and then we were back walking again. It had been raining on and off all day and each time her shoe plunked into a puddle, it sprayed a web of mud that clung to her socks. She pulled me along a little faster, maybe because I was falling behind or maybe for another reason.

And then suddenly we were there.

I knew because of the way she stopped. So abruptly that I accidentally crashed into her, sending the paper she was holding in her hand fluttering to the ground. I watched as raindrops landed on it, beading into pearls that then washed the letters away. She didn't seem to care.

We stood in front of a very red house. A crimson shutter dangled from the side of one of the windows and when we walked up the front steps, I waited for her to ring the doorbell. Instead she fished around in her pocket, took out a screwdriver and what looked like a paper clip, and huddled over the doorknob. Within seconds I heard a click, and then the big red door creaked open.

"Where are we?" I whispered. It was dark. I wondered if anyone was home.

"*Shhh.*" She put her finger over her lips. "This way."

She led me through the house as if she knew where she was going. As if she had been in this place before. We walked farther down the hallway until she found a door and opened it. I looked down into the depth of the staircase, but it was so black that I couldn't see to the bottom.

I shook my head, but her grip grew tighter and she dragged me down the steps behind her. The air was wet and heavy and smelled of dirty laundry. The windowpanes were painted red and covered in cloth, which made me feel like I was stuck inside a rotting tomato. She let me go and sat down on the ground, then wrapped her arms around her knees and began to mumble. Her voice was hoarse, as though she had been crying, and she stumbled over the first few words.

"This is the room from my dream."

"What are you talking about?"

She buried her face into her hands, rocking her body back and forth. Her lips were moving but no sound came out. I didn't know what to do, so I reached out and touched her hand, but she didn't respond. I shook her a little harder and then she moved her arms forward and started to crawl along the floor until she reached one of the cement walls. She stood up and lifted them above her head, slowly pounding the wall with her fists.

"Stop!" I yelled.

She kept hitting the wall over and over. She was determined, as if somehow she was going to be able to break through, but finally the assault got less and less intense until all that was left was the flat empty sound of a slap. She raked her fingernails across the concrete and then her body crumbled into a kneeling position.

I ran to her side and tried to get her to look at me. I needed her to tell me what to do. I needed her to tell me why she had brought me here. My breath quickened and I could feel the wetness in the air stick to my temples. My heart beat in my ears and I tried to remember about courage, but then I held my breath because I realized that it wasn't my heart that I was hearing.

It was footsteps.

With each step, the ceiling above me trembled, as if it were alive. Matilda whimpered as the footsteps got closer to the door of the basement. I looked around, trying to find a place for us to hide, but aside from some boxes in the corner, the room was empty. I didn't know what else to do, so I thought about Leah. About being the person you are supposed to be.

The letters coming out of me randomly floated through the dank air and then the footsteps stopped and everything was quiet. My sister was breathing heavily, like a child who was on the brink of sleep after a long tantrum. Then, suddenly, the door at the top of the stairs burst open.

The man cupped his hand over his eyes so that he could see in the darkness. As he came down, I took one big breath and the last few letters in my chest heaved out like stray coins at the bottom of a pocketbook. This time they floated up and suddenly I could hear Leah speaking to me.

Telling me that I had everything I needed. That I had always had everything I needed because my fate was in *my* hands. There was a carton on the ground that I rummaged through until I found it.

A hammer.

My knee scraped against one of the boxes as I climbed, but I ignored the sting. I reached the windows and ripped down the material covering them. Each pull let more light into the dingy basement and created a shredding sound that sounded like a shriek and the letters danced with delight.

I looked at the man and I looked at my sister and then I lifted up my arm and slammed the hammer into those red painted windows. I closed my eyes and I hit, listening to the painful sound of shatter, feeling the sensation of breaking running through every part of me, breathing slowly until finally it was quiet and there was nothing left to break. When I stopped, the letters were gone and all that was left were shards of glass showering the basement floor.

I could escape, but I didn't want to anymore. Instead, I took in a breath of the clean fresh air that was slowly filling the room. Sprinkles of rain hit my face and reminded me of glitter. It got very quiet until all I could hear was crying. But this time it wasn't Matilda who was crying.

It was the man.

First it was soft and gentle, like a baby. Then deep and guttural, echoing a pain so intense that the only way to contain it was through a scream. And that is what he did. His legs gave way from under him and he collapsed at the bottom of the stairs. He didn't cover his face, didn't hide behind anything. He cried until there was no voice left except for the quiet echo of air passing between his lips.

Matilda and I watched him in silence and I gripped the hammer tighter, but then I dropped it and it made a scraping noise as it landed on the floor. I climbed down off the box and Matilda looked up and so did the man. Then it got quieter than I have ever heard then or since.

It was at that moment that I understood about myself. That I am different because I see things that other people don't. No one moved and no one spoke, but it didn't matter because just like my letters, I could hear his words in my head. Pure and strong and sad. And I knew that he was crying for all the things that had been lost. He laced his fingers together and brought them to his face as though he was begging.

For forgiveness.

I watched him walk toward my sister, who was murmuring softly, like a kitten. She whispered something into the air, to me or to him I did not know.

"Matilda." Something about the sound of his voice made her look up and then she quieted. He lowered himself down to where she sat and extended his hand to me. There was something familiar about him; it was in his face or maybe it was his expression, or maybe it was the way he said her name, like he had been repeating it over and over in his dreams. We sat together, wrapped in a quiet that was occasionally interrupted by the clink of a pipe. We huddled in the corner of that dank and dark basement and it was only when I finally looked up that I saw it.

A crack of sunlight streaming through the air, hitting the shattered glass sprinkled on the floor and making it glisten like rubies.

Matilda

Sometimes I wish I never knew her secrets. I wished she had kept them all to herself. Maybe it's my fault for prying. For asking. For pushing until there was no other choice. For any of us.

I call them Tim and Therese mostly because it fits and even more because I know it bothers her even though she doesn't reprimand me. She knows that she deserves to be punished. Deserves to lose her title.

They are talking to each other now. Slowly and carefully, like walking across a thin sheet of ice, hoping that it won't crack and send them falling into the freezing water beneath. I live with my grandmother and spend time with both of them separately but not together. Not yet. There are words they want to say to me. I am just not ready to listen. Maybe soon if they are patient.

I spend a lot of time with Franny. We are tied to each other more strongly than most sisters. Maybe because of what we have been through or maybe because we choose to be.

We don't really talk much about her father. I tell her that without him, she wouldn't be here. Sometimes I think I should explain it to her better, and other times I know there is no way to explain. And I don't really need to because, in her own way, she has already made sense of it. Being with her reminds me that things are in the right place.

She is spelling a lot less now. I know because I don't see the letters flying randomly and angrily from her lips. Her face is softer and, when she speaks, her voice is shinier. We eat breakfast together some mornings at

Leah's house. We sit in her kitchen, which is now painted a buttery yellow and makes Franny's face glow like the sun. Leah always leaves us alone and I pretend that we are the only two left in the entire world. I wonder what Leah has told her about why she gave her away. When she talks about Leah, she smiles and I wonder if forgiveness can be that easy—if it is, I envy her. I also know there is a sadness for which she hasn't yet found the words. Doesn't matter, though, because I will be here for when they come.

Today when we finish eating, she asks me to take her to a park. Simply because she asks, I agree. It's a sunny day and we stand beneath the trees, hidden from view, almost like we don't belong, which . . . maybe we don't.

"We don't need this anymore," Franny says and hands me a book.

It is purple and bound by a rubber band so stretched it snaps at my touch. Inside are my notes to her. I pull one out and read through my promises and my despair and my brokenness. She has used a pen to trace over my letters so that now my words belong to us both. Words that remind us of who we were before becoming who we were meant to be.

She is looking at me, waiting for a response, and I nod my head. She hands me a box of matches and I take one and strike it. Nothing much happens except for the quick way it ignites. As the pages crackle and shrivel, a burning smell fills the air around us that reminds me of roasted peanuts.

We stand and watch as it rages and then quiets and when it is finished, we walk away, leaving what is left behind. We walk holding hands. We walk away and Franny doesn't turn back, but I do. I look up into the trees and see a twisted thread of smoke winding its way up above our heads, which then disappears into the cool blue air as if it was never even there in the first place.

Acknowledgments

I owe heartfelt thanks to Caroline Leavitt without whom any of this would be possible. She believed that my story was special and did not give up until I believed, too. To Holly LeCraw, for her guidance and support. To my agent, Anne Bohner, who took a chance on me. To my editor, Nicole Frail, for smoothing out all the rough spots.

Thank you to my father, who taught me that nothing is ever really yours except for the ideas in your head. To my mother, for her curiosity, her smarts, and her eternal optimism. To Talia, because she makes me laugh even when there is nothing to laugh about. To Rich, for his emotional and technical support and for still believing in magic. To Kristin, Roni, Jen, and Tamara, who cheered me on. To Maureen, Maya, Ruth, Roseann, and Elaine for reading and reflecting.

Finally, thank you to my children, who inspire me every single day.

Book Club Questions

1. Which of the characters in the novel did you despise or like and why? With which of the characters did you most identify?

2. What insights have you gained about people with autism? Why do you think the author does not use the term *autism* in the book?

3. Do you find that people who have secrets themselves are more likely to keep other people's secrets safe? Which of the secrets in the book, if revealed, would have changed the fate of the other characters?

4. Can you find references in the story to *The Wizard of Oz*? Do you believe that, like Dorothy and her red shoes, fate is in your hands? Or do you believe that destiny is predetermined and out of your control?

5. Are woman and girls in this book the victims of men? Is it unusual that the story is only told from the perspective of the women? Would the tone of the story have changed if the men had been given a more active voice?

6. What is it that draws Therese to Tim? And is it that same character trait that eventually breaks them apart?

7. How is Leah able to bring about Franny's transformation? What is it about Franny that helps Leah learn to trust herself?

8. What motivates woman like Therese, Leah, Sara, and even Barbara to suppress the voice of reason in order to gain love? Do you perceive it as weakness or strength?

9. Do you have questions about the intensity of Leah and Therese's feelings for one another? Can women forge such powerful connections with other women without romantic undertones?

10. Do you believe that everyone is capable of overcoming obstacles to become the person they are meant to be?